This book is dedicated to Laura and Aaron, the two best gaming buddies a guy could ask for. Toasty!

Level Up

A 'One Up' Novel

2nd Edition

Cover illustration by Sicarius8

(https://sicarius8.deviantart.com)

Title Font: Press Start 2P by Codeman38

Copyright © 2018 by Craig Anderson

Edited by Celestian Rince (https://celestianrince.com)

***

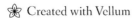 Created with Vellum

LEVEL 1: SURPRISE

"Seriously, I don't think it's possible to beat this final boss. He's burning through our extra lives again. I can't face another week like last week. Let's just use that cheat code I told you about and get this over with."

My brow crinkles at the very suggestion. "No, we're going to beat him properly. We haven't come all this way to cheat our way to the ending. I want a real sense of pride and accomplishment, not some hollow victory. I just need to level up more. We could go back and farm some low-level mobs, try and buff my stats. I only need 300 EXP to get to level 69 Rogue."

There's a hearty sigh at the other end of the microphone. "Seriously Marcus, I'm already maxed out. It's going to take days for you to catch up. Are you sure we can't just speed this along? I heard about this glitch that lets you craft infinite potions..."

"Absolutely not. What's the point in playing a game if you're just going to exploit the system?"

"To win mate. That's it. Kick arse, save the world and move on to the next game."

"Perhaps I don't want to rush to another game. Maybe I want to savour this one."

"You're killing me here. I never should have convinced you to join the scouts. You do know that scout's honour stops applying when you hit puberty."

"So any day for you then..."

"You're lucky this isn't a PVP zone. You'd be eating fireballs."

"Based on your aim in that last boss fight I'd only be worried if I was standing next to the guy you were aiming at."

Carlos stifles a yawn. "Ok, enough chit chat. One more try and then I have to go to bed. Tomorrow is a work day."

"You keep telling me you don't do anything in your new job!"

"True, but I still have to be there. They get annoyed if I get in after 10."

"10 a.m! I knew I should have applied for that sales job. Jenkins gets his lackeys to phone me if I'm not at my desk at 8:01."

Carlos' tone gets noticeably surlier. "Ugh, don't remind me of that arrogant bastard. I don't know why you keep putting up with him. I only lasted a year because you were there to stop me strangling him."

We're about to restart the boss fight when there is a thump on my door, making me jump. Before waiting for a response my Mum walks in. "I thought I heard voices. What are you still doing up?"

I pull off my headset. "Mum, I'm nearly 26 years old. I'm more than capable of deciding when I should go to bed."

"Good point, you're old enough to know better."

"We are only going to be five more minutes, we just have to beat this boss and then we can save." Could I sound any more pathetic. I'm like a five year old begging for a later bedtime.

Her expression softens. "Look, I know this isn't easy for you. I appreciate you helping me out with the mortgage. But don't you have that big meeting with Mr. Jenkins tomorrow morning? You don't want to be stumbling in there half asleep."

She has a point. "Ok, thanks Mum. Goodnight."

"Goodnight Marcus." With that she closes the door behind her.

I put the headset back on just in time to hear Carlos say, "Dude, you really need to move out. How do you not go mad?"

"Who says I haven't?"

"So you really think Jenkins is going to offer you that promotion in your meeting tomorrow huh?"

"He bloody better. He has been promising for months. I don't think I can keep going like this."

Carlos scoffs. "Classic Jenkins. He will just find a new excuse. Don't you remember when he did this to Andy? Kept stringing him along until he ran screaming from the building. I wonder what happened to him."

"He's working at the petrol station down on Smith Street. Apparently Jenkins convinced HR to fire him with cause, so it completely ruined his references."

"Why does HR always take his side? I swear he's hooking up with Miss Jones."

We both shudder at the thought.

"It's ok, it is finally all going to come together and all my problems will be solved. Just you watch."

"I'll practice my surprised face."

***

Mr. Jenkins smiles at me and says, "Marcus, thank you for coming this morning. I think we both know why I've asked you here."

Finally! I can start turning my life around, pay down the rest of Mum's mortgage and rent a place of my own. Maybe even go on a date. It feels like my life has been on hold for the last three years and it's about to get jump started again.

I realize he kept talking while I was dreaming of a better life. As I tune back in he says, "...quarterly reporting is becoming increasingly scrutinized by the higher ups, so I am going to need as long as possible to review before I present it to them. I'll therefore need it all wrapped up by this time tomorrow morning."

My brow crinkles in response and I swallow my excitement. "I'm sorry, what needs to be wrapped up by tomorrow?"

"The quarterly report. I want to be able to review it before the presentation. If you could have it to me first thing that would be a huge help."

I stare at him, choosing my next words carefully. "Are you sure you have the right person? I'm not currently working on the quarterly report. This is the first time you've mentioned it."

"Indeed. That's why I'm giving you all day today and all of tonight to get it done. I sent you last quarter's slide deck, you can use it as a starting point. It's really just plugging the numbers into the template."

I let out a sigh of relief. "Oh ok, well that I can do. Where do I get the numbers from?"

"I don't know, Brad did the slides last quarter. He might have some of the data queries saved. Check with him." He waits for me to rush off, but instead I stay seated. He says, "Is there something else?"

If I don't say something now they might not be able to catch me when I run screaming out of the building. "Actually yes there is. Is there any update on the promotion we discussed six months ago?"

It might be my imagination, but the air in this tiny corner office just got a lot cooler. Jenkins tenses up, as if he's getting ready to bolt. With his generous frame I am pretty sure I could outrun him, even if he has a head start. He sucks some air through his yellow teeth and says, "I have tried really hard to convince HR that we need an intermediate business analyst on the team, but they have pushed back on my current OPEX projections with the new position. As it stands we are running over budget for the quarter and we need to reset our bottom line and prove out our spending at this new staffing level before we can justify the additional expense. They did commit to opening up a new position at the start of the next financial year, when our budget is reset."

My voice gets a little louder, bouncing off the paper-thin walls. "That's six months from now!"

"Just to be clear, it would be a new job opening rather than a promotion. I am obliged to post it so that anyone on the team could apply."

"That's not what we discussed! You said the promotion was a reward for my excellent performance last year, and all the overtime I put in to keep us on top of everything."

"Unfortunately our hiring policy has changed. It's out of my hands. Tenure won't be taken into account in the hiring process. We don't want anyone accusing us of favouritism. If you'd like to discuss it with someone feel free to arrange a meeting with Miss Jones."

No thank you. People have a nasty habit of going into her office with a simple request and leaving unemployed.

I'm about to continue the argument when there's a knock on the door and Cindy strolls in without waiting for a response. She's wearing a lot more makeup than usual. If her skirt was any shorter it would be a belt. She places a large coffee cup on Jenkins' desk and flashes him a smile. "Hey boss. I was just grabbing a latte and what do you know they made me a white mocha by mistake. I know you drink those so I figured you might like it."

Jenkins pushes it away. "I'm afraid I can't have that, I'm lactose intolerant."

Everybody knows that. He never shuts up about it. It's why we don't do team lunches anymore. Well, that and the total lack of any kind of budget.

Cindy doesn't miss a beat. "What a coincidence, me too! It's made with coconut milk. Enjoy!"

She stares at me as if I just farted. "Oh hey Marcus. Sorry, I didn't know you were in here. I'll leave you both to it."

She saunters out of the room and I watch as Jenkins sips his coffee and smiles. I guess the word is already out about the promotion. It's going to be a long six months, especially if I have to compete with that level of arse kissing.

I can't just roll over and take this again. "I still don't understand the delay. I thought you said there was budget put aside this year for a more senior position?"

"Unfortunately that money had to be reallocated. My chair broke and I needed to buy a new one."

Jenkins swivels in his chair, as if to show off his new purchase. It makes his awful comb over flop from one side of his head to the other until it settles in something resembling the right place. The chair is one of those sloping ergonomic chairs that Silicon Valley start ups have. The type that costs several thousand pounds. He is literally sitting on my dreams, his fat arse suffocating the life out of them.

My left eye starts to twitch and my teeth clamp together to stop any words coming out. I stand up abruptly and he says, "Great talk. Don't forget about the quarterly report, and please don't neglect your usual tasks."

It's hard to talk through gritted teeth. "But I'm still working on the big presentation for the PDZ product launch for Saturn Corp you gave me yesterday. The deadline for that is end of day today. Did that change?"

He stares at me blankly. "No, I still need that presentation ready by end of day."

"But I have hours of work to do on it. How am I supposed to complete both of those tasks?"

"Work smarter, not harder! Honestly, an Intermediate Business Analyst would find a way..."

Oh god, it's started already. This is going to be my life for the next six months. I don't think I can cope with this. I dart out of the room before I leap over the desk and beat him to death with his fancy chair.

I sulk my way back to my desk and slump into my chair that is definitely not ergonomic. Antique perhaps. There are so many different stains on it that it looks like a pattern. It squeaks more than a busy afternoon for the Pied Piper.

Deep breath. I'm concentrating on the wrong things. Focus on the problem at hand. How am I going to get an entire day's worth of work done alongside ten hours of spreadsheets and graphs for the quarterly reports, without working all night?

I'm sure one of my colleagues will be happy to help. I've been a kind and patient mentor to all of them. The least they could do is get me out of this pickle.

I start with Brad. He's been here almost as long as I have and has only survived some of Jenkins' more ridiculous deadlines with my help. He's also the guy most familiar with the quarterly reporting. I sidle up to him as he's dumping a tea bag out of a still steaming cup. "Hey Brad, how's it going?"

He eyes me suspiciously and takes an extra-long sip of his tea. Eventually he responds. "Good thanks Marcus. Hey, could you help me out with something?"

"Actually I'm..."

"Could you grab my timesheet from the printer. Thanks mate."

Bastard. He knows I need his help and he's going to milk it for all it is worth. I sigh and say, "Sure, I'll be right back."

This should an easy task, but our printer spends more time jamming than a cheap cover band, and no-one ever tries to fix it. I stroll over and of course the red error light is flashing. I follow the on-screen instructions, opening door after door, pulling out trays with small green handles, searching for an elusive piece of paper that no-one has ever found. After carefully putting it all back together I close the final door and the light turns green just long enough for one sheet of paper to come through before the jam warning flashes back up. In my frustration I give it a good slap. The printer is from a time before plastic was invented, so it has the density of a small battleship. My hand immediately starts to hurt and I let out a choice selection of swear words.

I grumble my way back to Brad and slam the piece of paper down on his desk. "There you go."

"Thanks mate, appreciate it." He goes back to his screen, clearly hoping I've forgotten what I came to ask him for. Not today.

"I need your help with the quarterly reports..."

I'm barely able to get the words out when he holds up his free hand. "Sorry buddy, I'm totally swamped."

"But you know them better than anyone. I'm just trying to get a sense as to how to populate the slides. Jenkins said it would be pretty straightforward."

Brad laughs so hard a dribble of tea comes out his nose. He wipes his face with the back of his sleeve and says, "Good one. Those same slides have been used for at least a dozen quarterly reports. There is so much legacy data in there that no-one knows how any of the queries work anymore. It took me a week to cobble together as much as I could, and it took another week to make it stable enough that it didn't crash on the second slide. When does he need them by?"

"Tomorrow."

"Good luck with that!"

Bollocks. That does not sound promising. Before I can say anything else, Brad turns his back to me and opens up a spreadsheet. It's the same spreadsheet I've seen on his screen all week, something to flip to on the rare occasion that Jenkins bumbles out of his office. The lazy git is freezing me out.

I'll have to remember this the next time he gets stuck.

Jim is next on my hit list. I lean over the cubicle wall. It's slightly sticky and I peel myself off. Jim is sitting there with his feet up on the desk, playing on a portable games console. He's not trying to hide it, he hasn't even bothered putting headphones on. His tongue sticks out in concentration as his massive sausage fingers hammer at the buttons. I try to make polite conversation. "Hey Jim. What are you playing?"

He doesn't look up from the screen. "Doom." A heavy metal riff blares out of the speaker, followed by the sound of a chainsaw.

Of course he is. Tearing up demons is exactly how I imagine he likes to spend his mornings. "I don't suppose you know anything about quarterly business reviews?"

He glances up just long enough to give me a scowl. His resultant grunt sounds like it is intended to convey that no, he doesn't. Not exactly a massive shock. Jim is Jenkins' cousin, and purely coincidentally he is also our only Senior Business Analyst. The fact that he doesn't know a pivot table from a pool table is neither here nor there. I'd have more luck asking for help from an earthworm. Jim is many things, but competent is not one of them.

He leans back with a glide. I notice he's sitting in one of those fancy new chairs too. It should annoy me, but I've got more important things to worry about right now.

Unfortunately that only leaves one person, and it is such a long shot a professional sniper would pack up his stuff and go home.

I approach slowly, using the gauntlet of coffee machines and broken printers as cover. I don't want to give her a chance to run off before I can ambush her. I can hear typing, which is a promising sign.

There is no chance she would ever help me. I am her biggest competition for the promotion. She wants me to fall flat on my face. Still, I'm all out of options, so it's worth a try. What's the worst that could happen?

I slide into the entrance to her cubicle, blocking her escape. I do my best to smile casually at Cindy. Her desk is immaculate as always, with lines of pens and highlighters in order of colour. Every item has its place, and heaven help anyone that moves anything.

"How's it going?"

She smiles back sweetly. "Absolutely marvellous, thanks Marcus. How about yourself?"

Of all the responses I was expecting, that wasn't one of them. I stammer out, "Good thanks. So I need your help with something..."

"Of course. Whatever you need."

Now I am definitely wary. This isn't her style at all. Usually she can't wait to tell me how busy she is with very important work.

"Jenkins asked if I could work on the quarterly report, but I am swamped with other stuff. I don't suppose you could take a quick look at them to help me out?"

"Actually, I have some capacity this afternoon. Send me what you have and I will take a first crack at them. When do you need them by?"

"If you could just send me whatever you have by the end of day I can finish them up tonight."

She looks at me puzzled. "Isn't tonight your birthday drinks with Carlos?"

"How do you know that?"

"He invited half the office. Unfortunately I can't make it. Don't worry about working on the slides, I will make sure they are done and you have them first thing tomorrow. Consider it a birthday present."

There's a long pause while I wait for her to start laughing, but it never happens. I say, "Thanks Cindy, I really appreciate it. I owe you one."

"Nonsense, you would do the same for me Marcus. It's my pleasure."

Did I miss a memo? It is like the Cindy I know and love to hate has been replaced with her sweet and innocent twin. I certainly can't complain about the timing.

I skip back to my desk feeling a lot less panicked. If I really knuckle down and concentrate I should be able to get the Saturn Corp slides finished by the end of the day.

My desk phone rings. I pick it up and Carlos says, "Are congratulations in order?"

"You know damn well they aren't. Jenkins did exactly what you said."

His tone softens. "I'm sorry mate. I told you, the man's a weasel. It's time for you to start looking for something else."

"I know that. I'll start tomorrow. I just have a few last things to wrap up here today."

"At least we have drinks tonight to drown your sorrow."

"We almost didn't. Jenkins gave me a ridiculous amount of work to do, but luckily Cindy offered to help."

"Are you out of your mind? Don't trust her!" I keep forgetting he has a history with Cindy. They had something of a personality clash, in so far as Carlos has one, and Cindy doesn't.

"Must you always be so paranoid? She wants to do a nice thing for me so we can go for drinks. Maybe this is her attempt to turn over a new leaf."

"Mark my words, it's a stinging nettle."

"So who else is coming tonight?"

There's a pause before Carlos replies. "Just the two of us buddy, I didn't want a big group cramping our style. I'm going to be your wingman. Fire up the afterburner and hold on to your hat, it's going to be wild!"

So much for half the office. "Where exactly are you taking me?"

"It's a surprise!"

Oh great. I hate surprises. Especially Carlos surprises.

LEVEL 2: ACCESS DENIED

A car horn blares on the driveway, interrupting my intense staring at the PDZ slides. I pull myself out of the daze and check the clock. How is it already 10 pm?

Mum shouts up the stairs. "Carlos is here."

"Ok, tell him I'll be down in a minute."

A quick glance at myself in the mirror suggests that I could do with a lot longer. I'm still in my work clothes, which isn't a great start. My hair looks like a centipede curled up and fell asleep on my head. There are unruly tufts dangling everywhere. It is going to take an ungodly amount of gel to whip it into shape.

It's not the only thing that needs to get into shape. My arms have the definition of an 8-bit game. My six-pack is currently buried alive under a rippling layer of fast food and beers. Don't even start on my legs. I skipped all the leg days.

It doesn't take long to change into my only decent pair of jeans and a clean shirt. The big advantage of still living with my mum is the excellent laundry service. Never have I known anyone so ruthlessly efficient at ironing.

My hair takes longer as I desperately try to sculpt it into something resembling intentional style. After several failed attempts I give up and just ruffle it.

I jump down the stairs two at a time and land with a thud, almost rolling my ankle. I limp into the living room to find Carlos sipping a cup of tea from Mum's nice china. He says, "Why yes Mrs. Kennedy, I agree that it is a violent sport, and it's not everyone's cup of tea. Hockey has just always been a passion. Now if we could just get Marcus back on a pair of skates."

I plonk down next to him. "I thought we agreed after the last time that we wouldn't ever put me on ice skates again. I'm a big enough liability in shoes, there's really no need to strap sharp blades to my feet."

Carlos chuckles enthusiastically. He finishes his tea and places it daintily back on the saucer. "Thank you again Mrs. Kennedy for the delightful Earl Grey. Now if you will excuse us, we shall be departing. I promise to bring your son back in one piece."

He strides out of the room like we are on our way to the finest masquerade ball in all the town. I lean over and give my Mum a peck on the cheek. "See you later."

She says, "Don't be late and don't be drunk!"

"Love you too."

Carlos is already waiting in his shiny new BMW, the engine running with a soft purr. I still can't get used to seeing him in it. I climb inside and the new car smell hits me instantly as I sink into the plush leather seat. He flashes me a smile. "Would you like your seat warmer on?"

Seat warmer! My car doesn't even have a heater, it broke two years ago. I have to bring a thermos of tea to try and warm up the interior. I nod and he pushes one of the myriad of buttons on the dashboard. Within seconds my arse cheeks are toasty warm. I try to keep the envy out of my voice and fail miserably. "I still don't understand how you can afford this car."

"It's a lease, they are practically giving them away. Besides, it's good for my career. Customers don't take a sales guy seriously unless he drives a nice car. If I showed up in my beat-up purple Fiesta I'd have no chance."

"But you loved that car! Remember the aftermarket spoiler that created so much drag it lowered your top speed, and that ridiculous speaker you had in the boot that took up all the space and made our teeth hurt if you turned it up to full blast."

There were a lot of fond memories in that car, although also a lot of near death experiences. Carlos has never been one for following the rules. Unfortunately that also includes the rules of the road. Thankfully he's a lot more sensible now that his car is worth more than everything I own combined.

"So are you going to tell me where we are going?" I ask.

He takes his eyes off the road just long enough to waggle his eyebrows at me. "You'll see."

"Just promise me it's not the Kasbah."

There's no logical reason we would go there, every time we do we always swear it will be the last time. Just like ice skating.

"It may be a stop along the way. For old times' sake."

"We're going to more than one place?" I hate how old I sound right now, as if he just suggested we should climb Everest. Still, pub crawls are something I'm happy to relegate to my past, along with sweater vests and my brief dalliance with having a ponytail.

"Ok Grandpa, put your teeth back in, it's just a small pub crawl. You can take your foot out of the grave for one night."

I consider arguing with him, but since he became a sales guy he's become really good at convincing people to do stuff they don't want to. It's basically what he does for a living now. I'll have an easier time if I just go along with it and try to convince him to leave early instead. Who knows, perhaps I will even enjoy myself.

After several minutes weaving in and out of traffic we reach our first destination. The BMW looks very out of place in the car park behind the Kasbah. Every other car looks like it just came last in a demolition derby. Some of them are so old and rusty I can't be certain they haven't been abandoned here. No thief would risk tetanus to try and steal them. Carlos may as well scratch WANKER into the side of his car now and save the local hooligans the trouble. At least he would spell it right.

As we join the back of the line to get in I make an observation. "Everyone here looks rather young..."

Carlos does a cursory glance at the group in front of us. There is enough acne between them to coat a football pitch. He shrugs. "I don't know what you mean. They are the same age that we were when we started coming here."

"That was ten years ago! Don't you remember, we'd see guys our age and joke about how they should be at home with their wife and kids."

"Yes, well times were different then. Nowadays the kids are more enlightened, they wouldn't do something as crude as judge someone based on their age."

A new group of lads joins the queue behind us. One of them sneers. "Glad to see that the senior discount is attracting new customers."

It's the first of many such comments. We do our best to ignore them as the line slowly creeps forwards. Eventually Carlos turns to me. "So when are you going to stop working for Jenkins?"

The question catches me by surprise, mostly because I haven't really thought about it. I shrug. "I have no intentions of pursuing other opportunities at the moment. I'm quite happy where I am."

"You're in a rut. Jenkins will never take you seriously unless you stick up for yourself. He's taking advantage of your good nature."

Of course he's right. If that wasn't already blindingly obvious, today was the final nail in the coffin. Even so, I can't help but cling on to my last shred of hope. "I just need to impress him for the next six months and..."

"And nothing. He'll give that promotion to Cindy. She has more balls than you will ever have. You really need to grow a pair. It's time someone told you that."

I hum the tune to Happy Birthday and he laughs. "Ok fine, I'll stop giving you a hard time. You know it's just because I want what's best for you right?"

"If you wanted what was best for me we wouldn't be here!"

Right on cue the group in front of us is ushered into the building and we are left facing the bouncer. He looks as if someone has shaved a large angry ape and given up halfway through. He stares down at us and scowls. "You here to pickup your kids?"

Carlos laughs, but there's no sign that the bouncer is joking. His scowl stays plastered on his face as Carlos says, "No mate, we are just looking to have a quick one in here for old times' sake."

"Old times is right. You look like a pair of creepy perverts that are trying to pickup eighteen year olds. Sorry lads, I can't let you in. It's ladies night tonight, we have to protect our female guests."

We both glance at the line behind us. It's 95% guys. The few women that are scattered amongst them look as if they have been dragged here against their will.

I'm quite happy to turn and leave, but Carlos pulls out a crisp twenty pound note and tries to slip it to the bouncer with all the subtlety of a marching band. "Maybe you could check your VIP list and see if we are on there."

The bouncer pockets the note and glances at his clipboard. "Nope, I don't see any cradle snatchers on my list. Guess you guys should piss off back to the golf club."

It's the final straw. I've been pushed around all day by people abusing their positions of authority and I've had enough of it. I step up to the bouncer and poke him in the chest. "I suggest you give my friend his money back and let us in, or I'll be forced to report you for misconduct."

I wasn't aware that a human body could bounce. The bouncer skims me along the pavement like a skipping stone until I skid to a halt next to a bus stop. Carlos runs up beside me. "What on earth were you thinking?"

"You told me to grow a pair!"

"I didn't mean now! Are you out of your mind? You're lucky he didn't throw you into traffic."

I stand up and something rattles in my head. That's probably not a good sign. "I'm not sure lucky is the right word. I'll be writing a sternly worded letter to his manager."

"I'm sure he's quaking in his boots at the thought of your excellent penmanship." Carlos looks around sheepishly. "So should we just go to the next pub?"

I shake my head and the rattling gets worse. "I think perhaps we should just call it a night. I'd like to make it to my 26th year in one piece."

Even Carlos is going to have a hard time convincing me to change my mind, but he gives it a solid try. "But we haven't even had a beer yet. It can't possibly get any worse!"

That's when I hear her voice. It sends a shiver down my spine. I'm so overwhelmed with emotion that I'm barely able to process the words she is saying. "Marcus? Oh my goodness, are you ok?"

I close my eyes and pray that it is the concussion playing tricks on me. When I open them again I see her smiling at me, the glow of the streetlight behind her casting a glistening aura. She looks like an angel. Perhaps I really am dying. I can only hope. She reaches out and touches my arm, and I groan as I feel it. I'm still in the land of the living. She says, "I saw the whole thing."

There goes my last chance of maintaining any dignity from the situation. Of all the people that I didn't want to see me ricocheting down the street, Sarah would be top of my list. She'd probably be in the top three spots, that's how much I want to avoid what just happened.

I manage a weak smile and try to change the topic away from my recent street gymnastics. "Sarah? What are you doing here? I thought you'd moved to Australia."

Sarah brushes her strawberry blonde fringe out of her eyes and I feel a familiar pounding in my chest. It doubles in speed as she says, "I moved back a few months ago to join a startup here. I didn't realize you were still in town..."

Perhaps I was meant to be thrown by that angry bouncer. This must all be part of fates plan to get us to meet again. It's my birthday gift from the world. This feels like a story we'll be telling our kids one day. I'll be sure to make myself sound less pathetic in my version.

She looks at her watch and says, "I'm really sorry, I'm running late. Hey, do you still play video games?"

The noise that comes out of my mouth is supposed to sound like pfft, but it doesn't sound convincing enough so I drag it out until it becomes awkward. She just stares at me until I say, "Of course not! That stuff is for kids."

"Oh. That's a shame, I'm working on a really cool VR game at the moment and we had a couple of people drop out of tonight's focus group. I thought it might be the kind of thing you'd like. Never mind."

You've got to be kidding me. She's gorgeous, smart, and now she develops cutting-edge video games. Fate is really kicking me in the nuts on this one.

Carlos is smart enough to jump in. "Please ignore Marcus, I think he may be concussed. We love video games and would be happy to help out on your latest project."

She smiles at him. "I don't want to interrupt your evening if you already have plans."

"Not at all. We're just ticking a few things off Marcus's bucket list. It's his birthday tomorrow. He always wanted to be almost killed by a bouncer. Now that we can check that one off, our evening is wide open, isn't that right?" He stares at me and waggles his eyebrows. He's heard all about Sarah, including the pathetic story of that one time I tried to ask her out. I can see the look on his face. He thinks he's going to play Cupid. Unfortunately subtlety is not his forte.

I nod and Sarah beams. "That's great, you're really helping me out of a pickle. Are you sure you're ok to walk? It's not too far."

"Me? Oh yeah, no problem." I try a laugh, but it makes my ribs ache.

Sarah sets off at a brisk pace. Carlos says, "I'll catch up, just got to tie my shoes." He winks at me. It would be a lot more convincing if his shoes had laces.

I try to think of something to say, but no words come out. I'm not good at small talk. I'm not good at big talk either. Talking in general is an issue, especially as far as women are concerned. That applies tenfold when Sarah is involved.

I have a flashback to the first and only time I tried to ask her out. I went through the scenario a hundred times. I was going to casually drop into conversation that we should grab dinner some time. I was going for a delicate touch, no pressure, an offer she could politely refuse without ending our friendship. Instead I screamed, "YOU SHOULD DINNER!" in her face and bolted from the room. It took me three weeks until I could muster the courage to talk to her again. When she left for Australia I spent days searching for cheap flights down under, only to realize I could barely afford to eat, let alone jet halfway around the world. I never thought I would see her again.

And yet, here she is, walking right alongside me. It's my chance to make things right. I just have to find something we can both talk about. Perhaps I can find some common ground. "What is your game about?"

"I don't want to say too much and ruin the fun, but we are trying to recreate the massive scope and scale of an online RPG in virtual reality. We are using cutting-edge technology to massively increase immersion and make it feel as if you're really there, fighting along-side real people. We also have some pretty amazing artificial intelligence. Sometimes it is hard to tell the NPCs from the players. I think you'll really like it. There's skill trees, loot to find, card games to master and a whole bunch more stuff. You're going to be blown away."

How can I tell her I already am? She still looks stunning, even more so than I remember. Just seeing her again has brought all those long-buried feelings rushing back to the surface. This is it, my second chance. I'm going to grow a pair, just like Carlos suggested, and ask Sarah out.

I open my mouth to speak and no words come out, just a faint gargling sound. I do my best to pass it off as a cough. Sarah looks at me concerned. "Are you ok?"

"Never better. So what made you move back from Australia?"

There's a flicker on her face, a brief flash of sadness and then it's gone. She says, "I had a fiancee, but two days before the wedding I found out he was sleeping with his secretary and my best friend."

"You were best friends with his secretary?"

"No. Two different people. Needless to say I wasn't keen on sticking around. That's when this job popped up, right back in our home town. Talk about fate!"

"I'm so sorry, you didn't deserve that, but I am glad you found out before you married him."

"I suppose. I just wish men weren't such lying, cheating arseholes, you know."

"Yeah, really! Men are the *worst*."

Bollocks.

LEVEL 3: GAME OVER

Carlos finally catches up to us as we reach a large building at the university. He takes one look at us and says, "Wow, who died?"

My chances with Sarah. I give him a weary glance and announce, "Sarah was just telling me about her game. It sounds awesome, right up your alley."

"Bring it on! Let's show them how it's done." He glances up at the building, "So what are we doing here? Shouldn't we be in some hipster all glass video game company building that has ping pong tables and free booze?"

"This is where we test the game for now. We haven't optimized it for home computers yet, it requires a lot of raw computing power to run smoothly. The university has very kindly offered us time on their supercomputer, but only out of hours, hence the unsociable test schedule. They even lent us some old office space they weren't using, so I spend most of my nights here."

A young Indian guy stops us in the foyer. "Hey Sarah. I thought our testing tonight was cancelled?"

"Hey Raj. I found us a couple more guinea pigs."

"I wish you'd said, I just closed down the VR lab. It will take me some time to get it up and running again."

"Don't worry about it, they can use the headset in my office. I just want to get a fresh perspective from players that haven't already seen the game. Is the latest build stable?"

"We still have the issues on our fix list, but you already know about those. We also have a new glitch on the final boss. The latest patch was supposed to increase his health regeneration speed by 1.5, but someone forgot the decimal, so now it's increased by a factor of 15. He's basically unbeatable at the moment."

"Ok, we'll steer clear of him. These guys are fresh meat so we are going to be taking it easy. You can go home if you like, I can handle it."

"Are you sure?" He's already reaching for his coat.

"Yep, go spend some time with those cute kids of yours. I'll catch you tomorrow."

Raj is out the door so fast he's practically supersonic.

Sarah leads us through a cavernous space filled with VR headsets. There must be ten or fifteen, all hanging from a central pillar on the ceiling like a cyberpunk octopus. It is eerily dark and our footsteps echo through the dead space. There is no light source, just a vertical line of green LEDs blinking on the far wall, which we head towards. Sarah says, "Sorry about this, the overhead lights take forever to power up in here. It's just through here."

We come out the other side into a long corridor filled with offices. We pass one with the door cracked open and can hear someone mumbling to themselves in what sounds like Latin. We are almost past when the door beside me bursts open and a man says, "Who's there?"

Apparently when considering the correct response to the fight or flight reflex my body went for secret door number three, which is stand in the same spot and scrunch my face up like my poop is coming out sideways. Natural selection at work.

The man looks at me concerned. "Are you ok?"

Sarah jumps in. "Hey Professor Jasper. It's fine, these guys are with me. I'm just giving them the tour. I didn't expect anyone else to be here."

Professor Jasper pushes his thick rimmed glasses up his nose and looks around shiftily. "Yes, I'm running an experiment tonight. Ground breaking stuff. Will change the way we see the world. Now if you'll excuse me, I must get back to work."

The door slams shut without so much as a goodbye.

"He seems nice," says Carlos with a smirk.

"Yeah, he's a bit of a character, he has some pretty wild theories about the universe. Apparently none of this is real and it's all just some giant simulation."

"What does that make us, NPCs?" says Carlos.

"I guess so. The rest of the staff think he's nuts, but I find the thought kind of comforting. If none of this is real then you might as well make yourself happy and do what you love, right?"

"Right." I don't even know what that would be, but it certainly isn't Junior Business Analyst.

Two offices down we reach a door with Sarah's name on it. She fishes the key out of her pocket and ushers us inside. With a few flickers the light comes on to reveal a surprisingly large space. I was expecting a cozy cupboard, but there is room in here to swing a cat. One wall is a giant whiteboard and is covered in meticulous handwritten formulas, along with several sketches of cool dragons looming over mysterious dungeons.

Sarah picks up gloves and a VR headset off her desk and hands them to Carlos. "Just give me a minute to get the demo configured. I don't usually run the tutorial program, I need to make sure I have the latest version."

"Pfft, I can figure it out. Tutorials are the worst," says Carlos.

"Ok, well if you think you can figure out how to map your brain signals to your intentions on the fly then by all means skip the tutorial."

"What? Ok fine, I'll play along." He slips into the gloves before putting the headset on. His jaw immediately drops open. "Holy crap! These graphics are awesome."

Sarah smiles with a hint of pride. "Pretty cool huh. Try picking something up."

He does and he says, "How is this possible? I can feel it in my hands."

"Haptic feedback gloves. A small electric current stimulates material that can stiffen up to simulate you holding something. We can't fully simulate the weight yet, but it's a start."

Carlos sniggers. Sarah looks at me confused and I mutter, "you said stimulates and stiffens in the same sentence."

Carlos suddenly starts swinging his arms around like a windmill. I look at Sarah and she says, "Sword fighting tutorial. Everyone does that the first time. If he can just take a breath and calm down he will do much better."

Carlos shouts, "How do I move around?"

"It's the next tutorial. Patience."

I mutter, "Patience is not one of the skills Carlos has levelled up over the years."

Carlos suddenly starts jogging on the spot and Sarah ushers me back out into the corridor. She talks in a hushed tone, "I don't want to disturb him while he's playing, it will break his immersion. So what are you doing with yourself now?"

"I'm working at Master Systems as a Business Analyst." I decide to leave out the junior part of my title, it will only get my blood pressure up again. I need to keep the conversation focused on her before my anger starts to show. "How long have you been working on this game?"

"Just since I moved back a few months ago. I think we're really on to something here, like we are standing right on the edge of this amazing revolution. I always felt like games could be something more, it just took a while for the technology to catch up."

"I didn't even know you played games." I'm cursing myself. There is so much we could have talked about. What if that was my chance and I blew it.

"I didn't really. I was interested in them, but they were clearly designed by men, for men. It was all about shooting and dominance and putting your balls on another guy's face. That just wasn't for me. I wanted something more nuanced. Where you have to make hard decisions and those choices have real consequences."

I can't help but stare at her. She looks exactly as I remember her, that same frizzy hair, the line of freckles above her top lip, the flecks of grey in her blue eyes. I could close my eyes and draw her from memory, if I could draw worth a damn.

She catches me staring and looks away. I feel the urgent need to apologize, but then I'd have to admit I was gawking. Instead I say, "How are your folks?"

"Dad is doing ok, he retired last year. Mum on the other hand is on the warpath around this whole wedding fiasco. She's never been happier, she gets to pick up the phone and shout at Aussies all day."

Ah yes, Sarah's Mum. She drops hints with the precision and subtlety of a German bombing raid. The first time I met her she kept repeating the fact that I was Sarah's *friend* from university. Her inflection on the F word was like a knife to the heart and she hit me with a flurry of them, one after the other, testing my resolve. I had to hide in the bathroom for ten minutes to regain my composure. She is not a woman to be trifled with, particularly when her daughter is involved. I don't envy Sarah's ex-fiancee on that one.

There's something else she's not saying. I'm about to pry when Carlos starts yelling. We run back into the room to find him shrugging off the VR headset, a concerned look on his face. "Erm, Sarah, I think I broke your game..."

She rushes over to the computer and starts frantically typing. After a few seconds she says, "Don't worry, it's a known issue. The engine we used was originally designed for turn-based strategy games. Sometimes the game crashes and reverts back to the old ruleset. We are still working out the kinks. Do you remember what you were doing when it crashed? It will help with logging the bug.

It says in the log that you had 7,217 gold coins, so it looks like your inventory glitched out too."

Carlos looks around shiftily. "No, that sounds about right. I may have been exploiting a pricing issue with your merchant. He sells sticks and rocks for 1 gold coin each, which can be combined to make arrows, which he buys back for 4 gold coins. I may have repeated that process a couple of thousand times..."

"We left you alone for five minutes!"

He stares at the ground. "I'm sorry."

"Don't be. We've been testing this game for months and nobody found that exploit. I'll get that patched right away. I should hire you!"

He perks up again. "Damn straight, but I already have a cushy gig. I'll let you know if that changes. The only thing I couldn't figure out was how to decapitate the enemies."

"Yeah, our game is rated 15, so there's violence and nudity, but no decapitation, graphic sex or swearing."

"Hey Marcus, sounds just like your average week!"

I give him the look that reminds him he is supposed to be on my side. As usual he completely ignores it. "Mate, you've got to try this game out, it is amazing even without all that cool stuff!"

Sarah hands me the gloves and I slip them on. They are still warm from Carlos' turn. Then she helps me into the headset, tightening the straps to hold it into place. I am plunged into darkness and I instinctively grope around, finally landing on something soft and warm. I give it a squeeze. These gloves are amazing, it is as if I am holding something. I hear Sarah's voice over the headset, "Could you stop groping me please."

I hear Carlos' distinctive chuckle behind me and feel the blood rushing to my face. He's not going to let me forget that for a while. The sad part is, that's the most intimate I have been with a woman in a long time.

I'm just starting to feel sorry for myself when icons appear around the peripheral of my vision. I see a standard life bar, a blue magic bar underneath it and something that looks a lot like my inventory. Sarah's voice comes back in my ears, "Wave your hands. You should see them represented in the game."

I do as I am told and am surprised to see realistic equivalents floating in the game world. She says, "Ok, I'll boot up the tutorial. Don't move, the system has to scan your resting brain waves."

There's a tingle in my scalp and a green checkmark appears on the screen. Then a message appears. It says, "Prepare to defend yourself."

A sword materializes in front of me and I instinctively reach out to pick it up. As soon as I do a knight comes around the corner and runs straight at me, his sword raised above his head. I start flailing my arm and remember Sarah's tip from earlier. I take a deep breath and wait for the knight to get into range. I lunge forwards and skewer him before he can hit me.

He doesn't look best pleased. A hint comes up about how to hold my sword up to block and I get to practice it a lot as he starts wailing away at me. My health is being slowly chipped away. I can't stand here blocking forever. That's when I get a new prompt:

To parry, try blocking at the exact moment you are hit. It will negate all damage and build up a multiplier to make your next hit more powerful.

Sounds good. I do exactly what it said, but I can't figure out the timing. I go too early and it only counts as a block, then I try too late and get a sword in the face. Thankfully this is the tutorial, so my health keeps replenishing, if this was the real game I'd be dead already.

After a dozen attempts I finally get it right and there is a *ching* sound. The damage multiplier ticks over from x1 to x2, which is a big improvement. I hit the knight once and the rest of his life vanishes.

I'm still feeling smug about it when my health starts to disappear again. I turn to find a guy behind me stabbing me in the back with a dagger. Sarah's voice comes over the headphones. "Don't forget to always be looking around so you don't get ambushed. This guy is too close for your broadsword, you'll need to fight him hand to hand."

I open my hand and the broadsword disappears. As my attacker prepares for another attack a prompt briefly flashes on the screen, but I don't know what to do and I get stabbed again. I shout to Sarah, "how do I click on the prompt?"

"You don't. You just have to think it."

Next time I am ready and I think *disarm* as the prompt appears, flipping my hands up in what I feel is a very convincing attempt at realism. The knife falls out of the knight's hand and he turns and runs away.

The next prompt tells me to walk. I move to take a step forward, but it flashes up *just think about moving*. I do that and jump as my character takes a step forward. I think about running and he sets off at a pace I couldn't maintain ten years ago, let alone now. I shout out, "this is creepy!" It's really hard not to move my legs.

A platform appears in front of me and it says *try jumping*. I do as I am asked and immediately plummet to my death. Sarah says, "The system is still synchronizing with your brain waves, so there can be a slight delay. It might feel a bit like lag in an online game. That will improve with time."

I scrunch up my face and try again. This time I manage it. Next up is a fallen tree at waist height. The prompt says *combat roll* so I think about it. The screen spins and I find myself on the other side of the log. It is very disorienting, but I'm confident with practice I could get the hang of it.

A new message appears. *Tutorial complete. Loading demo.*

I find myself in a field of wheat, which sways gently in a virtual breeze. I reach out my hand and run it through the swaying plants and I jump as I touch one. Please don't let it be another part of Sarah. She comes back over the headset, "Pretty cool huh. That's the haptic feedback. There's a sword behind you. You're going to be needing it."

I spin and see a sword sticking out of the ground, its blade glistening in the sunlight. I reach out and wrap my hands around the handle. I brace myself to pull it out of the ground, but it has no weight and I nearly topple over. It is absurdly long. I swish it at the wheat stems and they fall to the ground decapitated. "This is amazing!"

Carlos shouts in the background, "Right! Have you tried throwing a fireball yet?"

As soon as I think *fireball* a flickering light appears in my left hand and grows into a small ball of flames. I haphazardly toss it into the field and it immediately sets fire to the dry plants. The fire spreads quickly, threatening to engulf me. I shout, "Sarah...a little help please."

There's a giggle in my ear and dark clouds appear instantly in the sky, pouring rain onto the fire and extinguishing it with a puff of smoke. She says, "try not to burn all my hard work to the ground!"

I'm still marvelling at the realism when a flashing green arrow appears on the screen. A small red circle appears in the bottom red corner. As I focus on it a menu expands to fill the screen.

New Quest: Bring 7 chickens to the cook in the tavern.

I hear the faint sound of clucking in the distance. I set off slowly. I'm still finding my feet. It feels very unnatural to move around without moving my body or pushing a button, but I can see the potential. With practice, this could bring a new level of immersion. I only have to think about running and my avatar picks up the pace.

As I crest the hill I see a group of shady characters approaching. They all have their weapons drawn. One of them shouts, "there's the warlock. Grab him and we can collect the bounty."

The goons stare at each other and one says, "Do we need him alive boss?"

The leader sneers at me. "These magic folk can be tricky. It will be easier to drag a dead body back to town."

They fan out and move towards me with surprising speed. The tutorial is certainly over. I wave my sword at them ineffectively as the nearest one lunges towards me. I attempt to dodge but I react too slowly. I'm almost expecting to feel the blade pierce my skin, but it passes right through me, taking a chunk of my health bar with it. Sarah's voice is back in my ear. "Don't forget to parry. You can build up a pretty significant damage boost if you get a few in a row."

I try to do as I am told, but I still can't get the timing right. I'm getting stabbed over and over while my opponents dance around me, landing blow after blow. One of the bandits laughs and wipes my virtual blood off his blade. "He's even softer than I expected."

Cheeky bastard!

I don't mean to get angry, but it's hard not too. I've been pushed around all day and now these A.I. goons are getting in on the act. Well they've messed with the wrong warlock! I concentrate and my left hand bursts into flame. With a flick of my wrist it arcs through the air and sets one of my attackers alight. He runs around screaming as his friends all take a step back. Who's soft now!

A flashing icon catches my attention and I glance at it. It says, "ultra attack is ready."

It's time to get my warlock on. I look at the remaining guys and think how great it would be if my ultra attack was something that would teach them a lesson. That's when I see the shadow on the ground and hear the almighty screech. We all look up in unison as a two hundred foot dragon bursts through the clouds and rains fire. I hold my hands up to my face as the fire hits, but my health bar doesn't budge. I guess I am a fireproof warlock. My assailants are not so lucky, they are reduced to smouldering piles of ash.

Sarah says, "Wow, most people save that for the boss fight, but sure, why not vaporize five square acres of land to kill three level 1 grunts..."

I guess I got a bit carried away. I'm about to remove the headset when my scalp starts to tingle again. It's a tickle at first, like a static shock, but it keeps growing in intensity. I grab at the headset as the screen flickers and goes black. I pull upwards but nothing happens. Sarah has strapped me in tight. I say, "Something's wrong. Can you get me out of this?"

"Sure, just give me one second, the game has crashed. There's some kind of CPU spike on the servers. I just need to isolate the issue before it wipes our whole partition. Carlos, can you get him out."

I feel another pair of hands fumbling with the headset. "How is this stuck on so tight? I didn't have a problem getting it off, it must be caught on something."

My whole head is aching now and I resort to a very graceful dance that I am sure looks even more ridiculous than it feels. I've almost got the helmet off when a surge of power hits and buckles me at the knees. As I fall to the ground I hear screaming and realize that it's coming out of my mouth. That's when everything goes dark for real.

***

I open my eyes slowly and am surprised to see Sarah staring down at me, her face a picture of concern. The lights shine behind her, she looks like an angel. The only thing missing is the halo.

I try sitting up and the whole room spins. I rub my temples, which only marginally helps. "What happened?"

"You died!"

"I know that, the screen went black. I mean what happened in the real world?"

"You died! For real." Her expression suggests she's deadly serious.

"I'm sorry, what?" I look around and see Sarah clutching a small white box that has wires coming out of it. I follow them to my chest and am surprised to see my shirt is undone and someone has shaved patches of my chest hair.

Carlos runs into the room. "The ambulance is on the way!" He skids to a halt when he sees me. "Holy shit, you're alive!"

I feel my pulse race. They aren't joking. I was dead. Like, dead, dead. There was no heaven, no angels, no pearly gates, not even a hot-tub full of sulphur. There was just nothing. I didn't even know I was dead, until I wasn't. What the hell. Just when I thought this day couldn't get any worse.

Professor Jasper bursts into the room. "Is everyone ok in here? I heard screaming."

Sarah starts to cry and tries to explain between sobs. "Marcus was in the game when the CPU utilization went off the charts. There was some kind of power surge down the cables and he got electrocuted."

Professor Jasper shakes his head. "Actually my dear he got shocked, the term electrocuted only applies when someone dies from the electricity. It's a common misunderstanding."

She waves the defibrillator at him. "I know what electrocuted means."

He stares at me bewildered. "Holy shit!"

I get to my feet, my knees still wobbling. "Yeah, that's putting it lightly." I rub my eyes. My peripherals are still blurry, there are white spots creeping around the edge of my vision and no amount of eye rubbing is making them go away. It's like there is something there that is trying to come into focus.

A paramedic comes running into the room. She takes one look at me and says, "Holy shit! Sorry, I mean, please sit back down sir." She pulls a variety of instruments out of her bag and starts prodding and poking me. When she is satisfied that I am in-fact still alive she ushers in her partner with a stretcher. She shines a light in my eye and says, "There are no signs of permanent damage, but we'll have to run more tests at the hospital. You'll need to spend the night so we can keep an eye on you. Is there someone you'd like us to call?"

Oh god. Mum is going to lose her mind over this. It's taken me my entire life to get her comfortable with the idea that I can leave the house unaccompanied. What's she going to be like when she finds out that I died tonight? It's going to be *years* before she lets me leave the house again. Carlos already has his phone out to dial her, but I say, "Wait! Don't call her. She'll only panic and come running to the hospital. I'll tell her tomorrow, when I have had a chance to compose myself."

Carlos taps away on his phone and nods. "Ok done. I've told her you're drunk and are crashing at my place."

"You couldn't have told her I picked up?"

Carlos smiles. "I wanted to make it believable."

"Sarah, can I borrow that defibrillator for a second..."

The paramedics share a look and plonk me onto the stretcher. The second I lay down I feel tired. I mutter something about getting some rest, and then the room fades out of view again.

LEVEL 4: RESPAWN

The smell is the first thing I notice when I wake up. It smells clean, like a vat of hand sanitizer. There's also a rhythmic beeping in the background, and the sound of muffled conversations.

It takes me a moment to remember where I am. I sit up to find Carlos asleep in a chair beside me. His snoring is making my headache worse. I hit him with my pillow until he reluctantly opens his eyes. "Morning. What time is it?"

I look around until I find a clock. "It's 8:30am."

As I say the time my heart races. I'm late for work! Is dying a valid reason for a day off? I can't help but feel that Jenkins may not think so.

I continue looking around the room. Something still isn't right. My vision is off. There's all sorts of junk floating around in my eyes. It must be a side effect of the electric shock. I'm about to mention it to Carlos when a doctor walks in. She doesn't look much older than me. She smiles warmly and picks up the chart at the end of my bed. "Good morning Marcus. How did you sleep?"

"Well thanks. I feel much better."

"The good news is that all your test results came back and there is no sign of any lasting damage. You're a very lucky young man. Any aches, pains, other noticeable side effects?"

I blink a few times. "Actually, my eyes still don't seem quite right."

She pulls out a tiny flashlight and ambles up beside me. She holds open my eyes and shines the light in them, making me flinch. After a few seconds she says, "no signs of any burst blood vessels or anything else to worry about. If it doesn't improve in a couple of days you should book an appointment with an optometrist."

"Ok, I will do that. Am I free to go?"

"You are, but take it easy. You had a major shock last night. It's not unusual for new side effects to develop as time goes by. If you start feeling dizzy or getting chest pains you need to call 999 or come back here immediately, is that clear?"

I nod and the cute doctor leaves the room. Carlos says, "You really gave us a fright last night. I'm glad to hear that everything is ok. Sarah was very concerned for your well-being." His eyebrows waggle.

"She felt responsible. She was probably worried about the PR nightmare. Imagine if one of the beta testers was killed while playing the game."

Carlos' eyes light up. "That would be awesome! Imagine how many people would line up to buy it if you had a news segment about how the game is so realistic that someone died while playing it. You'd have a license to print money."

"Only you could find a way to turn my tragic death into a marketing opportunity."

Carlos pops an imaginary collar. "What can I say, it's a gift."

"Shouldn't you be at work?"

He laughs. "There's no-one on my team around at this time in the morning. You think Jenkins is missing you yet?"

I find my phone on the bedside table and try to turn it on, but it is dead.

Carlos says, "Yeah I tried to get that working for you, I think the zap killed it, or the battery might just be dead."

"I need to go to work."

"To work? Are you out of your mind? You *died* last night. Jenkins will manage without you for one whole day."

"I feel fine. There are some things he is expecting me to wrap up today. It's important."

"You know you really should go home first. You don't exactly look top-notch at the moment."

"I don't have time for that, I just have to finish up some slides and then I'll take the rest of the day off."

Carlos shakes his head. "Honestly, I worry about you. Grab your stuff, I will call a taxi."

"No! Every time you call we end up with the crazy taxi driver that is always talking about killing his ex-wife."

Carlos puts his phone down. "Already requested. Taxi is on the way. I'm sure it will be a different guy this time."

***

"And then I would move the body in the dead of night to this pig farm which is just down the road. Everyone knows you can't go to jail if they can't find the body."

"Fascinating, you have clearly given this a lot of thought. It's the next left after the lights." I give Carlos a look and he just laughs.

We fight to be the first out of the taxi. Carlos chucks him a tenner and says, "keep the change."

As he wheelspins away from the curb I say, "why do you insist on always tipping him?"

"Is he the kind of guy you want upset at us?"

"Point taken."

We walk into the entrance of Master Systems and I see Cindy walking into the lift clutching two coffees. I chase after her, shouting for her to hold the lift, but she must not hear me as the doors slam shut just as I reach it.

"I suppose I should go show my face. Let me know how it goes with Jenkins." With that Carlos wanders off towards the sales department. He looks just as scruffy as I feel, but the difference is, he can pull it off.

The lift takes forever, but eventually it comes back and I take it up to the twelfth floor. A couple of my fellow passengers give my outfit the once-over, which makes me self-conscious enough to at least tuck my shirt in. I'm not sure much else can be done to improve matters other than a full-body hazmat suit.

I'm barely out the lift when the applause starts. My colleagues apparently feel it is appropriate to highlight my tardiness, despite the fact that Jim isn't here yet and won't be for at least another hour.

Brad pats me on the back. "That must have been one hell of a party. Sorry to miss it. Jenkins is looking for you and heads up, he's pissed."

Oh great. I rush over to Cindy's desk. "Please tell me you got those slides finished."

"Slides? What slides?" She smiles, but it is not an innocent smile, it is the look of a snake that just injected you with poison and is waiting for it to take effect.

I refuse to believe what is quite clearly happening. Perhaps it is a simple misunderstanding. "The quarterly review slides for the board meeting. You said yesterday they were almost done."

"I have no idea what you're talking about. Why would I do those slides, Jenkins asked you to do them." She speaks loud enough for several other people to hear.

Yep, there it is, the paralysis is kicking in. Time to get out of here before she coils herself around me and squeezes until a promotion pops out.

Panic sets in. I'm good in a crisis, but this is way beyond that. Jenkins was expecting those slides an hour ago, and I haven't even started them yet. This is going to require some kind of miracle.

Jenkins bursts from his office like a whale breaching the surface. He takes one look at me and says, "My office. Now."

This is not going to go well. I quietly slink into the room and take a seat while Jenkins slams the door and says, "I am not impressed. I told you how important it was to send me those slides first thing this morning, and an hour later you come strolling in looking like you're fresh from the nightclub. Cindy informs me you were out drinking last night. Do you consider this acceptable behaviour?"

I manage to blurt out, "I was in an accident last night, they had to resuscitate me at the scene. I came here from the hospital."

I thought that might slow him down, but no such luck. "A likely story. If you died last night, why are you here?"

I really want to answer that, but honestly I don't know. Why am I here? Why was my first thought upon waking this morning that I was late for work? You would think dying would give me some life-altering perspective, but I'm still the same downtrodden peon I was yesterday.

Jenkins keeps talking. "I thought so. Consider yourself lucky that I need those slides from you. Send them through to me, then you will go home and get changed. I expect you to make up the hours you have missed this morning over the weekend. Is that clear?"

"I can't." Before I can explain his face flushes and his voice drops. "If those slides aren't in my inbox in the next 10 minutes I will be sure to tell the board of directors who is responsible. Then I'll have a chat with my friends in HR. Good luck getting another job when you're fired with cause."

There it is, that familiar fear. That the last 3 years of torture will be for nothing, that I'll be tossed aside and have to start over. I can't let that happen. This has to mean something, it has to go somewhere.

There's just one small problem. I can't send him slides I don't have and I am certainly not ready to go home and face my mother. There is no point in saying anything else, I may as well just sit out the clock and wait for the inevitable. I quietly slink out of Jenkins' office and plonk myself back at my desk.

I guess I should start job hunting. Perhaps this is it. Rock bottom.

It's only uphill from here. I nudge my computer awake and a new popup fills the entire screen. It looks almost 3D.

Choose role

Oh no, not another systems update. The last time the IT guys rolled out something like this it took my computer down for the better part of a day. I don't have time for this. I scroll through the list looking for Business Analyst. There are a lot of joke entries, including archer and barbarian. The IT guys don't get out much. Someone is for sure getting fired for this.

Eventually I find BA. It tells me my role specializes in pivot tables, pie charts and data analysis. Thanks for pointing out how utterly pointless my job is. I should have picked middle management, then I could have specialized in a constant stream of pointless bull-shit and unrealistic deadlines.

The update completes and I am left staring at the spreadsheet that Jenkins sent me yesterday. It taunts me with its unstructured data, pivot tables inside pivot tables and an SQL query that would put some novels to shame. This is it, the spreadsheet that killed my career.

I'm about to close the file when a new prompt appears on my screen. It says *Use data analysis?*

That's odd, I have never seen that option before. It must be part of the new update. I click yes out of curiosity. The numbers all rearrange themselves instantly into clearly marked and labelled tables. It even generates appropriate graphs. I now know exactly what I am looking at. I have no idea how it even did that, the data made absolutely no sense, and yet here it is laid out clear as day. I take back everything I said, I am buying the IT guys a beer next time I see them.

There is suddenly a lifeline, a chance to save my job. The question is, do I want to? I think I do. I'm not going to let Cindy win and I'm not going to give Jenkins the satisfaction. I'll leave here when I am good and ready.

I feel something I haven't felt in a long time. The urge to fight back.

I copy the graphs over to the slides and in six minutes the quarterly review deck is good to go. I email it to Jenkins, feeling proudly defiant. I get a curt "I need twelve copies." as a response. He just can't let me have my moment.

The red paper jam light blinks back at me. I don't know why I was expecting today to be any different. If the printer could smirk, it would. We do our dance, the trays sliding in and out from memory, following a process I have done a thousand times. A single sheet of paper comes out and it jams again. As usual I give it a good slap, only this time the printer slides across the room and crashes into the wall, leaving a sizeable dent. I stare at the damage and immediately leg it before anyone sees me. What the hell was that?

I send the print job to the sales office, which is the only office in the whole building that seems to own a consistently working printer. Annoyingly I don't have access to that office, so I have to ping Carlos to bring them up. He appears a few minutes later with a bemused grin on his face.

I grab the slides from him. "You're a lifesaver."

"I feel more like a paperboy. Did Jenkins forgive you for being slightly tardy and your less than stellar appearance?"

"Actually he's sending me home to change just as soon as I give him these printouts."

Carlos beams. "Excellent! I'll call a taxi. We can pick my car up on the way."

"Wait, don't you have to work?"

"What? No, my boss already saw me so he knows I am working today. Job done. Let's go."

"Can you at least call a different taxi company?"

"Of course. I'll meet you in the lobby."

I pop the printouts on Jenkins desk. He doesn't even look up, he just says, "go home and change."

I walk towards the exit and Cindy says, "leaving so soon?" She's really enjoying this.

"Yeah, Jenkins said the slides were so good I must have been up working on them all night. He gave me the rest of the day off. Don't work too hard." I stroll into the lift with as much swagger as I can muster.

***

"And then I would rent a wood chipper and invite her over to get the last of her stuff. She's got a bad knee, so it would only take a nudge for her to have a nasty fall. Hey presto, Bob's your uncle, no more alimony. No-one would suspect a thing."

Except any person that has ever been in this taxi. If I smile any harder my cheeks might seize up.

We ask the crazy cabbie to drop us off around the corner. Carlos waits until he is sure he has left. "I swear I called a different place! Can a taxi driver work for more than one company?"

"I suspect not, but who is going to tell him that? Let's just get your car and pretend we didn't hear any of that."

As we round the building Carlos lets out a gasp. I'm not sure what exactly I was expecting, but it certainly wasn't the empty shell of Carlos' car. There's barely anything left, no radio, no seats, no steering wheel, no wheels, no car doors. Who on earth steals car doors? Surely it would be more efficient to just steal the rest of the car at that point.

Carlos is still staring at the carcass of his pride and joy when a couple of local youths approach us. One of them says, "Oy, is that your car?"

He nods and the kid laughs. "What kind of idiot leaves a BMW parked here overnight?"

He's still laughing while his mate gives Carlos and I the once-over and pulls a small blade out of his pocket. He snarls. "If you're driving a car like that you must be minted. Hand over your wallets."

"You've got to be kidding!" Carlos looks like he might thump the guy. I quickly step between them. "I'm sorry, we've had a bit of a rough night. Now's not really a good time for a mugging. Can you come back later?"

He waves the knife at me. "You want to die?"

"Actually I already died today, so how's about you and your mate piss off and leave us alone." I don't even know why I said that. It's been a long day and it isn't even noon.

His friend tries to convince him to leave, but our mugger is having none of it. He flips the knife from hand to hand and says to his mate, "keep an eye out for the coppers. I'm going to teach these city boys a lesson."

He takes a step towards me and something flashes up in the centre of my view. I barely have time to read it when he lunges. *Disarm?* My whole body moves in one fluid motion. I circle out of the way of his attack and kick the knife out of his hand with a snap. It arches in the air and lands in my other hand, which is behind my back. I slowly hold the knife out in front of me and they both turn and leg it.

A new message flashes up on my eyes:

+10 EXP

Am I having some kind of episode? Is it normal that I am seeing things? The doc did say I may feel the after effects for a while, but surely this isn't normal?

Carlos says what I am thinking. "What the hell just happened?"

"I have no idea. I acted on instinct."

"Instinct? Are you secretly a ninja?"

"You've known me most of my life and you spend almost every evening at my house, when do you think I'm squeezing in ninja school?"

He shrugs. "You went away to university for a few years. Maybe you went to train with the monks in the mountains?"

"The only way I was like a monk at uni was my celibacy. Now please stop talking. I've got a headache."

I close my eyes as the pain builds. It feels like my head is going to split open. Even with my eyes shut, the blurriness around the edges of my vision is starting to come into focus. I gasp as I realize what it is. I have a health bar and a variety of other icons. I frantically rub my eyes and shake my head, but they refuse to go away. When I open my eyes, I find them overlaid over the real world.

Carlos says, "Are you ok? You're acting strange, even for you."

There's something familiar about the HUD. I have seen it somewhere before.

It's from Sarah's game.

My heart starts to race and I take a few deep breaths before I can get any words out. "We need to go see Sarah. Right now."

"Actually I think I'm going to stay here and call the police to report the utter decimation of my beloved beemer." This is the closest I have ever seen him to crying. He picks up his number plate and cradles it like a newborn.

"Sad as this is, I need your help. I think something is wrong with me. I mean like seriously wrong. I might not make it as far as Sarah's, but I really need to talk to her. Your car can wait, it's not going anywhere."

He stares at the wreckage and lets out a sigh as he tosses the number plate onto the roof. "Ok fine. Come on."

LEVEL 5: LEVEL UP

We are barely in the door of the university when the receptionist says, "No begging in the lobby. Don't make me call security."

I guess we do look at little worse for wear at the moment. I definitely don't want any burly security guards to try to escort me from the building. I don't know how it would go and I'm in no rush to find out. I give the receptionist my best smile and say, "We're here to visit Sarah Aran. We are old friends of hers."

"I'm afraid Miss Aran isn't accepting visitors today. There was an incident last night and she has had to clear her schedule."

Carlos steps forward and prepares to turn on the charm. It would probably work a lot better if he'd showered recently. I'm fairly confident there isn't a panic button under the receptionist's desk, but if there is she'd be hammering it right about now.

I grab Carlos by the arm and say, "Please let Sarah know that Marcus popped by to see her. Tell her it's urgent." With that I drag him out of the building.

As we round the corner he says, "What was that? I thought you desperately needed to speak to Sarah, and then at the first sign of trouble you immediately give up."

I'm not listening. I'm staring at the ground. There are a couple of sticks that look different to all the rest. There is the faintest glow around them. I pick them both up and head over to the side entrance. I rub the sticks together and just like that they become the perfect lock-picking set. I have no idea how to pick locks, but it feels like I should. I randomly jam both sticks into the lock and wiggle them about. Carlos watches me and says, "What on earth are you doing?"

"I'm picking this lock."

"Using twigs you found on the ground? Are you sure you're ok? Perhaps you should have a lie down."

"The direct route didn't work. I want to avoid a fight. I figured there would be a stealth route."

I jump as a small green bar appears, with an arrow that bounces back and forth inside it. Oh bugger, it's a quick time event. I'm not exactly feeling speedy in my current state, but after a couple of attempts I get it figured out and the door opens with an audible click. Carlos is as shocked as I am. Before anyone sees us, we sneak inside and find ourselves back in the corridor that I died in last night. There's no sign of Sarah.

As we huddle in the corner Carlos says, "Mate, you've got to tell me what is going on. In the last hour you've disarmed a knife-wielding maniac and followed it up with a spot of breaking and entering. I know it's your birthday, but you're a bit young for a midlife crisis."

I'm about to tell him everything when a lab tech turns the corner and spots us. He starts hollering and in seconds there is security everywhere. We are totally surrounded. I can feel a deep urge to challenge them to hand-to-hand combat, which makes absolutely zero sense. Before I engage in mortal combat Sarah appears, looking like she hasn't slept a wink. "What are you both doing here?"

"I need to talk to you."

"Right now?"

"It's urgent. It's about last night."

She stares at the group of people around her and says, "It's ok, I know these guys. I asked them to pop by, they must have just gotten lost. I'll take it from here."

The security guards begrudgingly disperse, clearly disappointed that they didn't have a chance to practice their particular brand of justice. Sarah ushers Carlos and I into a side room and locks the door behind her. She does her best to keep her voice low as she says, "Are you out of your minds? This is a high security computer lab. The equipment in this room alone is worth millions of pounds, and you're breaking in? Are you trying to go to jail?"

"Something happened to me last night."

"I know Marcus. Our lawyers are already drawing up a settlement, just hold tight for a few days. If they hear that you've been snooping around here you might panic them into trying to drag this through court. Nobody wants that."

"A settlement? That's not what I am here for. Something is wrong with me."

She looks at me, eyebrows raised. "I'd say you're in pretty good shape considering you were dead a few hours ago."

"I'm seeing things. Video game things."

They both stare at me like I'm a crazy person. Carlos says, "I think we might need to get you back to the hospital..."

"It feels like I am still in the game and none of this is real."

Carlos laughs, but Sarah stares at me with fear across her face. She says, "What do you mean this doesn't feel real?"

"I'm seeing a HUD, with a life bar and other icons. A guy tried to mug us this morning and a prompt flashed up for me to disarm him. I broke into your lab using two sticks I found on the ground and a quick time event. It's like this whole thing is one big game."

"I'll be right back. Do not leave." Sarah bolts from the room.

Carlos is staring at me. I'm expecting more words of concern for my health, but instead he says, "So if you're stuck in a video game, does that make me an NPC?"

"I have no idea what any of it means."

"Can you learn new skills and gain experience just like an RPG?"

"I don't know. It seems that way."

His whole face lights up. "That sounds awesome! What skill shall we level up first? You've already started getting to grips with lock-picking, but that's not exactly a great everyday skill. We should try something less traditional. Maybe this is finally your chance to learn how to flirt with women! We can get you levelled up, if you know what I mean." Oh god, now he's winking at me. This couldn't possibly get any more humiliating. No wait, he's still going.

"All the way to level 69 baby! You can show them how big your skill tree is..."

I was wrong.

Sarah comes back with a guest. Professor Jasper is staring at me with a mix of fear and curiosity. He walks towards me slowly, reaches out his index finger and pokes me in the abdomen. I say, "Ow!"

He says, "Interesting, you can still feel things. That's a good sign, or possibly not. Sarah mentioned you were having some hallucinations about reality. Can you describe them for me?"

His eyes are locked onto mine, watching intently. I explain the same things I already told Sarah and Carlos.

When I am done he says, "Fascinating." He turns to Sarah. "When exactly did the accident occur? Please be precise. Was it when I heard the screaming, or before that?"

Sarah moves to a screen on the wall and taps a few icons. After a moment she says, "The game froze just after midnight and the power surge happened a few moments later."

Jasper grins. "Do you know what this means? My experiment was a success! I have proven without doubt that none of this is real."

Carlos pokes me in the arm. "Feels pretty real to me."

"Of course it does, we believe what we are programmed to believe. You are simply responding to stimuli. Are you familiar with the theory that the world is in fact one giant simulation? That we are merely computer programs running on a future civilization's ancestor simulator?"

I glance at Sarah. "Yeah, it may have come up in conversation. Sounds a little woo woo to me."

Jasper glares at me, horrified. "I assure you it is quite the opposite of woo woo! It is based firmly in both science and statistics. We can hypothesize that advanced civilizations would want to study their ancestors, perhaps to understand decisions we made or even just for their entertainment. Assuming that computers continue to improve on the same linear progression it is highly feasible that the computer power required to do this will exist in the near future. Because a future civilization could theoretically run thousands or millions of these simulations, simulated lives would number in the trillions. Therefore it is far more statistically likely that we are in fact denizens of a simulation, rather than actual flesh and blood organisms in the one true universe. If we were virtual beings that simulated the real thing, we would think, act and behave as if we were the real deal. From our point of view it makes no difference if we are real or virtual, because the virtual world would *be* our reality. With me so far?"

My headache is coming back. Carlos says exactly what I am thinking. "What does any of this have to do with Marcus seeing video game stuff?"

"My experiment was attempting to *prove* that we are in fact living in a simulation by triggering a chronal incident. If our reality is running on a computer, it is theoretically possible to influence that computer's performance and see a degradation in reality. I did that by putting a strain on the simulation, using the university's supercomputer to process impossible math equations. I then monitored time to see if reality slowed down. At just past midnight I detected a blip in time, but before I could quantify it the simulation shut me down by frying the supercomputer. The one that you were attached to. In that exact moment, when the simulation was at its most vulnerable, you died."

Sarah is the first one to speak. "You broke reality, and reality fought back, and somehow Marcus got caught in the crossfire?"

"Precisely. He was in a game within the simulation when it broke. I suspect the system tried to restore him to that same state when he was revived, not understanding that he was no longer in the game. The rest of the world lost a few seconds of reality, but for Marcus those few seconds contained a crucial transition. Computer programs are not infallible, bugs and glitches happen all the time."

"Let's say I believe you, and this is all just one big glitch in reality. How exactly do I make it stop?" I ask.

"How do you make any game stop?"

Carlos says, "You win, or you die."

"Precisely. There is no reason to suspect that the rules will be any different. However, there may be some complications. The simulation is trying to reconcile two different sets of rules. There is no way to know how it will do so. It could choose rules at random, it could slowly blend the virtual rules with reality, or anything in between."

There's really only one question I need to know the answer to right now. "So if I die, do I die for good, or do I restart?"

"No way to know I'm afraid. You could die and find out?" This is said so matter of factly I'm not sure if he is joking.

"Ok, so that's out. I've already hit my death quota for this week. How do I win?"

"There should be a quest list. It usually just lists the open quest items. The end goal in the game is to beat the end boss, but there are a lot of optional quests along the way. Can you get into any menus?" asks Sarah.

I try. It is a very strange sensation. The menus overlay onto my vision. Selection is handled simply by thinking about the option I want. It takes some getting used to, but slowly I figure out how to navigate.

Several of the menus are nonsensical, but a couple prove interesting. One opens my inventory and shows a phone, a wallet, two sticks and a pack of cards. It is laid out in a grid, with each item taking up a single space.

The next menu to catch my eye is simply titled Stats. I open it and gasp. There are pages and pages of stats here, for my entire life. I scan through the list and a few choice entries jump out at me:

- *Hours spent asleep: 75,324*

- *Number of women slept with: 1*

- *Number of missed opportunities for sex: 13,456*

- *Number of times sexual frustration was self-resolved: 8,923*

Yeah, I'm going to stop reading those now.

I keep searching until I find what I am looking for. Quests.

I excitedly proclaim, "I've found a quest list!"

Current quests:

- *Conquer your fears (0 of 4)*

- *Complete a legendary armour set*

- *Defeat the Dark Lord*

- *Earn the love of a fair maiden*

The last one really makes me panic. Fighting monsters and flinging fireballs is one thing, but who said anything about love? Could this get any worse?

That's when I see the timer. It says *40 hours 43 minutes.* As I watch the minute counter ticks down to 42. I say, "Sarah, does your game have a time limit?"

"Oh, yeah. The build I was working on was for VR arcades, there was a hard time limit. We had it set for a couple of days in our version though."

"What happens when the timer reaches zero?"

"The game shuts down and you lose all your progress."

Bollocks.

LEVEL 6: SMALL THEFT AUTO

Professor Jasper wanders off to run more tests. He seems positively thrilled at the thought that the entire universe is completely made up. As soon as he leaves I say, "So he is clearly insane."

Carlos says, "Well one of you is. You are the one seeing a video game HUD. Either this is all real and you've gone bananas, or what he said is true."

"Why are you so quick to believe him? If he is right then none of this means anything."

"Not at all. Maybe all the real humans died thousands of years ago, and we are all that is left of them. Or maybe there are millions of Carloses out there, leading virtual lives, some rich, some poor, some famous, some happy, some dead."

"Now that is a terrifying thought. So what is the point of it all?"

"What was the point of it all before?"

In a perverse way he's right. Does it really change anything? The world is no less real today than it was yesterday. Well, apart from being trapped in a video game.

That needs to be my focus. I can't live the rest of my life like this. If I am going to have any chance of winning the game in the required timeframe I need to understand what it is exactly that I am up against.

I need a plan.

"Sarah, do you have the rules for your game written down somewhere? In a design document perhaps?"

Her laughter echoes around the office. When she stops she says, "Sorry about that. We are an indie studio, documentation isn't really our strong suit. I'm pretty familiar with the game though, what do you need to know?"

I have so many questions, but I need to establish the basics. "How do I level up? What are the criteria for gaining EXP?"

Sarah thinks for a moment before answering. "We use a graded EXP system. You only need a couple of hundred EXP for the first ten levels or so, but after that it starts to ramp up. Most standard tasks will give you EXP, defeating enemies, visiting new areas for the first time, trying out new equipment. The biggest source of EXP comes from completing quests. Every level grants a skill point, which can be used to improve stats on a skill tree. The first point in a skill tree grants a special ability, and then after that every 5 points will get you a new skill."

"Ok, sounds like pretty standard stuff. I need to get my level up so I am less vulnerable. Let's find some low-level mobs so I can farm some easy EXP and get a few upgrades under my belt."

It's not the most sophisticated plan, but it is a start. Doing something has got to be better than sitting around contemplating the fact that the universe isn't real and we are all just 1s and 0s. I feel like that should bug me more, but like Jasper said, it really doesn't make all that much difference. The world is no less real today than it was yesterday, even if I now have HP to worry about.

We haven't even made it out the front door when a gentleman stops me. "Young man, I need your assistance. Can you please fetch me a latte. I had one too many beers last night and would prefer to avoid driving."

I'm about to tell him to take a hike when a new notification appears, making me jump. I glance at it.

New side quest - See you latte.

You've got to be kidding me. I thought I would be slaying dragons and vanquishing demons. Instead I'm going to conquer this guy's hangover.

Carlos says, "Oy mate, bugger off, we are in the middle of something here. Go get your own damn latte or find some clueless intern to do your bidding."

The man turns to walk away and I shout after him, "Hold on. I'll get you a coffee. What kind would you like?"

He turns back to face me but his expression remains neutral. "I only drink lattes from a small artisanal coffee shop on the other side of town called Grinds of Yore. I shall wait for you here."

Oh right, because the point of a fetch quest is to force you to trek all over the place. An arrow appears on my HUD, pointing the way.

I start to walk and Carlos and Sarah chase after me. Carlos says, "What are you playing at? We are supposed to be getting you some EXP. Now's not the time to be fetching coffee for some random dude..." He stops talking and smiles, "This is a side quest isn't it!"

"It sure is. Sarah, can I have more than one active side quest at a time?"

She nods and I continue. "We should see if there are any more, I don't want to be hiking back and forth all over town."

"Are these worth decent EXP?"

"Yes, but we had a declining EXP reward for subsequent side quests, so each one will reward you with less EXP. We didn't want people to ignore the main quest and get massively OP. Let's find a few more to round us out."

Fine by me, I don't want to spend the day being a glorified errand boy.

I step out of the building and see them everywhere. People just milling around, with little blue dots above their heads. After a deep sigh I set off to chat to all of them, and before long there is a long list of side quests for me to fulfill, each more mundane than the last.

There's only one small problem. "Can we take your car Sarah? Carlos is having some mechanical issues with his..."

She shakes her head. "I don't have a car. I ride my bike to work."

"I'm guessing it's not big enough for the three of us."

"It would be a little cozy." She thinks for a moment. "Perhaps we could borrow someone else's car?"

Carlos' face lights up and he says, "How do you get around in the game? Is there fast travel?"

"We hadn't implemented fast travel yet. The only thing we had to help speed up going from one area to the other was horses. We had some more legendary mounts too, but you had to capture those."

"And how did one go about acquiring a horse? Did you have to buy it, or tame it, or could you steal one from someone else?"

Sarah picks up where Carlos is going. "You could steal them from outside the taverns. As long as a royal guard didn't witness you stealing it wouldn't register as a crime."

He turns to me. "Excellent. We are going car shopping."

Carlos leads us to the university pub. They look in much better shape than Carlos' car, in so far as they still have wheels. Carlos heads straight to the flashiest red sports car, a big grin on his face. He gestures to it and says, "Sir, your steed awaits."

I stare at him blankly until he says, "No time to waste, get out your magic sticks and get this door open."

"I can't steal someone's car!"

He turns to me. "Sure you can. You heard Sarah, it doesn't count as a crime unless someone sees it. Chop chop."

"Can't we just get in a taxi?"

Carlos slaps me hard in the face and I see my health bar lose a sliver. He says, "You need to think like a video game. Normal rules don't apply right now. You are the hero in this game, you can do whatever you like with impunity. Now let's hurry up, these random items aren't going to fetch themselves."

"But this isn't a horse. Who knows how the rules will apply."

Carlos chuckles and points at the front of the car. "Way ahead of you buddy."

I move around the front and groan. It's a Mustang. This is just crazy enough to work. I get out my two sticks and rub them against the lock until the bar appears again. It takes me a few tries, but then the door springs open with a satisfying click and I get a new message:

Lock-picking upgraded to level 2

I move on to the ignition, but this lock must be harder as the zone to land the arrow in is smaller and the arrow is moving quicker. This is going to require all my concentration.

I'm just getting the hang of it when someone shouts, "Oy! Get out of my car!"

Oh shit. I immediately jump out of the car, but Carlos shouts from the passenger seat, "You're the hero remember! You need this horse to complete your quest. What would you do if this was a game?"

The owner of the car is approaching fast and he's not smiling. He is also at least twice my size. He doesn't wait for an explanation, he punches me right in the face. It hurts like hell and takes a worrying chunk off my health bar. I can't take many more hits like that. I stagger backwards and try to regain my composure.

I've never been in a fight before, at least not one where I was intending to fight back. Normally my special move is to look pathetic until my opponent starts to feel bad about hitting me, but something tells me that's not going to work in this scenario. A new status has appeared above this guy's head. Apparently he's a level 10 brawler. His health bar is far longer than I would like it to be.

I remind myself that I am the hero and I punch the guy as hard as I can. At first it doesn't look like it is doing anything, but I try a few more times and see a small notch in his health bar. Each hit is taking off one point at a time, and he has 50 health. I shout back to Sarah, "What are the odds of a level 1 character beating a level 10?"

"Pretty slim. He only has to hit you a couple of times to kill you and it would take you all day to take him down. Your best strategy is evasion. If you can, try hitting him from behind, sometimes that triggers a stun animation."

I wait for him to try and punch me again and I combat roll out of the way. It feels ridiculous and I am waiting for him to run over and kick me like a football, but instead he stumbles and stands there, giving me a chance to hit him. I punch him in the back of the head, but nothing happens.

Several people walk past, but nobody pays any attention to the full-on street fight that is happening. I'm rolling more than a hippie in Amsterdam, but not a single person has stopped and got their phone out. My attacker keeps making the same lunge for me and I keep darting out of the way and jumping up to give him a quick punch in the back before he can turn around. After several hits he suddenly starts to wobble on the spot when I hit him and Sarah yells out, "Quick, he's stunned!"

I hop back into the car and start to wiggle the sticks. I shout out, "how long do I have?"

"Just a few seconds."

The bar bounces back and forth. In my peripheral vision I see the car's owner shake his head and turn on the spot, trying to find me. It is now or never. I stop the arrow dead centre and the car roars to life. I floor it and we lurch out of the parking lot. I shout out, "He's going to call the police."

"That's not how our NPCs behave. If you can get out of his line of sight he should forget all about it."

I stare in the rearview mirror and sure enough, as soon as he becomes a dot on the horizon he shrugs and casually strolls into the pub.

I catch sight of myself as I stare into the mirror. There is a large welt forming on my face and there is certainly going to be a black eye. Being a hero is hard work.

Carlos hollers, "Wow! That was a close one. Nice work on the stun. We need to get you trained up in combat pronto. How is your health bar?"

"Not great. Just over half left."

Carlos turns to Sarah. "How do you regain health in the game? Are there potions or healers, or is it handled via items?"

"Both actually. Food can be used to recover health but it won't remove status effects. You'd need to go to a base for that."

I notice a phone charger, so I fumble my phone out of my pocket and get Carlos to plug it in. After a few seconds it comes back to life, along with a lot of voicemail notifications. I'm going to guess that I really don't want to listen to any of those.

"STOP!" yells Carlos and I spank on the brakes. I turn and he points at the glowing sign declaring a drive thru is just around the corner. He says, "We need you at full health, we can't risk you being ambushed and getting killed before we've even gotten started."

I point at my face, "You think a cheeseburger is going to fix this?"

He shrugs. "It couldn't hurt."

We drive up to the window and I order a quick bite. Carlos orders some ridiculous combo meal.

"I didn't see you getting punched in the face!"

"Doesn't mean I can't be hungry."

Sarah refrains from ordering anything. She still seems on edge.

I take a big bite of my burger and hear a sound effect as my health bar refills a portion. I quickly polish off the rest and am back at full health. I take a peek in the mirror and am surprised to see my black eye has gone. I find myself wondering just how much I could heal this way, and then immediately hoping that I don't have to find out.

LEVEL 7: COMBAT TRAINING

I hand deliver the man his latte. He smiles and says, "Thanks! This is exactly what I was looking for. Here's your reward." He hands me a gold coin that looks like it would be worth a small fortune if it didn't immediately vanish in my hands. I get an update that 2 gold coins have been deposited into my account, plus a handful of EXP. Then he smiles and walks away.

Carlos says, "So we aren't going to talk about the fact that he just stood in the exact same spot for two hours waiting for you to return with his coffee? That guy is clearly either an NPC or the worst employee ever."

"Based on Jasper's theory we are all NPCs," says Sarah. "That reminds me, I should go check in with him, he's going to want an update on our progress today. What level did you say you are now Marcus?"

I do a quick check. "Level 4. Those last couple of side quests didn't even make a dent. It is definitely time to go do something else."

"Where have you been putting your skill points so far?"

"Actually I haven't yet. I've been saving them up. I want to get a better feel for the combat before I start putting points into skill trees. I don't know where I need the most help."

"That sounds like a very sensible approach." She turns to leave and then spins back. "I won't be long, can you both stay out of trouble?"

"Of course. We'll wait right here."

Sarah is barely around the corner when Carlos exclaims far too loudly, "You've still got a pretty huge crush on her huh."

I make a shushing motion. "What is the matter with you? She's only down the hall. That's not the kind of thing you just blurt out."

"You're about as subtle as a swift kick to the nuts. If she has eyes, she's noticed. Are you going to tell her how you feel?"

My mind goes back to my quest list. How on earth am I going to meet that final objective? I splutter out, "Hell no. I don't want to make it weird. She's just out of a serious relationship. I'm just going to work on our friendship."

"Congrats mate, you've maxed out your friend zone skill."

"Don't do that. You know how I feel about her."

Carlos is about to spout some sage wisdom, or more likely another helping of utter bollocks, when my phone rings. I glance at the screen and the icy chill of panic sets in. It's my Mum. In all the excitement this morning I have totally forgotten to call her. She is going to absolutely flip her lid. I put on my best sick voice and answer the phone, "Hey Mum."

"Hey sweetie. How goes the adventure?"

I've already got my passionate tale of a sudden virus locked and loaded, so it takes me a moment to say, "I'm sorry, what?"

"I just assumed you were out somewhere having an adventure with Carlos."

How does she know I'm not at work? That is such a Mum trick. "Yeah, we aren't working today, we have a few things to take care of."

Here it comes. Which variation of the lecture will it be, the one where I ruin my entire career or the one where I need to be more respectful of other people's time. Perhaps she will mix things up and go with a combo.

...any minute now.

At first I'm concerned that we have been disconnected, so I say, "Hello?" in that way that only people not expecting a response can say it. Mum replies, "I am glad to hear that things are going well. You should go check out the darker side of town, perhaps you'll find what you are looking for over there. Remember, I'm here if you need a place to rest and heal up." She sounds strained, like she is talking under duress. I want to ask more questions, but she hangs up on me.

Oh no, it's worse than I thought. Carlos sees the look on my face and says, "How much trouble are you in?"

"A lot. My Mum didn't tear a strip off me. Something is seriously wrong."

It takes him a moment to fully appreciate the implications of this. "Wait, she's now the hero's Mum. That means she's basically going to just ignore all the horribly dangerous stuff you're doing and spout nonsense and exposition."

"What does that mean? What has happened to my real Mum? We have to go check on her." I turn to leave.

"Hold up. She's in character. That's not going to stop while the game is still going on. The good news is, there's no reason for it to continue when the game is over. The best way for you to help your Mum is to win the game."

That makes a twisted kind of sense. Of all the things that have happened today, this is the one that hits home the hardest. Mum is a pain in my arse, but she is reliable and consistent in her admonishment. It is like she has been taken away from me, replaced with this artificial automaton. I could hear the fight in her voice though, my Mum is still in there somewhere, straining to get out. I'm not sure if that would be a good thing right now.

My phone rings again. Maybe Mum has broken free of her programming and is phoning back to tear me a new one. I answer it and hear the screech of an enraged Jenkins, "Where are you? It has been hours since you left to get changed. Are you planning on coming back?"

I put on my sick voice, the universal one used by every employee no matter what fictional ailment they are coming down with. "Sorry, I meant to call you, I've suddenly come down with something."

"This is unacceptable. I will be raising the matter with HR."

The line goes dead before I can say anything else. Carlos sees the look on my face. "Jenkins?"

"Yep. He's pretty pissed."

"Screw Jenkins."

"But..."

"But nothing, you are the hero of this game. Since when does the hero have to put saving the world on hold to pop into the office? Jenkins isn't going anywhere."

He's not wrong. Let HR do their thing. What's the worst that can happen?

I'm still contemplating that when we hear screaming outside. Carlos and I both share a look and we run out of the building to see a young woman surrounded by youths in hoodies. One of them is tugging at her purse as she desperately holds on to it. There is no-one else around. She spots us and screams, "Help me!"

I pause. They all have health bars above their heads. A quick scan informs me they are all level 4 ASBOs except the guy tugging at the bag, who is a level 6 Hooligan. He is going to be a problem for me, but I can't just leave a young woman to be mugged. Time to put my combat skills to the test.

I roll up my sleeves. Carlos places his hand on my shoulder. "Are you sure about this? There are five of them."

I smile. "Then it's a fair fight."

"What can I do to help?"

"Get me some food. I'm going to need it."

An open top bus pulls up out of nowhere with a full orchestra on the top deck. They frantically start playing a rousing number that gets my blood pumping.

I run over and smack the first guy in the face. It catches both of us by surprise. I have never hit anyone unprovoked before. He loses a chunk of health and staggers around as his friends all turn to face me. I've played enough games to know how to manage a mob. Don't leave anyone at half health, because an enemy with a sliver of health is just as dangerous as a healthy one. We trade punches, but I'm doing a lot more damage than he is and a couple of well-timed blocks on my part help to mitigate most of the harm. After a few hits he collapses, unconscious, just as his friend reaches me. I ignore the EXP notification, now is not the time for distractions.

The new guy swings at me and I combat roll out the way. As I am standing up another one reaches me, so I roll a few more times until I have created some space. To anyone watching, this must look absolutely ridiculous. I get enough distance from them that I should be able to dart in and out and chip away at them. I try flinging a few fireballs their way, but nothing happens.

I'm still staring at my left hand wondering if there is an on switch when I realize I have made a critical mistake. I turned my back on the mob leader. The first I learn of it is 50% of my health disappearing. I turn to see him flailing nunchucks around like a ninja. Mob management 101, never take your eye off the primary threat. He swings at me again, but this time I get the disarm prompt. I catch the nunchuck in mid-air and pull the leader towards me. He staggers and I spin and flip him over my shoulder. He lands with a thud and I am still holding the nunchucks.

What. The. Hell. I'm a badass.

A new prompt pops up.

New Weapon acquired. Nunchucks.

Oh yeah. I flip them effortlessly around. I have no idea how I am doing this, it is as if I have been training my entire life. Usually I'm barely coordinated enough to carry two drinks, let alone wield deadly weapons.

The muggers are unperturbed by my new-found mastery and charge me one at a time. It's much easier to manage them now that

I'm armed, the nunchucks do a lot more damage than my fists. It only takes a few hits to take down each guy, until only the leader remains. I don't know how hard he hits without his nunchucks, but I don't have the health to find out. I can't afford any mistakes.

He's smarter than his friends. He hangs back warily as I twirl the nunchucks around. We circle each other a couple of times, until my back is up against a bus shelter. Then without warning he lunges at me. My back is pinned against the wall, I can't dodge. I block the hit and roundhouse kick him into the bus shelter. It's the first time in my life my foot has been above my head. He slides down the wall with a squeak.

+ 50 EXP. Level 5: Angry Toddler

As abruptly as it began the orchestra music stops and the open top bus drives away. I guess the fight is over.

I pop the nunchucks in my pocket, they may come in handy later. Then I scoop up the handbag and return it to the young lady with a smile. "Excuse me, I think you dropped this."

She swoons. "My hero. How can I ever repay you?"

"Your smile is thanks enough."

Level up - Charisma level 2, Awkward teenager.

She plays with her hair. "Are you sure there is nothing else I can do for you?"

Carlos appears by my side, clutching an armful of snacks. He whistles through his teeth at the pile of unconscious teenagers. "I could only find Doritos and Mountain Dew, I hope that's ok."

The moment is lost and the young lady turns and walks away. A stat flashes up.

Number of missed opportunities for sex: 13,457

I turn to chase after her, but she has already vanished. I resist the new urge to punch Carlos. "Your timing is impeccable as always."

"So what did I miss?"

"I know Kung Fu!"

He deepens his voice, "Show me."

I throw a few punches. He doesn't look too impressed, so I try to show off with a roundhouse kick, but Carlos steps forwards at the last second. I kick him in the head. The pop and crisps fly everywhere as he falls to the ground. Carlos scrambles back to his feet, rubbing his temple. "Bloody hell, what are you playing at? I was just trying to do that cool scene from the movie. If you want to kick the crap out of someone I am sure we can find you more teenagers."

"Sorry, my bad. Obviously I'm still working out the kinks."

"Yeah, well so is my chiropractor after that little episode. I'll be sending you the bill."

I scoop up a packet of Doritos and set to work on getting my HP back to 100%.

I'm still busy stuffing crisps in my mouth when Sarah comes running over. "What happened here?"

"Combat training." I sprinkle her with crisps as I talk.

"I left you alone for five minutes! You can't just go around beating up kids."

"They started it!"

She gives me a glance that looks eerily like something my Mum would fire my way. She nudges the pile of groaning bodies. "It looks like you finished it. I assume you got some hands-on exposure to the combat system?"

"Kind of. One of them pulled a weapon on me, but I got it off him. As soon as I held it in my hands I knew what to do."

Sarah nods. "Yeah, the more you use a weapon, the more moves you will learn with it. Just be aware that weapons can suffer damage and will break with enough use. Also, I have no idea what will happen if you use a sword on a person in the real world. I suspect we don't want to find out."

"There's something else. I tried to use magic, but nothing happened."

"What level are you currently?"

I do some quick checks. "I levelled up from all the EXP I got schooling those thugs. I'm now level 5."

"Unless you are a magic class, magic doesn't unlock until you're at least level 10. We wanted to make sure players were comfortable with the weapons first before we let them start chucking around balls of fire."

"Do you think magic will work in the real world? Won't it break physics?" asks Carlos.

"Well if this is a simulation then physics are simply a set of programming rules, which we have already shown can be rewritten. There is an easy way to test though. Try jumping."

I instinctively stare at my feet. "I'm sorry, what?"

"Jump. As high as you can."

I crouch and launch myself into the air. To my surprise I leap several feet. I land in a heap to the sound of Carlos saying, "That was awesome!"

"It appears the simulation is favouring the physics of the game world for you, at least as far as certain actions are concerned," says Sarah.

I get back to my feet and dust myself off. "Ok, I'll have to keep that in mind. I wonder what other rules are temporarily re-written? For example, are we sure that I will die if I run out of health? Maybe I would respawn?"

"It's unlikely. The game is a rogue-like, when you die it is game over." She thinks for a moment and says, "Actually, that's not entirely true. One of the programmers snuck in an easter egg where if you complete special challenges you can earn an extra life."

"That sounds very useful right about now. What kind of challenges?"

"Mini games."

Carlos and I both groan. Mini games are the worst.

"Where are we going to find a bunch of annoying, impossible skill games?"

Carlos smiles, "I know just the place."

LEVEL 8: 1UP

As we climb out of the stolen Mustang I hesitate. "This feels like a waste of time. We should be focusing on the main quest."

"Do you want to be caught off guard by a mid-level boss and be dead forever? Cause if so we can carry on picking up coffees and tampons, or whatever random crap the next NPC wants."

He has a point. I see the looming, rickety Ferris wheel up ahead and my legs lock up. "I hate the fair."

Sarah gives me a look. "Who hates the fair?"

"Oh god, please not the story..." groans Carlos.

I ignore him. "I was only a little boy when my parents first brought me to the fair. We went on the bumper cars and ate candy floss, all the usual things. Then they tried to get me to go on the Ferris wheel. I'm scared of heights, so I wasn't thrilled at the idea, but they convinced me we would be up and down in no time at all. As the wind picked up and the clouds rolled in..."

Carlos interrupts. "They got stuck. They were up there for a long time. He wet his pants. Massive childhood trauma. The end."

I glare at him and he says, "Sorry mate, but we don't have time for your Shakespearean rendition."

"I was going to leave out the pant wetting part!"

"That's the best bit. Who cares, you were like five or something."

Twelve is almost five.

I don't want to go anywhere near this place, but Carlos is right, it is too big of a risk to be wandering around without any extra lives. I'm just going to have to man up and get over it.

I take a step towards the fair and walk right into an invisible wall. Carlos and Sarah both keep walking, I have to shout after them. "Guys. I can't come in."

"Seriously mate, get over it, everyone pisses themselves every now and again," says Carlos.

"No, I mean I physically can't go in there. Look!" I press my hands up against the invisible wall. That's what I notice the message:

You must be level 6 or higher to enter this area.

I relay the message to my companions and assume that is the end of it. Carlos has other ideas. He shouts across the road at two very large bikers who are quietly minding their own business. "Oy, you two. My mate here just told me both your wives were lousy in bed. He said he's sticking with your Mums from now on, because of all the experience they have. With dicks."

I glare at him and he shrugs. "You need the levels. Have fun!"

***

"That was not fun. You are a total arsehole." I'm holding a handful of teeth. I'm not sure how many of them are mine. Carlos hands me a Mountain Dew to help me heal up. Can teeth grow back?

"You seem to be getting the hang of the combat, but you shouldn't have let them punch you in the face so many times."

"Thank you sensei, I shall heed your words of wisdom passed down from the ancient times."

"Hey, at least you made it to level 6. Have you figured out what you're going to spend your skill points on?"

Actually I haven't. It is too hard to choose. There are so many cool-sounding skill trees with even cooler abilities. I take a quick look at the strength tree. Each new skill point adds 10% to my damage output, with the first special ability being a flaming uppercut. That sounds pretty epic!

On the other hand I really could use more life at the moment. My health bar is dangerously short and I'm still pretty rubbish at combat, as demonstrated by my fistful of molars. Each new level will give me 10% more health. The first ability doubles the effectiveness of food items. It is the sensible option, playing it safe.

I simply can't decide, so I do what comes naturally, I pick a bit of everything. A couple of points in health, a couple in strength, and I leave two spare, just in case. I don't get any cool abilities, but it should make me a better fighter. Slow and steady wins the race.

I try walking into the fair again, and this time there is no invisible wall. A part of me is disappointed, I was hoping for an excuse to go somewhere else. Anywhere else.

We head straight to the nearest game. It is knife throwing. The man running the stall looks like the kind of guy that you would cross the road to avoid. He smiles, revealing a gappy grin. "Roll up, roll up and show off your skills. It's easy to win. Simply get the knife to stay in the centre of the target, like this."

He whips a knife at the target and it sticks there with a satisfying thud. He makes it look easy, no doubt from a lifetime of practice. He picks up three knives and holds them towards me. "Only a quid, boy. Easy peasy, lemon squeezy."

Carlos throws a fiver at him. "Here you go, that should cover a few practice throws."

I take the knives and a new status immediately flashes up.

New Weapon acquired. Throwing Knives.

I can tell just by feeling them that they are weighted awfully. I balance one on my fingertip and can feel the centre of gravity is all the way at the back of the handle. These aren't designed with accuracy in mind. I'm going to have to compensate.

As soon as I stare at the target a reticle appears. It swerves around like a drunk uncle at a wedding. I try to ignore it and throw the knife by sight, but my arm is having none of it. A bar fills a blip and then the knife topples out of my hand onto the floor. The carnie grins even more. Apparently the bar is the strength of the throw.

I try again, concentrating hard to fill the power bar. The moment it reaches the top the knife flies out of my hand, but the reticule is nowhere near the target. The knife gets embedded in the abdomen of one of the prize teddies and the carnie scowls. "You're paying for that teddy boy!"

Ok, so it's all about timing. I flip the last knife in my hand absentmindedly and wait until the perfect moment as the reticule swings back towards the middle of the target. I power up my throw and release it right as it is over the centre. The knife flies out of my hand with enough force to embed into the target up to the hilt.

+ *10 EXP*

1 UP 20% complete

Not bad for a newbie. The guy looks less impressed. He tugs on the knife, trying to pull it out of the target. Eventually he gives up and grabs the bear that I eviscerated with my previous throw. He tosses it to me and says, "One prize per person per day."

He turns back around and tugs on the knife and I spot an opportunity. I reach over the counter and grab a handful of throwing knives, which I put in my pockets. There is no way they should fit, but they slip in without a fuss. I tentatively try walking. Success, I don't get stabbed in the thigh. Interesting. I check and I can see them on my inventory.

We hit up several more booths with similar results. Ring toss, basketball throw, even hook a duck has its own mini game. I'm almost there, but I still need one more to get my extra life.

We round the corner and there it is. The darn Ferris wheel. I don't want to go near it, but the last game is nestled in its shadow. The test your strength machine. For obvious reasons I have never used one of these before. I swallow my fear and walk towards it. Carlos pays and the guy hands me the hammer. He is a big bear of a man and he is straining to hold it out with two hands. He drops it into my hands, clearly expecting me to topple over.

New Weapon acquired. Battle Hammer.

There is almost no weight to it. I can easily brandish it with one hand. The guy stares at me wide eyed, enough that I have to feign struggling to hold it. I stare at the metal pad I am supposed to hit and a quick time event starts. I hate quick time events. My reactions just aren't what they used to be. I get the first two prompts, but I miss the third one and the hammer comes crashing down on the carnie's foot. He lets out a howl and hops on the spot, and then a life bar appears above his head.

Level 9 Carnie.

Uh oh. I shout, "Run!" Carlos and Sarah are smart enough to dart in the opposite direction to me. The Carnie reaches out to grab me and I combat roll out of the way, his bear hug narrowly missing me. I swing the hammer at him out of pure instinct, but he grabs it in mid-air and tugs it away from me.

Disarmed.

No fair! That's my trick. He hefts the hammer up over his head and I roll left as it turns the ground where I was just standing into a crater. I don't need to check the stats to know that one hit from that hammer is going to be enough to finish me off. Time for a tactical retreat.

I try to run through the nearby crowd, but people are getting in the way. They seem nonplussed about the large angry man chasing after me. If only I could get above them. That's when I remember my new jumping ability. I tense my legs and leap on top of the nearest booth.

Now we're talking! I hop from booth to booth with ease. I even throw in a flip for good measure. Mr. Hammer Time is having none of it though, he storms through the crowd, shoulder barging everyone out of the way. I'm having so much fun I don't notice that I've reached the last booth. I turn back and there he is, ready to swing. As he crashes the hammer into the flimsy wooden poles I leap to the only thing close enough, a swinging basket on the Ferris wheel. It hauls me up into the air as the booth collapses below.

The Carnie is not happy about my narrow escape. He grabs on to the next carriage. With some creaking and protesting from the ancient machinery his feet leave the ground. He is right behind me and we are going in a circle. I pull myself up on top of my carriage and wait. When we circle back around towards the ground I will jump down and get a head start on him. That's when the Ferris wheel grinds to a halt, leaving my carriage swinging precariously at the pinnacle. I make the terrible mistake of looking down and my knees wobble in response. I'm too busy trying not to throw up to read the message that flashes up.

Flying High - 1 of 4 Fears conquered. 25% complete.

+ 100 EXP

Level 7: Tenderfoot

I scan around, looking for a way out, but there isn't one. The carriage suddenly lurches to the left and I turn to find the Carnie pulling himself up. It's at this moment that I notice the wagon of hay on the ground. It looks a couple of inches deep, certainly not enough to break my fall. I don't know if there is fall damage in this game. I guess I'm about to find out. The Carnie looms over me, ready to shove me off the edge. I reach into my pocket and grab the first thing I can find. As I leap off the carriage I spin in the air and toss the throwing knife, catching him right in the shoulder. A sliver of his health disappears, but I wasn't looking for damage, I wanted the stagger. He wobbles, tries to regain his balance, and then topples backwards off the Ferris wheel and lands with a crunch on the Test Your Strength machine. The small metal ball flies up the tower and rings the bell at the top just as I land in the cart.

I should be dead, or at least have several broken bones, but instead I step out of the cart and brush some hay off my shoulder. A new notification appears.

1UP 100% complete. Extra life gained.

Sarah and Carlos come running over to check if I'm ok. I brush them away and rush around to see the body of the guy I just killed. I'm shocked to find him standing back at the Test Your Strength machine with a neutral expression. He makes eye contact with me and smiles. "Fancy proving your manliness?"

"No thanks. Are you feeling ok?"

He laughs. "I'm a little hungover. Is it that obvious?"

"No, no, not at all. You are the picture of good health. Have a nice day."

"You too. Come again soon."

Either he's not the sort to hold a grudge or he has returned to his default programming. I place my hands on my knees and breathe a deep sigh of relief as Carlos and Sarah appear by my side again. Carlos says, "Are you sure you're alright?"

"Yep, I'm good. Actually, I'm great. I got the extra life, so now I'm safe from any surprises. As a bonus I chipped away at one of the main quests. I'd call that a resounding success."

"Ok, so what's next?" asks Carlos.

"We need to get you more skill points. Abilities are the fastest way to improve your DPS in the early game. That means we are going to need more combat," replies Sarah.

"Perfect. I know just the place!" He beams.

I do not like the sound of this.

LEVEL 9: EINE SCHLÄGEREI ZWISCHEN BETRUNKENEN

Carlos hops back into the Mustang clutching a bag from the local sports store. I raise an eyebrow. "Dare I ask what you just bought?"

"It's a surprise."

"Is this the kind of surprise that might use up my only extra life?"

I was joking, but his sheepish smile suggests this may be closer to the truth than I would like.

Sarah revs the engine with a big smile on her face. "Ok, so where to next?"

"The Sozzled Hedgehog," exclaims Carlos.

"Never heard of it. Is it new?"

"Nope, it used to be The Hammered Badger, but Health and Safety shut it down when they found half a Labrador in the freezer, so they renamed it. The new name is far more fitting, what with it being full of drunken pricks."

I give Carlos a look. "You're kidding right! Nobody in their right mind would go near that place. It is full of football hooligans."

He waggles his eyebrows and I catch up. "No, not a chance. I am not starting a bar fight."

"You need levels, they need a scrap. It seems like a win-win to me. You've already fought muggers, bikers and a carnie today, surely you can handle a bunch of drunks."

"I was defending myself. It's very different from instigating a fight."

"You're still not getting it are you. This is just a game. These guys are another mob to be used for EXP gain and farming loot. When you play a game do you spend your time obsessing over the back-story of every low-level minion you fight? Or do you wade in there without a moment's hesitation."

"Based on that logic I should just beat up random people on the street."

"Now you're getting it! We don't have the luxury of time for you to deliver lattes all over town for diminishing returns. If you're going to boost your levels quickly you're going to have to engage in less than savoury activities. Those are always the ones that reward you the best."

"I'm afraid he's right. We were proud of our combat system and we stacked the rewards to encourage players to use it," says Sarah.

I want to argue more, but we pull in to the Sozzled Hedgehog car park. It is packed, considering it is two in the afternoon. I hop out of the car feeling apprehensive, but then Carlos reaches into the bag and pulls out an item that takes me to full on panic attack. I yell at him, "There is no way I am wearing that in there, they will tear me apart before I make it to the bar."

"That is kind of the point. Look on the bright side, at least they will instigate the fight. That way your scout's honour can stay intact."

He holds out the offending article and I reluctantly accept it. I get a status update.

New chest armour: German football shirt. +5 defence, +5 efficiency. Special ability - Provocation

"At least stay out here."

"And miss the action. No chance! How about you Sarah?"

"This doesn't look like the kind of place a young lady should be hanging around outside of by herself."

"So it's agreed, we are coming in. Let the games begin!"

I swear he's enjoying this.

Sarah and Carlos walk several feet behind me as I gingerly step into the bar. I'm expecting to be lynched immediately, but nobody is looking at me, they are glued to the projection screen at the front of the room. An England game is on the tv. That explains the full car park. A quick glance confirms they are playing Germany. Of course they are. I make a mental note to murder Carlos if I make it out of this bar alive.

There's a huge cheer and I clench my fists in anticipation. Someone shouts, "what a dynamite header! Treasure this moment lads, we are finally going to show these Germans who's boss."

I risk a glance at the screen. England just pulled ahead 2-1 with only five minutes left to play. If they can just hang on then everyone should stay in a good mood and I can sneak out of here quietly. I could try and bolt now, but I don't trust Carlos not to make a scene and force my hand. Better to try to lay low and blend in. I saunter up to the bar. "I'll take a pint please."

The barman hands me a flagon of ale the size of a small child. "That will be five gold pieces."

"Five gold pieces? Can I pay with a tenner?"

He looks at me confused and repeats his request. "That will be five gold pieces."

I have no idea how to proceed. I only have a couple of gold. I need to find three more gold pieces before this guy decides to kick off. There is a vase on the bar, the kind that would normally contain some kind of loot. I pick it up and chuck it on the floor in the hopes that it is full of gold. Instead a thick cloud of grey dust fills the air. The barman's face goes from perplexed to enraged. "What have you done to Mildred?"

Oh bugger. I turn and run for the exit, but the barman shouts, "Oy Jimmy. Lock the doors. He hasn't paid."

A guy as wide as the doorway blocks the only way out. He cracks his neck left and then right. Then he moves on to his knuckles. Each crack sounds like a tree falling down. His hands are the size of wrecking balls and look just as dangerous. I hold my hands up and back away slowly. "This has all been a big misunderstanding. I'm happy to pay, I just realized I have left my wallet at home..."

Jimmy smirks. A very long health bar appears above his head.

Level 14 Bouncer.

This couldn't get much worse.

An angry groan ripples through the pub. I take my eyes off Jimmy just long enough to glance at the TV. Germany just equalized and the patrons are not thrilled about it. That's when I hear someone shout, "Oy Kraut! Are you lost?"

So much for me being low profile. I start backing towards the nearest wall as the crowd of drunken football supporters all wheel around in unison. I catch a glimpse of Carlos and Sarah making their way to the far corner of the room, where they are the least likely to get showered with my blood splatter. Jimmy is still approaching me, but now he's being more cautious. No point in bruising up his knuckles on my face if the locals will do his job for him.

One of the scrawnier-looking blokes steps out in front of the pack. He shouts over the din, "Alright lads, let's not do anything we regret. We should invite our new friend to sit and have a drink with us and watch the rest of the game."

He reaches out and I get ready to defend myself, but he places his hand around my shoulder and walks me towards the TV. The crowd parts and I find myself surrounded. Someone vacates their seat and just like that I find myself at a table of gentlemen whose tattoos paint a vivid picture of xenophobia and violence. There is a large assortment of drinks on the table. It's not entirely clear who is drinking what, but drinking it they most certainly are. Someone slams a pint down in front of me and says, "Drink up mate, you'll need this."

I take a loud sip just as the final whistle blows. It's a draw. I'm not sure if I should be relieved or frightened. My new friend confirms it's the latter. "Penalties. You know what that means. You have to drink a pint for every penalty your team scores."

"Funny story, I don't actually support Germany."

A lot of eyes narrow. "Then why are you wearing a German football shirt?"

Yeah, this is going to be hard to explain. *For a dare* sounds like something that will get me a swift kicking. *Ironically* is not a word that this crowd is going to understand. *To get into a massive pub brawl* makes me sound like a crazy person. Scratch that, *Because I am trapped in a video game* is the crazy person answer. I stare at him blankly before I say, "It's laundry day."

That gets a few chuckles, but the guy isn't laughing. He is watching the screen intently as the English player steps up to take his penalty. He slams it into the top left of the net and the pub erupts in cheers. Everyone at my table downs their drink immediately and retrieves a fresh one from the pile in the centre of the table. Then they all go quiet as the German steps up. I find myself praying that he will miss, but he feigns going left and at the last second slots it right. Typical German efficiency. He doesn't even celebrate, he is far too sensible. I wish I could say the same. I find myself with a pint glass at my mouth as someone tips up the bottom. Can I get drunk in a game? I guess I am about to find out.

Back and forth they go, both teams scoring their penalties. I'm finishing up my fourth beer as the English player steps up. He's the team captain, the hero they all need. I mutter a prayer that he will bring this victory home. The goalkeeper goes left, he kicks it right and the crowd is on their feet, but there is a loud clang as it bounces off the goalpost.

I watch as the German captain steps forward, no signs of pressure or fear. He hammers the ball into the back of the net like it's no big deal. Little does he know he is signing my death warrant. All at once, everyone turns to look at me and their expression is one of pure rage. The four pints are just starting to kick in as the first guy screams and takes a swing at me.

There's no room for evasion. I can't combat roll my way around the pub. Instead I block and take the hit. I can hear Sarah shouting over the ruckus, "Marcus, you need to parry. If you block they will whittle you down."

It is good advice, but hard to follow when twenty blokes are all simultaneously trying to kick your teeth down your throat. I'm paying no attention to levels, health or anything else. I am just trying to survive. Easier said than done.

A drunk guy staggers towards me and takes a swing. I try blocking just as he is about to hit me, but my timing is off and he smacks me right in the face. He goes in for another hit, but this time I get it right, and his punch is deflected with a *ching*. I punch him quickly while I'm doing double damage.

I try several more parries, but most of them end with me getting punched in the face. Now is not the time to perfect my technique. I scavenge from every surface, leftover chips, a half-eaten burger, the dregs at the bottom of Doritos packets, anything to keep my health up.

I notice that some of them are holding back, watching me. They are judging me, letting others take the hits so they can learn what I am capable of. Well it's time I brought the fight to them. I have to wrap this up quickly as the booze is starting to kick in.

I reach into my pocket and pull out the nunchucks. The drunks are at least smart enough to back away, but not smart enough to leave me alone. I whirl the nunchucks around to show them I know how to use them. That's when Jimmy steps forwards.

He raises his fists and darts towards me like a pro boxer. I swing the nunchucks and they connect perfectly with his head, but instead of him going down, my nunchucks snap in half. Damn, I forgot about weapon damage. Jimmy grabs me by the throat and hauls me up over his head. He tosses me like a rag doll over the pool table and straight through a trophy cabinet filled with glass and the spikiest trophies ever made. I slump into a heap below the cabinet, a solitary hit left on my health bar. Before I can get up the last remaining trophy wobbles and topples over, landing on my head and killing me instantly.

Everything starts to fade to black. I can still hear talking in the background, but I can no longer move. That's when the prompt appears:

You Died.

Continue? Y/N

1 Life remaining

What the hell? I'm dead. Again! That has to be some kind of record. Now I'm really going to murder Carlos. I've barely had my 1UP an hour and thanks to his idiotic plan I already have to use it. It's not like I have a whole lot of choice.

I hit Y, praying that this works. All of a sudden I am back on my feet with full health and only a slight twinge of pain in my back. Jimmy looks confused to see me back on my feet, but he's more than happy to put me down again.

I can't keep fighting like this. Defence is not working, there are too many of them. If I am going to make it out of this pub I need to take the fight to them. I grab a pool cue from the rack.

New Weapon acquired. Bo staff.

Bingo. I run into the crowd and go full Musou. Drunks go flying as I twirl and spin, the bo staff an extension of my body, keeping them at a distance. The moment I stop I regret it, as the room keeps spinning. The beer is kicking in. I have to end this fight now before I barf.

Thanks to my renewed assault there are only a few left standing, and of course Jimmy. I know how much damage he can do now, so I need to be more strategic in my approach.

I'm still considering the optimal strategy when I hear the shouts for help. I look over and see a couple of drunks cornering Sarah and Carlos. At this point they don't care who they punch. Anyone not wearing an England shirt is fair game. Jimmy lunges for me, but I roll out of the way and he crashes into the wall, temporarily stunning him. I reach into my pocket and pull out two throwing knives, which find their targets. The two drunks scream as they find their feet pinned to the ground.

I turn back just as Jimmy shakes it off and takes another swing at me. There's no room for error. I roll just in time and punch him in the back of the head, stunning him. I follow up with a flurry of hits from the pool cue. It shatters, but Jimmy still has a few hits left on his health bar. He's too tough for me to take down with my bare hands. I need a new weapon. I scour the room, but there's nothing.

That's when I spot the new blue bar under my life bar. With all the EXP I gained from wailing on these drunkards I've finally earned my magic. Just in the nick of time.

"Eat fireballs!" I proclaim and thrust my left hand at Jimmy. He stares at me blankly and nothing happens, not even a spark. He takes a swing at me and I only just manage to dodge it in time, rolling backwards to avoid any further attacks. I shout at Sarah, "My magic isn't working. It says I have MP, but when I try nothing happens."

"Check your current spell."

I don't exactly have the luxury of time for an extended menu browse right now, but there's nothing else to hit him with. I dart to the other side of the room to create some distance and hop into the spell menu. There's no sign of fireballs, lightning bolts or ice blasts. Instead I have a spell called *Pivot tables*. What the heck?

Jimmy is almost upon me and I am out of options, so I select the spell and cast it in his general direction. One of the nearby tables swings around and hits him squarely in the face. He falls to the ground in a heap, his life bar depleted. Carlos runs over and says, "What on earth was that?"

"Don't ask." I look around at the piles of unconscious hooligans and say, "We need to get out of here before the police arrive."

"You're not going anywhere!" I turn to see the barman standing on the bar wielding a shotgun. "You'll pay for what you did to Mildred!"

The funny thing about a bar is that it can also be used as a table. I concentrate and the bar flips up 90 degrees, flinging the owner into the fruit machine. Gold coins come tumbling out and with a sigh I go back to scoop them up. I make sure to leave five of them next to the cash register. Then I carefully step over the piles of unconscious bodies and out the front door as quick as I can.

When we reach the car I grab Carlos by the shoulders. "What kind of stupid plan was that?"

"I don't see the problem. You made it out in one piece."

"In one piece? I died! I had to use up my only extra life. It sure would have been nice if I could have held onto it for ten bloody minutes."

"It's fine, we'll just get you another one."

Sarah shakes her head, "Actually, that was the only one. We didn't want to spoil the suspense of the game. That was more of a fun easter egg."

"Well there's no sense dwelling on it. What's done is done. On to the next quest."

I do want to dwell on it, but it won't do any good. Being mad at

Carlos won't bring my 1UP back. Instead I say, "Can we just get out of here. I don't want to be around when they finally wake up in there and find their precious drinking hole destroyed."

"Actually, we treat indoor locations as an instance in our game, so as soon as you go outside they get reset." says Sarah.

I watch as a couple of guys walk into the pub. There are no cries of distress, nothing at all to indicate that anything is wrong. I turn back and say, "I'll be back."

I can't help myself, I have to see it with my own eyes. I walk back into the pub and everything is exactly as it was when we first entered, even down to the barman. I toss a gold coin at him and say, "here's a tip mate."

He pockets the coin and smirks, "I have a tip for you too. If you'd like to walk out of here alive I suggest ditching the shirt."

Oh right. I jog back out of the pub, right past an oblivious Jimmy. Sarah says, "Satisfied?"

"I believed you, I just wasn't sure if the same rules would apply in the real world. We should still get out of here, I need new clothes and a top up on my health."

"To the drive thru!" says Carlos.

LEVEL 10: WARS OF GEAR

There is a rather large bag of cheeseburgers in front of me. I'm not even hungry, but I keep eating them until I am back at full health. In between mouthfuls I voice my frustrations. "I don't get it. The only spell I have right now is the ability to pivot tables, which isn't exactly earth-shattering. I can't wait to unlock animated slides and requirement writing. The end boss will be quaking in his boots when I shower him with magic PowerPoint slides. How come I don't get any cool magic?"

Sarah thinks for a moment. "Usually magic spells are assigned to particular classes. Did you pick a class?"

"No I don't think so." That's when I remember the new menu on my work computer. "Wait! I think I selected Business Analyst."

"That explains it then. Business Analyst obviously isn't a class in the game, but it looks like it has blended it with your real-life job description."

"So you're telling me I'm not going to be flinging out lightning bolts? Can I change my class?"

"Only if you're willing to die and start again."

"Perfect. Useless magic it is then."

Carlos laughs so hard he almost chokes on a burger. I say, "This isn't funny! I'm supposed to be a badass warrior. I literally just died unlocking my magic ability and this is what I have to play with. How am I supposed to beat anyone with spinning tables?"

"Games give you what you need to succeed. We just don't know why this will be useful yet. It's probably for the best, if you were going around tossing out fireballs imagine the insurance premiums. You'd have firefighters following you everywhere."

I guess he has a point, that would be a bit of a liability.

"So what am I supposed to do now? Every time I get into a fight there's always a guy a several levels higher than me that takes off huge chunks of my health. It's making group combat too big of a risk."

Sarah eyes up my clothes. "You're still using low-level gear. At the very least you need to boost your defence. That will give you more of a fighting chance against the bigger foes. It's the quickest way to buff your stats."

"Ok, so how do I get better gear? Is there a shop that sells the good stuff?"

"There is, but it's not going to give you the kind of stat boost you're looking for. You need gear that is purple and up. In the game you have to get them from a stronghold, and they are usually well-guarded. We wanted players to have to work to access them."

Carlos scoffs, "Can't we just pay money to unlock them? Time is of the essence here."

She glares at him. "Of course not, we'd never put something like that in our game, it would completely unbalance it. The only way to get them is through skill."

"That seems like a catch-22, to get the better gear so you can survive against tougher mobs, you have to fight your way through this mob..." I let out a sigh.

"Actually, not all of the strongholds are combat-oriented. Most of them are stealth missions."

I shudder. Stealth missions are the worst. "Is the stealth instant failure if you got caught?"

"No, but every guard would immediately know where you are and attack all at once, so it rarely goes well if you're spotted."

"Ok, that doesn't sound like a viable option. Too risky."

Carlos scoffs. "I'm getting tired of saying this. You need to stop being you. This is a role-playing game, you need to inhabit the role of a warrior hero. Someone that charges in to battle first and asks questions after the dust has settled."

"That didn't exactly work out great in the pub did it?"

"Oh my god, are you still going on about that?"

"Which part, the bit where I died? Yeah, it's going to take more than half an hour to get over that."

"Well if you don't want to die you should do one of these missions. As you just learned, the biggest risk to you right now is getting jumped by an enemy that's double your level. The only way to solve that is to upgrade your gear so they aren't one-shotting you. The longer you wait, the higher the chances of you running into an unbeatable foe. You're an analyst, tell me, does risk aversion and inaction help in a time-sensitive situation or is it more of a liability?"

Damn it. I hate to admit it but he's right. The longer I sit around not doing anything the more danger I am in.

"Ok Sarah, where might we find one of these strongholds?"

***

I lurk until the armoured car appears at the jewellers across the road. Two of the guards step into the store, leaving at least one more inside the van. I amble up to the back with my two trusty sticks in hand. It only takes a few seconds to open the door, much to the surprise of the guy sitting in the back reading the paper. I make short work of him and drag him over to the nearby alley that Carlos and Sarah are hiding in. They help me switch into his clothes. Nice, he has level 2 trousers.

Sarah says, "Remember what we talked about. The guards won't be able to see you if you're in the shadows. If they hear anything suspicious they will come to investigate. If you're spotted you have a few seconds to disable the guard before they raise the alarm and all hell will break loose."

"Ok got it, shadows good, alarm bad."

I amble back over and climb into the van, pulling my cap down over my face. The two guards return and a small hatch opens. A box of cash is slid into it and the guard bangs twice on the side of the van. I pull the case in and bang twice in response.

I open the case and am disappointed to see it only contains thousands of real world pounds. That's not much use. I was hoping for gold coins. I'm just going to have to hold out for the main prize.

After a couple more stops a voice comes over the intercom and says, "Ok Frank, we are on our way back to the bank. Try not to fall asleep back there."

I push the intercom button and grumble an unintelligible response.

We drive for several minutes before we stop again. There is a muffled rumbling that sounds like a garage door opening. Then the van tilts as we go down a ramp, before coming to a stop at the bottom. This is it. Time to get my stealth on. Be one with the shadows.

The back doors open and the two guards stare at me. Their faces turn from friendly to angry as one of them shouts, "Hey! Where's Frank?"

So much for stealth. As the nearest one reaches for his walkie talkie I dive out of the van, knocking them both to the ground in the process. I quickly knock them both out and leave them tied up in the back of the van with gags stuffed in their mouths. Not exactly a great start.

I use Frank's security pass to buzz into the next room. There are inexplicable pillars of shadow dotted around the room, despite the fact it is the middle of the day and the room is otherwise well-lit. There are several guards walking aimlessly in circles. I overhear one of them say, "are you sure this is what they want us to do? Just walk in circles like this?"

The other guard says, "Yep, the HR lady was very specific. Just follow the path they showed you. Only deviate if someone calls an alarm. No breaks either, we have to work straight through. I hope you wore comfy shoes!"

"This job makes no sense. The payroll alone must be astronomical. What are we even guarding?"

"Don't know, don't care. As long as the cheques clear, I'm happy."

I try to run to the nearest shadow and my footsteps echo around the room. It sounds like I'm wearing tap dancing shoes. A couple of guards swivel their heads in my direction. Despite the fact that there are half a dozen guys walking in here one of them says, "Thought I heard footsteps..."

I spot a pile of cardboard boxes in the corner of the room. They would make the perfect disguise. I sneak over and pull one over myself in a crouch. I crawl out of the shadows, thinking I'm some kind of super genius, when a guard says, "What the heck is that?"

Shit! I speed crawl back into the shadows and peer out of the tiny eyeholes as he comes over to investigate. He's so close I could reach out and punch him. I resist the temptation, there are four other guards in the room and I don't yet trust my ability to take them all out before one of them manages to raise the alarm. Instead I hold my breath, but after a few seconds the guard shrugs and goes back to his previous patrol route as if nothing happened.

I sit in my box for a couple more minutes until I am certain that everything is back to normal. The more I watch the guards, the more I see the pattern they are taking. If I time it right I should be able to get through without any of them seeing me. I hop from shadow to shadow, hiding behind pillars and waist-high walls, being careful to move slowly, to avoid my clomping footsteps. This is too easy!

I stroll through the exit patting myself on the back for cracking the stealth level. I'm expecting to find the advanced gear, but instead I am in another large room full of even more guards walking in circles. How many guards work here?

I watch them all orbiting and can't find a route through. I must be missing something. Perhaps I have to take a couple of them out to create some gaps? That's when I notice the beam six feet up that cuts diagonally through the room. Sarah didn't say anything about acrobatics. I take a moment to drop a few of my spare skill points into agility, just to be safe.

I run up the nearest pillar and flip up onto the beam like a gymnast. I slip at the last minute and manage to grab on with one hand. Dropping now would land me in the middle of a group of guards. A prompt flashes up and I instinctively select it, and with no effort I pull myself up onto the beam. Yesterday I could hardly lift the TV remote without pulling a muscle, and here I am today doing one-armed pull ups.

The beam is not very thick, but I feel confident right up until a graded bar appears in the middle of my vision with an arrow bouncing from left to right. I don't react quick enough and it dips into the red zone and I almost topple back onto the guards below, catching myself at the very last moment. I try again, this time keeping the arrow in the correct zone. Once I reach the other side I have to time it perfectly to slip between the guards and into the next room, where hopefully my prize awaits.

Wishful thinking. This room is two stories, with guards, security cameras, three drones and a sweeping laser grid. This is getting ridiculous! I'm busy hiding in the shadows when a guard comes round the corner with a dog. It is sniffing the air and straining against its lead. I press myself into the darkness, but the dog keeps dragging its owner towards me. I realize too late that the rules have changed. The guard says, "Who's there?" and pulls out a torch and a gun.

Bugger.

I launch myself out of the shadows and tackle the guard to the ground. I knock him out with one punch as the dog starts barking. Every guard in the room suddenly turns to see what all the noise is about. So much for stealth. There's no way I can take them all on without taking some serious damage. I reluctantly pick up the gun and get a status update.

New weapon acquired. Sleeping darts.

Interesting. I cringe as I point it at the dog and pull the trigger. Thankfully the status update was right and a small dart knocks the dog out instantly. A quick check confirms I have nine darts left. It's time to say goodnight to some guards.

The first guy that comes to investigate sees the prone form of his comrade and rushes to help. He doesn't get his walkie talkie out until he is right next to me. I shoot him with a dart from the shadows before he can raise the alarm. He falls on top of his friend, snoring loudly.

One by one the rest of the guards come to investigate and they all go the same way, until there is a mound of unconscious bodies. Why does every stealth mission always end this way?

The laser grid has a large red OFF button on the wall next to it, which is something of a design flaw from a security standpoint. I take out the drones with a couple of throwing knives. I think that's everything. As I move towards the exit I hear a groan from the pile of guards and fire what is left of my sleep darts into the mound until the noise stops.

I walk through the door, and there it is, in a glass case. I'm not sure what I was expecting, but a purple hoodie was not it. I'm sure if I look hard enough I'll find a glass cutter or diamond-tipped letter opener in the room, but instead I punch right through the case. The hoodie doesn't look anything special, in fact it looks like it's from a charity shop, but as soon as I put it on I get a message.

Legendary Hoodie of Godiva. + 40 Defence

Now we are talking. I am about to walk back the way I came when

I notice an obnoxiously large air vent on the wall. You've got to be kidding me. I pull off the grate and clamber through it, popping out just above the garage that I started in. Rookie mistake, always look for the sneaky shortcut!

I walk out of the garage and find myself several streets away from where I started. I'm about to call Sarah and Carlos when a scruffy man in a trench coat jumps out of the nearest alleyway. I'm about to ninja punch him into next week when he grabs his coat and flings it open. I can't close my eyes fast enough and am expecting to see homeless dong, but instead the inside of his coat is full of items. He snarls, "Welcome! What are you buying stranger?"

I glance at his stuff. There is a ridiculously large sword, a crossbow, several hand grenades, a garishly-coloured mushroom, a whole roast chicken and several different coloured herbs. As I glance at each item the stats show up. That's when I spot the solid red shoes. I glance at them.

Legendary Shoes of Cursus Velox. + 20 Speed. 30 Gold pieces.

I only have 20 gold left from the fruit machine. I'm about to leave when the merchant says, "Anything to sell?"

I check my inventory. I only have sticks and a couple of throwing knives. It's not going to be enough. That's when I remember the pile of unconscious guards. I say, "Give me a minute."

A few of them are starting to wake up, but it's nothing a swift punch doesn't solve. I rifle through all of their pockets. It feels a little sordid, but I really want those shoes. I have a lot of random items now, far more than my pockets should hold, but in they go without a problem until my inventory screen is full. As soon as that happens I can't even pick up anything else, it's like there is an invisible box around it. I head back outside and start to flog it all to the merchant, who offers me paltry sums for everything.

When all is said and done I have 31 gold and I hand it over for the shoes. With a crooked grin he says, "Pleasure doing business with you."

As soon as I put the shoes on I feel different, like my feet are tingling with a mild electric current. I try to take a step forward and run full speed into the wall, taking a chunk off my health. I jump back to my feet and shake it off before trying again, a lot more slowly this time. Even moving slowly is a sprint. These may be more trouble than they are worth. I'm not going to be able to do any nuanced movement.

I pull out my phone and call Carlos and Sarah. They are still several streets over. Carlos says, "Give us a minute and we will come pick you up."

"No need, I'll be there in 2."

Moving slowly may be an issue in these things, but let's see how quick they can go. I point my feet in the general direction I'm heading and try to sprint. The world becomes a blur and in just a few seconds I see Carlos and Sarah appear on the horizon. I skid to a halt next to them and Sarah says, "Nice! Shoes of Cursus Velox? Have you figured out how to walk normally in them yet?"

I shake my head, afraid to move anything else in case it results in me plowing into another wall. Sarah laughs and says, "Yeah we had problems in testing, the speed boost was dialled in too high and testers kept barfing. We had to add a toggle switch so players could turn them on or off."

I stare at my new shoes and a toggle appears. I flip it to *off* and suddenly I can move normally again. What a relief!

Carlos pokes at my hoodie. "This thing doesn't look worth much. Was that the best they had?"

"Yeah, I'm afraid the selection was rather limited. I had to knock out twenty guards to get this."

He shrugs. "I guess every little helps."

That reminds me, I should have gotten some EXP for all those takedowns. I check my stats and sure enough I'm now level 12. The best part is, that means more skill points! There are so many cool things I am going to spend it on, it's going to be hard to choose. I hop into the menu and drool over my options, but then a quicktip catches my eye.

Upgrade magic to unlock new spell.

Finally! I'm going to get something less useless to spend my MP on. I have just enough skill points to get to the first spell unlock. I can't see what the spell is, so I guess it is going to be a surprise. I spend my skill points and wait to see what epic new magic I just got.

Pie Chart. Throws pies.

You have got to be kidding! I spent my skill points on this? Is there a refund option?

I select it and aim at the nearest wall. "This better be good!"

I cast it and a cream pie flies out of my hand and splats against the wall. It slowly slides down the wall. Carlos ambles over and gets a finger full of cream. "Wow, that's a delicious new spell you have there. Does it do any damage?"

"I don't know. Care to help me test it?"

"No thanks! I'm still sore from the kung fu demo. I'm sure we'll find some goons soon enough."

I'm still fuming when my phone rings. It's work. I'm about to ignore it when Carlos takes it out of my hand and answers, "Marcus' phone? Yeah, he can't come to the phone right now, he's busy saving the world. Can I take a message?" He nods his head. I am expecting to hear tinny screaming coming out of my phone, but instead there is quiet chirping. Carlos' expression goes from jovial to concerned and he says, "Of course, I will let him know. Thank you."

He hangs up the phone and stares at me with a look of genuine fear. I wait for him to tell me what is going on, and when he doesn't I say, "What is it? You can't just answer my phone and not tell me what they said."

"It was Miss Jones."

He doesn't need to say anything more. My heart starts to pound and I resist the urge to turn my new shoes back on and run as far as I can in the opposite direction. Sarah looks at us both bemused and says, "Who is Miss Jones?"

"She is the head of HR at Master Systems. She said Marcus has to go in immediately."

"Ok, so what's the big deal?"

"She's terrifying. I have seen grown men coming out of a meeting with her bawling their eyes out. They call her the Executioner. If you end up in a room with her it means you're already terminated," says Carlos.

"Ok, so just don't go in then. What's the worst that can happen."

If only it was that simple. I finish reading the status update that just appeared and says, "I don't have a choice. It just popped up as a new main quest item."

LEVEL 11: THE EXECUTIONER

Carlos hugs me as if I'm about to walk the green mile. I say, "You'd better get out of here before she sees you playing hooky."

That's enough to make him release his grip and jog back to the car. I barely get to wave at Sarah before the car screeches away, leaving me all alone.

I try walking into the building, but my security pass isn't working. That's not a great sign. I push the intercom and the crackly voice of the receptionist says, "Master Systems, how can I help you."

"Hi, it's Marcus Kennedy. My pass doesn't seem to be working."

The door buzzes open without another word. As soon as I enter reception, a security guard appears. "Please follow me sir."

He leads me down the corridor towards HR. The walls are covered in motivational posters from forty years ago that look as tattered as the morale around here.

DETERMINATION

ENDURANCE

INTEGRITY

We stop at a frosted glass door and the security guard knocks once and scurries away before there is an answer. No doubt he's on his way to my desk to retrieve my meagre possessions.

I consider running again, but then I will never complete my quest. I grit my teeth and stand my ground until the door slides open. Miss Jones is smiling. That's a bad sign. I've never seen her smile before. It looks almost reptilian, her eyes dead of emotion and her lip quivering as if she has to expend effort to hold it there. She gestures to the seat opposite her desk, which has been host to more terminations than an electric chair.

I take a deep breath and sit down. There's a bowl of mints on her desk that look like they have been there since the building was erected. Miss Jones waddles back to her seat and strains to fit into it, her carefully tailored pant suit crinkling as she wedges herself in. She smells faintly of cat food and hair spray. She stares at me as if she has never met me before, despite the fact that I've been in here half a dozen times to complain about Jenkins.

After a lengthy pause she says, "Mr. Kennedy. Can you please tell me why you believe it was ok to abandon your job today?"

"Of course. There was an incident last night..."

She interrupts me, "Yes, we are aware that you were out drinking last night. I would also like to understand why you think it is ok to get drunk on company time."

"Company time? It was 10 pm, and I didn't actually have a..."

"Your role requires you to be on call twenty four seven, therefore all time is company time."

Ok, it's on. I'm not going to sit here and be assassinated. "Well you only pay me for eight of those hours."

She reaches up and pulls down a binder the size of a concrete slab. It looks like it weighs about as much as one too. She opens it with a creak to reveal well-worn pages. She caresses each page as she turns it, as if it's her favourite novel. Eventually she stops and scans a page until she says, "Chapter 17, Section 4, subsection 9 of the employee handbook states, and I quote, 'resources represent the company at all times and must behave in a manner that is fitting. Failure to do so will result in penalties up to and including termination of employment.'"

"Ok. I'm not sure how that applies. I didn't even drink."

"So how do you explain your absence from work this afternoon young man?"

"If you'd let me explain..."

"Mr. Jenkins says you have been increasingly hostile lately. It sounds to me that this is some petty act of rebellion because he refused to give in to your demands to be promoted."

I clench my fists. "Increasingly hostile? I've done every ridiculous thing he has asked me to. I work twice as hard as anyone else on the team. Three times now he has promised me a promotion, and then found an excuse to put it off."

"Ah I see, so you think you're better than everyone else, is that it? This must be causing the air of superiority he mentioned. I'm afraid we can't tolerate this kind of behaviour, it is bad for morale."

Now I'm really angry. I struggle to keep my voice level. "You think *that* is what is hurting morale? How about our manager taking three hour lunch breaks while we do his work for him? How about him taking credit for everything we do and throwing us under the bus the moment there is a hint of a problem? We've had seven team members burnout in the last 12 months. I'm the longest serving member on the team and I've only been here three years. It seems to me that I am not the problem here."

Her eyes narrow. She's honing in on her prey. "I've heard enough. We won't tolerate this kind of toxic attitude here at Master Systems. According to Chapter 9, Section 12, subsection 19, I am terminating your employment effective immediately, without severance pay or references. Your things will be dropped off at the address we have on file for you."

I should be devastated, but I'm not. I don't even want this job. I haven't wanted it for at least 12 months. Getting fired is probably the best thing that could happen to me, but I am not going to let that happen. If they think I'm just going to roll over and take this laying down, they've come to the wrong place. "I've complained a dozen times about Jenkins and you did nothing. He complains about me once and I get the boot?"

"Goodbye Mr. Kennedy. We are done here."

I stand up and slam my hand down on the desk, making her jump. Before I can say anything my hand brushes against the employee handbook and a prompt appears.

Use Data Analysis?

I select Y. In seconds I extrapolate every useful piece of information from the dusty binder. There are twelve sentences in the entire 500-page document that have any meaning or value, but they are all I need.

I sit back down and kick my feet up on her desk. "Actually Miss Jones, we are just getting started. Can you please explain to me why you believe it is ok to ignore Chapter 4, Section 3, subsection

9 which states that an employee must be given two verbal notices and a written warning before a termination based on behaviour can be considered?"

She flips through the pages until she finds the section I am referring to. As she scans it her face starts to redden. She stutters, "This is dismissal with cause, the standard guidelines don't apply."

"Ah I see, well Chapter 24, Section 3, subsection 5 lays out the reasons for dismissal with cause and I fail to see one that applies to my situation. I can recite them to you if you'd like? Or I can tell you seven ways you are currently violating our dress code."

She slams the binder shut, a scowl leaking out from under her carefully measured expression. She hefts up the tome and places it carefully back on the shelf. I think she's going to shout for security, but instead she turns and slaps me right across the face. The sound echoes in the tiny room. My health bar loses 25% instantly and a health bar almost as wide as she is appears over her head.

Level 20 Bureaucrat.

I wasn't expecting a fist fight. I'm not prepared for this at all. I try to turn and run, but the door is firmly locked. She is at least twice my size and also a woman. Hitting her is going to be an issue.

I'm busy being all chivalrous when she throws a handful of stress balls at me. Instead of bouncing harmlessly off me they hit with the force of squishy cannonballs. If I wasn't wearing this hoodie I am pretty sure I'd be dead already. I can't just stand here and take it, I won't last 10 seconds. I'm going to have to fight back.

Prepare to eat pies! I cast my newest spell at her, the pie hitting her right between the eyes. It's hard to tell if it did any damage, certainly not enough to be worth throwing another one. She wipes whipped cream off her face with a scowl.

I grab a handful of mints and jam them in my mouth. They crunch between my teeth and a fraction of my health returns. I glance around the room, looking for anything I can use as a weapon. My best option is a large pot plant in the corner. Unfortunately Miss Jones has seen it too, and she uproots it in one tug. She swings it at me and I only just manage to duck out of the way in time. There's no room in here to roll around, if she backs me into the corner I'm going to get pot planted to death. That is not how I plan on going out.

She takes another swing at me. I wait for the prompt, and there it is. I select it and immediately disarm her. I heft the pot right at her and it explodes, showering her with mud and ceramic. It does a decent amount of damage, but it's not much use to me now. I fling it at her and she dodges with surprising speed as the pot plant embeds itself in the far wall.

She reaches out and tries to grab me in a bear hug. I only just manage to break free. That's another way I'm not planning to die today, smothered by a middle-aged lady covered in cat hair. I need to keep her at a distance.

So much for that idea. She grabs another handful of stress balls and gets ready to fire them my way. I instinctively pick up the employee handbook to shield myself. It absorbs most of the impact, but she charges at me like a bull in the world's smallest china shop. There's nowhere to run. I have to time this right. Just before she makes impact I smack her across the face with the manual and the rest of her health bar evaporates as the binder explodes, showering the room with paper. It seems the only thing more effective than facts against HR is using their own rules against them. I guess I found her weak spot.

Breaking the rules - 2 of 4 Fears conquered. 50% complete.

I'm waiting for her to pass out, or better yet dissolve, but instead she straightens her collar and says, "You've made some excellent counter arguments. I may have been hasty with your termination. Let me have a conversation with Mr. Jenkins and fill him in on our discussion. For now, please consider yourself employed here."

It's a hard fact to celebrate. "Thanks, I guess."

I see a flashing icon on the ground next to where Miss Jones was felled. I walk over to it and see that it is a new ability.

Passive: Bullshit detector.

What on earth does that do? I pick it up and it gets added to my move list.

Miss Jones wipes whipped cream from the corner of her mouth and then stares at it, confused. I try the door again and it slides open easily. I get out of there as quick as I can, grabbing a handful of mints on my way.

I find Carlos and Sarah waiting for me around the corner. Carlos pulls a chunk of pot plant out of my hair. "How did it go?"

"It got a little heated, but we worked it out."

He looks genuinely impressed. "How did you convince her to give you another chance?"

"I hit her with the employee handbook."

"Nice! I didn't realize that thing was worth the paper it's written on."

"You'd be impressed with how impactful it was."

"Where to now?" asks Carlos.

"Drive thru."

He laughs, "did you work up an appetite arguing for your job?"

"There may have been a minor physical confrontation."

He slaps me heartily on the back. "That's the spirit! I wish I could have seen that."

If you'd told me this morning that I would be beating seven shades out of the head of HR with a pot plant I'd have laughed in your face.

Perhaps dying wasn't so bad after all...

LEVEL 12: STACK OVERFLOW

As we sit in the fast food car park Carlos says, "We are almost at the end of the first day. We need to speed this up. I think we're going to have to find some bugs."

"I should be offended, but based on your last time playing the game I'm going to assume there are plenty more exploits to find. What do you have in mind?" asks Sarah.

"I just need a solid hour in the game to test out a few theories." He glances over to Sarah, "You could take Marcus to that thing we talked about while he was in with Miss Jones."

"What thing?" I don't like the sound of that. Since when are these two making plans without me?

"It's a surprise," states Carlos. "You're going to love it."

Somehow I doubt that.

We drive back to the university. Sarah and Carlos run off to her office, leaving me in reception. I slump into the nearest chair. I should be exhausted, but I feel totally fine. Still, it's nice to sit for a moment and not have to worry about fighting for my life.

I'm minding my own business when I see a familiar face peering around the corner at me. I say, "Hey Professor Jasper. Are you ok?"

He doesn't say a word, but he frantically waves me to him. I walk over and he drags me into his office, slamming the door behind him. "Are you winning?"

"Erm, I don't know exactly yet. It's a bit early to tell."

"It is imperative that you win the game."

"Well yeah, if I don't I'm dead, so I'd say it's pretty high on my to-do list. Why the sudden concern for my well-being?"

"Because I believe there may be more at stake here than we realize. Look at this." He spins his screen towards me. It is covered in random lines of code and scrambled text. I say, "Wow, that's fascinating. What is it?"

"It's the simulation code. The rift in reality has made the simulation unstable. I have found a way to see behind the curtain, so to speak."

So there it is. The code that runs the universe. I should be in awe, but I still don't know what difference this makes. I didn't need any more convincing.

"Is this a good thing? Can you stop what is happening to me?"

"Alas no, I can only see the code, I can't modify it. That would be like trying to hack into MI5 using your calculator. I can only see fragments, snippets here and there, but even then something isn't right. Look at this." He points to a block of code that is a different colour to the rest. As I watch it slowly expands, one line at a time, filling more and more of the screen. I say, "I'm going to need a little help deciphering this."

"That red section is the game code. It is spreading. I thought it might stay contained in your general vicinity, but that isn't true. It's trying to make the whole world your play space. If you can't beat the game it will overrun the entire simulation."

"What then?"

"There are two possible outcomes. Either the entire world will continue as the game in your absence, a world without a player. Alternatively the simulation will become corrupted beyond repair and will be deleted."

"Wait, you're telling me that if I don't beat the game, either way the entire world is screwed?"

"Precisely. Your decisions are no longer your own. You are fighting for the survival of the entire planet. You must therefore do everything in your power to win, no matter the cost."

Well that's just marvellous. Just what I needed, something else to worry about. From my point of view it doesn't really change anything, either way I would be dead, but do I really want to be the guy that is responsible for ending the whole world?

"Are you sure about this?"

"Of course. The data doesn't lie."

"Well that's just marvellous. Thanks for this little pep talk, it's been a real motivator."

"Glad I could help."

He goes back to staring at his computer as if we'd been politely discussing the weather. Now I'm really starting to panic. How can I deal with this kind of responsibility?

I walk down the hall to Sarah's office. Carlos is still in the game, a daft grin on his face. Sarah looks less impressed. She says, "He's found 37 bugs already."

She looks at me more closely and her expression folds into one of concern. "Are you alright?"

"Yes, I'm fine, the day is just catching up with me." I know I should tell them, but what will it achieve? This is my burden to carry.

She's still staring. She knows something is wrong. I need a diversion.

I glance at her screen and Carlos is dual-wielding pistols. "I thought this was a medieval fantasy game?"

"It is. We've used a commercial engine though and I guess some of the generic assets are still available. Carlos found a way to stack overflow the inventory system and next thing I know he has pistols. There are no bullets defined in our game, but it doesn't seem to be slowing him down."

I watch as the guns shoot out a barrage of fireballs. He then draws a six-foot sword made of ice. I look at Sarah and she says, "It is supposed to be six-inch dagger. I still don't know how he broke that one."

Carlos slices through a mob of skeletons with ease, each swipe freezing his enemies in place. As the others try to grab him he uses the frozen corpses to block their attacks. He back flips into the air, raining down fireballs like a one man meteor storm. The rest of the mob are turned to ash before he hits the ground. Sarah stares at me and I say, "He had a misspent youth."

"We've had an army of testers working on this game for months and they didn't find any of this stuff."

"Yeah, it is kind of his thing. He likes to break stuff. If it was him in this mess instead of me he would probably be level 50 by now. He'd have also blue screened the universe. He's crashed more games than you've had hot dinners."

Carlos hears me and removes the headset, a huge grin plastered all over his face. "Mate! I have so many ideas for how we can speed up your progress. Give me another hour with this and I'll have you as a level 50 ninja warlock by breakfast."

"That's great." I'm going to need all the help I can get, now that I'm the saviour of the universe. I can't believe what I am about to ask. I feel dirty even saying it. "Do you think you can help me figure out how to maximize my EXP and gold coins? We are going to have to min/max this if we have any chance of completing all these quest items."

"On it!" He puts the headset back on, leaving me alone with Sarah. She says, "Carlos and I had a chat. We think we have figured out another one of your fears and we've come up with the perfect way for you to face it." She checks her watch and says, "We have to go right now if we are going to get there in time. We can leave Carlos here, he seems happy in the game."

"Are you going to tell me where we are going?"

"Nope."

"Why not?"

"We both agreed you wouldn't come if you knew where you were going."

"Now I really want to know."

She stares right at me. "Do you trust me?"

"Of course I do!"

"Then shut up and get in the car." There's a hint of a smile creeping in as she does her best to maintain her serious face.

We drive across town. It's exactly how I imagined it all those years ago, just the two of us, off on an adventure together. In my fantasy Sarah was wearing something more revealing and I had more muscles, but I will settle for this reality. If that's what I can call it.

As we are driving Sarah turns off the radio. "What happened to you? You just fell off the face of the earth after university. I half expected you to be running your own company by now, and instead you're slumming it as a junior Business Analyst."

I see Carlos has been blabbing again. I wonder how much he has told her. "My Dad got in a car accident and I took the first job I could find to help pay the bills. I guess when he passed away I never stopped to reevaluate what I was doing with my life. It's only recently that I've been questioning why I'm still working there."

She takes her eyes off the road long enough to make eye contact with me. "I'm sorry to hear about your Dad. I didn't know."

"Accidents happen. It took me a long time to come to terms with the fact that it was just bad luck. Could have happened to anyone. He was in the wrong place at the wrong time. It was simply a bad roll of the dice. Or perhaps it was preprogrammed. Who really knows how any of this works."

"How did your Mum take it?"

"It's made her afraid of everything. Every time I leave the house she is convinced it is the last time she's going to see me. She's getting a little better, but it's been hard on both of us."

"Carlos said you're still living with her. Have you thought about moving out?"

I laugh a little harder than necessary. "I would love to, but work isn't exactly paying me the big bucks. By the time I've helped Mum with the mortgage and bills there isn't much left for me to think about buying my own place. The good news is she only has four years left on the house until it's all paid off."

"That's a long time to put your life on hold."

"It's not like I am turning down a bunch of better offers. It works for both of us."

I'm not sure I can keep talking about this, not just because of the mood it is putting me in, but because it is reminding me how much it hurts to lose someone you care about, and now everyone I care about is relying on me.

Sarah suddenly swerves left and pulls the car into a pub car park. As she turns the engine off I say, "Are we stopping for a cheeky pint?"

"Not exactly. Come on."

"What are we doing here?"

"You'll find out."

I reluctantly follow her, the feeling that this is some kind of elaborate trap still lingering. As soon as we walk in the door I see the banner and turn to leave, but Sarah grabs my arm. "We figured we needed to deal with your fear of rejection."

"Rejection? I'm not afraid of rejection!"

"Then why won't you ask a woman out? Carlos said you keep chickening out every time you guys go out together. It's been years since university and he said you haven't had a single relationship. It's time to get over it."

It has suddenly become a lot easier to decide who is going to live and who is going to die. If Carlos survives the end of the world I'm going to kill him. "Maybe I'm not interested, did you think about that?"

"Sure, but I don't think that's it. There's something stopping you. You need to get out of your own way. You're a great guy, you deserve to be happy."

"I'm very happy!"

"Are you telling me if you had died yesterday that you would have strolled up to the pearly gates content that you had lived your life to the fullest?"

I open my mouth to spout a witty retort, but nothing comes out. The truth is, she's not wrong. What would I have left behind? A pile of half-finished video games, a dozen spreadsheets and a mountain of regrets. It's not really the legacy I had imagined.

I could turn and run, I have the shoes for it. Something keeps me here though. I *have* been afraid of commitment. I saw how broken my Mum's heart was when Dad passed away and a part of me vowed to never let myself be that vulnerable. Perhaps it is time to put that behind me. Knock one more fear off the list.

I stroll through the double doors before I can change my mind, underneath the banner that says *Speed Dating Tonight!*

LEVEL 13: SPEED RUN

A young lady with a clipboard is grinning far too enthusiastically as we approach her. She says, "Are you two here for tonight's event?"

"What? No, just him." Sarah goes an interesting shade of red. I guess I am not the only one with commitment issues.

The lady checks her clipboard. "I'm afraid that's not possible. We already have more men than women. I can't let the ratio skew any further." She turns to me. "Perhaps you could try again next week?"

"Sorry, there won't be a next week if I can't get over my fear of rejection." I meant that to sound sarcastic, but now that I think of it I sound suicidal.

The hostess is now looking at me, very concerned. Sarah can see we are about to get kicked out so she says, "Ok fine, I'll do it. I will bring up the numbers for the ladies if you let my friend take part."

The hostess looks torn between letting me anywhere near a woman and improving her ratio. After a few seconds she says, "Ok fine. Read these forms and then someone will show you where to go."

I scan the form. In essence, if I like someone I should tick the box next to their name. If I'm not interested I put an X. If we both tick then our contact details get shared. When the bell rings we move on to the next person. Sounds simple enough.

Sarah takes a seat with the rest of the girls. There are only five of them. I find a group of anxious-looking guys, at least a dozen, all standing around chugging their drinks with the enthusiasm of teenagers that have found the key to their parents' liquor cabinet. Several of them are wearing suits and the others are at least wearing shirts. If I had known we were coming here perhaps I would have changed out of my hoodie. Still, the only other item of clothing I have to equip, I mean wear, is my Germany football shirt and I think that has caused quite enough trouble for one day.

As I stroll up to the group one of the guys wearing a bright red shirt looks at me and scoffs. "Is it laundry day?"

A couple of the others chuckle. It's been a long day, so I fire back. "Yeah, the washing machine on my yacht is on the fritz again and Jeeves didn't have time to make it to the dry cleaners yet. You know how it is. Just can't find the help these days."

That gets a bigger laugh from the group and the guy downs his pint before sizing me up. His tone changes. "You think you're funny, how about we step outside?"

A tiny health bar appears above his head.

Level 3 Try hard.

One punch and he'd be toast. I wave him away. "Sorry buddy, I'm not much of a fighter. Save your energy for the girls."

He still looks like he might go for me, but then a larger guy in an orange shirt places his hand on his shoulder. "It's not worth it T.J. He's right, save your energy."

"He's disrespecting me Earl. The guy's a wiener. I should teach him a lesson."

"The girls are watching."

T.J. glances over at the tables and huffs before backing down.

One of the other guys sticks out his hand. "Ignore him, he's an idiot. I'm Charles. Is this your first time speed dating?"

I glance down at my outfit. "How did you know?"

"You have the look of fresh meat. Don't worry, the girls will dig that. I can give you some tips if you'd like?"

What do I have to lose? "Sure, I need all the help I can get."

"Don't try too hard, you will come across as desperate. If the first question the girl asks is what do you do, then that is all she cares about. Giving the wrong answer to that question will immediately take you out of the race. Feel free to be creative with the truth for that one. If she mentions an ex-boyfriend or recent breakup then that means she is on the rebound and out to get him. Tick those ones even if you don't fancy them, they usually just tick every guy. Finally if they ask you to buy them a drink tell them to take a hike, the drinks here are ridiculously overpriced because they know the guys are trying to impress. If all else fails just don't say anything. Women love it when you let them talk, it rarely happens. That should be enough to get you started. Any questions?"

"You sound like you've done this a lot. Does it work?"

"If it worked I wouldn't have done this a lot."

"Good point!"

"It depends what you're looking for. If it's just a bit of fun and possibly a quick fling then I'd say it's more effective than trying to pickup in a random bar, because you've already filtered out most of the girls with boyfriends and husbands. If you're after true love then you've come to the wrong place," he says.

I stare across the room at Sarah as she wriggles uncomfortably in her seat. Maybe Charles is wrong, maybe this is exactly where I will find true love.

A bell rings and the guys all finish off their drinks before rushing to sit at a table. Charles grabs me by the arm and says, "No need to rush old chap." He waves at the barman. "We'll get two beers here."

"Both on your tab Mr. Rock?"

He nods and the barman pours our drinks while I watch the rest of the guys fighting over the limited number of seats. T.J. shoves another bloke and the next thing they are having a full on punch up in the middle of the bar. Earl goes wading in to try and break them apart.

Charles chuckles and hands me a pint as security drags all three of the troublemakers out of the building. "Happens every time. There's always one that wants to show everyone he is the alpha male. We should thank them really, compared to them we will seem like civilized gentlemen. Cheers." We chink glasses and wait for our turn.

Charles points at an older gentleman. "Check this guy out. He's dying out there."

I overhear the guy say, "Hi, I'm John. I am 64, recently divorced, no kids. I work in sanitation."

Charles shakes his head. "Don't be formal like that, listing off your attributes like bullet points. It makes it sound like you're applying for a job. You want to be light and breezy. Don't overshare, far better to be mysterious."

I scan the room. "Like that guy?"

The guy I point at has a shaved head and is wearing a suit and tie. He isn't saying anything, instead he is sitting in silence and staring at the girl. She wriggles in her seat uncomfortably.

"God no, that guy is way too intense! He looks like he would rather murder her than date her. Maybe go for something a little bit in-between."

The buzzer comes far quicker than I was expecting and suddenly I'm up. I leave Charles at the bar and sit down at the first table. The woman sitting there takes one look at my outfit and marks an X on her card without saying a word. Not a great start. I try to think of something sweet or witty to say. Instead I sit down and stare at her blankly. It goes on for so long it becomes awkward. This is usually the part where I would run, but I'm stuck in this seat until the buzzer goes.

I try to think of something to say, but my mouth is suddenly constipated. Nothing will come out. I don't know what my problem is. I try to force out the words, but instead I let out a low groan.

Eventually she says, "Are you ok? Do you need the toilet?"

I can do this. I just have to say something nice about her, a compliment, anything to break the ice. Anything at all.

"You have a face!"

Nailed it.

She doesn't even bother pretending any more. She pulls out her phone, no doubt to tell her social media followers what a disaster speed dating is turning out to be.

I just need to give myself a pep talk. Come on Marcus, remember what Charles said. Play it cool. She's just a person, a regular, run-of-the-mill girl. "I don't even fancy her."

Wait, did I say that last bit out loud?

Now she's scowling. She says, "*You* don't fancy *me*?"

"I'm really sorry, you're just not my type."

"Like you can be picky."

Now it's my turn to be offended. "I'll have you know I have very high standards."

"What, and you're saying that I don't meet them? What exactly should I change? Perhaps you'd like it if I lost some weight, or maybe I should get a boob job? Is that the problem? You're just like my ex! You'd prefer someone with breasts so large they block out the sun, is that it? Maybe I could put on a bikini and play some volleyball for you?" She's shouting loud enough that the other couples around us have stopped to stare.

I need to do some damage control. I wave over a waiter and say, "We'd like a couple of drinks here please. My treat."

"Oh I get it, perhaps if you get drunk enough you can drop your standards, is that it?"

Please oh please can someone push the buzzer.

She turns to the waiter. "I'll have a bottle of champagne and one glass please."

That's going to cost me.

The buzzer sounds, bringing sweet release. The girl says, "Just so we're clear, I wouldn't date you if you were the last guy on earth. I'd prefer to die alone."

That should do it. Any minute now I'll get my status update.

Nothing.

Why didn't that register? It was certainly humiliating enough. Maybe this isn't one of my fears after all. Or perhaps I have to get rejected by all of them. That's going to be fun. One down, four to go.

I vow to do better. I just have to stop trying and start talking. This is all just a game, stop thinking, start playing.

I have barely sat down at the next table when the new girl says, "What was that all about? Is that your ex or something?"

"What? No, we just met."

"Wow, she was *so* mad at you. I assumed there was a history there."

"What can I say, it's a skill I have."

She smiles. "Impressive."

"I'm Marcus." Oh good, at least I managed to get out my name this time. Progress!

"I'm Claire." She holds out her hand and I start to shake it, but then I forget to let go and it becomes awkward. Eventually she pulls her hand away and says, "Is this some kind of *treat them mean, keep them keen* act?"

"No, this isn't some calculated ploy to exploit your insecurities. I'm just really bad at dating."

"I'll say. So what made you come speed dating?"

"I'm here with a friend. It was her idea." I glance over at Sarah and a pang of jealousy hits me. The guy she is with is making her laugh.

Claire looks at me and says, "Friend huh. Seems to me like you'd prefer it was something else."

"What? No! Don't be silly."

Claire stares at me until I crack under the pressure. "Is it that obvious?"

"Only to someone with eyes. Why don't you tell her?"

"She just broke up with her fiancee. She kind of hates guys at the moment."

"All the more reason to let her know how you feel. Or would you prefer to wait until after she's met someone else?"

"It's not that simple."

Claire places her hand on mine. "Perhaps it's not that complicated. How does she feel about you?"

"I have no idea, I only just met up with her again. There was something there once, maybe, a long time ago."

"Then you owe it to yourself to let her know. What's the worst that can happen?"

"She can reject me, stomp all over my heart, and then the world will end." I really need to stop saying that, people are going to think I am completely insane.

"I'll make you a deal. If that happens, I'll go out on a date with you. But if you don't tell her I'm going to have to mark you as an X.

I don't date quitters." She picks up her pen and spins it around her fingers. "So what's it going to be?"

I've been so distracted this whole time I didn't even stop to look at Claire. She's cute, with flowing red hair and a patch of freckles on each cheek. Any other day I'd kill to go on a date with a girl like this. She's right, I have been fighting for my life all day and I am still here, but I'm still too afraid to tell Sarah how I feel.

The buzzer sounds. I turn and say, "Thanks Claire, I really needed to hear that. It's been a pleasure meeting you."

"You too Marcus. Good luck." She makes a show of ticking her card.

I walk right past the next girl, and the next one, all the way to Sarah's table. Charles is about to sit down, but he sees me coming. He instantly pulls back the chair and says, "Do you mind taking my spot old chap, I desperately need another drink."

"Thanks Charles. I owe you one."

"Nonsense, I can see you're a man on a mission. I don't want to stand between you and your destiny." He flashes me a wink and pulls me aside. "Do you need protection? In case things go well?" He subtly palms me a condom. I don't want to make a scene so I quickly slip it into my pocket. Then he whistles and strolls off towards the bar.

I sit down and Sarah says, "What are you doing?"

"What I should have done a long time ago."

There it is. The raw fear, the real deal. That deep ache in the pit of my stomach. I care about Sarah and I'm about to confess how I feel. I've been waiting to do this for years.

Her eyes widen and she says, "Wait, no..."

Nothing is going to stop me now, not even Sarah. "I really like you. As in, I fancy you. I've thought about you a lot over the past 3 years, and what I would say to you if I ever saw you again. I get that you're still getting over the last guy, but I have to know if you feel the same."

Bit the Bullet - 3 of 4 Fears conquered. 75% complete.

I wait for her response, my heart pounding in my chest. I'm the hero in this story, this is the part where she falls lovingly into my arms and we live happily ever after.

Sarah groans. "You bloody idiot. What have you done?"

I'll be honest, it's not the response I was expecting. "Excuse me?"

"You've made me the love interest!"

It takes me a moment to comprehend what she is saying.

Oh shit. I'm about to grab her and drag her out of the room when I notice we are surrounded by waiters. They slowly tighten the circle around us until there's no escape. One of them reaches out and grabs Sarah. She screams and he drags her through the group. They close the gap immediately.

The tallest one says, "Lads, I heard this guy sent a bottle of wine back earlier for not being fruity enough. Let's be sure to thank him."

Health bars pop up everywhere. These guys are tough and there are at least a dozen of them. I can still hear Sarah screaming in the distance. If I move quickly I may be able to catch her.

I run at the wall of crisp white shirts and bounce right off. They keep moving towards me, my available space getting squeezed. I try to leap over them, but they reach up and grab my ankle, dragging me back to the earth with a thump. Actually, several thumps.

I try to parry, but I still can't get the timing right. Instead I block. Each hit doesn't do much damage by itself, but there are so many of them. My health bar is slowly being eroded by the onslaught.

Group management 101, don't get surrounded. I flick my left hand and a flying table carves me a gap in the crowd, allowing me to get out of the centre of the circle. They still stalk towards me, but at least now I can put my back to the wall if I need to.

I reach into my pockets but I have nothing of value except a couple of sticks and a condom. I really need to stock up on weapons. For now I'm just going to have to improvise. I take down three of the closest attackers with a flurry of kicks and a few solid punches, but they just keep coming. There are too many of them. I need a distraction. What is it that waiters want more than anything else in the world?

There is something of value in my pockets after all. I pull out my remaining gold coins and toss them into the group. "Here's a tip, thanks for the great service."

The waiters stop their attacks and scramble to scoop up the money, starting a couple of fights amongst themselves. This is my chance.

I'm about to leave when one of the waiters grabs me from behind. He's a big guy and he lifts me clean off the floor, my legs flailing around ineffectively. I'm still trying to figure out how to break free when there is a loud crash and pieces of glass shatter around me. The big guy slumps to the ground and I see Charles pouring what is left of the champagne out of the broken bottle and into a flute. He takes a sip and says, "looks like you needed protection after all old chap."

LEVEL 14: A WALK IN THE PARK

I flip on my speed boots and spiral outwards from the pub, hoping to get lucky. After four laps I skid to a halt. There is no sign of the guys that took Sarah. It's as if they vanished.

I have no idea what to do next, I just know that I need to save her. Carlos will know what to do. I sprint back to the car and tear off towards the university. I could follow the streets, but time is of the essence, so I drive as the crow flies, ignoring traffic lights, down pedestrian side streets and straight across a football pitch. There's a tatty football that's been discarded in the middle of the pitch and I can't help spin the wheel hard left to flick it into the goalposts.

Ten minutes later I burst into Sarah's office. Carlos is still there, headset on, his tongue sticking out in concentration. I yank the headset off and he says, "Dude! Never break immersion like that, not cool."

"They've taken Sarah."

"Taken her? Where? Who?"

"I don't know. I told her that I cared about her and just like that she was snatched. She seemed to know it was going to happen."

Carlos groans. "I just got to that part of the game. The moment you show romantic interest in another character the game targets that individual and kidnaps them. It's meant to give you motivation to keep moving forward."

"It's working! How do I get her back?"

"I don't know. I tried to save mine and accidentally shot her in the head with an arrow, so I may not be the best person to ask. The game told me where to go to save her though, it was a new quest."

Of course! I check my quest long and sure enough there is a new entry:

Quest: Damsel in distress

I select it and an arrow points the way. I turn to leave and Carlos says, "Are you sure you're ready?"

"It doesn't matter if I'm ready, they have her right now. They could kill her before I even get there."

"That's not how games work. They won't do anything until you get there. It's a scripted event. They won't hesitate to kill her once you get there though, so I'll ask again, are you sure you're ready?"

I think back to the small gaggle of waiters that almost killed me. "I need weapons."

"Ok, let's deal with that. What level are you?"

"I just turned 15."

That's when I see the flashing notification. I click on it and it says:

Party system now available.

I stare at Carlos and an option appears above his head.

Add new party member? 2 slots remaining.

I should ask first, or at least give him a heads up, but for a moment I forget this is the real world and I hit yes just to see what happens. Carlos starts blinking rapidly. "Something's happening! I think I joined the game."

"Oops, sorry about that, it asked if I wanted to add you. I should have checked first."

"Are you mad? Of course I want in on this. Let's go kick some arse."

I go to leave when I notice his health bar. "We can't. You're still a level one. I can't take you anywhere, you're going to get murdered by every grunt we bump into. We're going to have to get you levelled up and fast."

He smiles. "No problem. I found some pretty interesting exploits in the game. I'm curious to see if they work in the real world. Give me an hour."

"I'll come with you."

"Nope. The game shares EXP evenly between all party members. If you come it will take twice as long. You should focus on a different quest. If you want better weapons you need to find a blacksmith. In the game they have all the best stuff. I'll warn you that you can't just buy the legendary ones, the blacksmith always needs you to do some pointless side quest."

Just what I need, more quests to do. I'm already struggling to keep on top of the main quest. Still, I can't rescue Sarah in my current state, the best piece of gear I have is a tatty purple hoodie. I need something offensive. Something other than Carlos.

He says, "Meet back here in an hour?"

"Are you sure you are ok to go out there alone?"

He does a back flip and starts shadow boxing. "Yeah I think I can manage. I've had more practice in the game. See if you can get some good kit for me while you're at it."

As Carlos is walking out the door I shout after him, "Where can I find a blacksmith?"

"Where else. The Smoking Anvil."

***

The Smoking Anvil is an old man's pub. It smells like pipe smoke from ten feet away, even though smoking has long since been banned inside. The car park is full of beige Volvos and two-seater sports cars, for those who are still working through their mid-life crisis.

I crack the door open and peer inside. There is a full-sized snooker table dominating the centre of the room. Golf is currently playing on the TV, which is tucked away in the corner. Music from the sixties is blaring out of an old-fashioned jukebox. I spot at least a dozen kinds of local ales on tap.

The moment I cross the threshold the patrons all stop and stare at me. An elderly gentleman approaches me. "Are you looking for your Dad sonny?"

"No sir, I am after a blacksmith."

The jukebox skips with a scratch and everyone stops what they are doing. A large bearded gentleman steps out from the shadows. "What are you looking for?"

I'm not really sure what the answer is when it's a crowded pub. Presumably asking for high-tech weaponry is out. I say, "I've heard you're the man to see if I need to upgrade my equipment." I throw in a wink.

"Please stop whatever it is you're doing with your face. I can't help you right now, I have to go pick up my daughter Mary. Unless you can do it for me?"

That sounds suitably pointless. "Of course. Where is she?"

"She's in the park just down the road. Bring her back here and I should have everything ready."

Simple enough.

I turn on the speed shoes and within ten seconds I am in the park. There is a rugby game in full swing, catching the last of the sunlight. There's a yoga club, fire breathers, even an impromptu archery class. A crowded park seems like a bit of a dangerous place to be shooting arrows, but who am I to argue.

I spot the blacksmith's daughter standing all alone. I know it is her because she's as tall as he is and wearing a chain mail dress. She looks more than old enough to walk down the road to the pub. I stroll up to her and say, "Your dad sent me to get you."

She nods and I turn to leave, but she just stands there. I take a few steps, then I go back and say, "Just follow me, ok?"

She does. Kind of. She makes it three steps before she veers off to the left for no apparent reason. She is walking at a snail's pace, so it is not hard to catch up to her. I walk alongside her. "It's actually more this way..."

She ignores me and keeps walking, right into archery practice. An arrow misses her by an inch, landing in the centre of the target with a thwack. That's when I realize what is going on. I'm in an escort mission. Escort missions are the worst!

She continues her glacial pace while the arrows rain down around us. I orbit her like a tiny planet, desperately trying to change her course away from the mortal danger. I can see a shot lining up and it's going to catch her for sure, so I leap in front of it like her bodyguard. My hoodie absorbs most of the impact. I only lose a small chunk of health as the arrow clatters to the ground. That was close. Too close. I pull my hood up and dance around in front of her, blocking the shots of the archers, who seem perfectly content to keep loosing arrows despite someone clearly being in the firing line.

We are almost in the clear when I take an arrow right in the knee. I hobble off and yank it out with a squeal while Mary stops to smell some flowers. I limp back into danger and drag her out of harm's way. I shout, "Stay right there." She stares at me, oblivious.

I stop and take a look at my knee. It's not bleeding, but it's going to be sore tomorrow. I really need to find myself some legendary trousers, these level 2's just aren't cutting it. I poke my finger right through the hole.

I look up to find Mary has gone again. That's when I hear the commotion. She has wandered onto the rugby pitch. 30 angry guys are charging into each other in the mud, and right in the centre of it is Mary. She has sat down in the middle of the field for reasons known only to her. She starts making a daisy chain.

I crank up my speed shoes and run out onto the pitch. I try to grab Mary and drag her away, but she is heavy and refuses to cooperate. That's when I get tackled. A chunk of health disappears and I feel my teeth rattle as I hit the ground. The guy looks at me and says, "Are you mad? Get off the pitch!"

I run up behind Mary and go full speed with my shoes, but she is hard to shift. It's like trying to push a monster truck up a hill. Mud and grass goes everywhere, but eventually we get to the other side. She suddenly picks up speed, right towards the fire breathers. There is ten feet of clear space on either side of them, but Mary walks right down the centre. I try to shield her from as much of the flames as possible and by the time we are out the other side my hoodie is looking rather worse for wear. There are entire patches where no more purple is visible. I'm a charred mess.

At least we only have yoga left to navigate. We are through the worst of it now.

I've no sooner thought that than one of the yoga students pulls out a knife and charges right at us. I try to hit her, but she is very bendy and keeps dodging out the way. She takes a swing at Mary and I manage to get between them. I try to parry, but I muck up the timing again and take a knife between the ribs for my trouble. It takes a nasty chunk off my health and hurts a lot. The yoga ninja leaves it stuck there and pulls out another one from goodness knows where. While I am pondering that particular mystery her mates join in. I proceed to beat the crap out of seven women in yoga pants. This gets the attention of the rugby players, who don't take too kindly to it. I have to turn on my turbo shoes and sprint in and out of danger, taking swings at guys the size of small lorries in between stealing food from a couple's picnic basket. Their sand-wiches are the only thing standing between me and certain death. The entire time this epic battle plays out, Mary continues her leisurely amble towards the Smoking Anvil.

***

The door to the pub creaks open and I limp in. I hold it open for Mary, who casually strolls in and says, "Hey dad."

"Hey sweetie." He turns to me. "Any trouble?"

I'm busy removing a knife from my ribcage. When I pull it out there is a disturbing whistling sound coming from my chest. I use the knife to trim the feathers off the arrows that are sticking out of my back before I yank them out. I turn back to the blacksmith. "No, it was a walk in the park."

"Happy to hear it. I've got everything setup. As a thank you please help yourself to a free item."

He's setup a makeshift stall in the corner of the pub. None of the regulars seem too fussed about the large pile of weaponry stacked on a table. I take a closer look and smile. There is all manner of bladed instruments here, long swords, broadswords, battle axes, even a hammer. The fancier ones have gold trim and jewel encrusted hilts. I check out the stats for each and do some quick comparisons. I'm about to pick a very shiny scythe when I notice the locked wooden box on the corner of the table. I turn to the blacksmith. "What is that?"

He smiles. "That's the mystery item. You don't know what it is until you choose it."

I look at all the other weapons, so many murderous options. I should play it safe, go with what I know, optimize my offensive capability. That's what a sensible player would do. I'm a sensible guy.

"I'll take the mystery box."

I have no idea why I did that! This better be something good. If it's a KLOBB or something equally useless I'm going to be pissed.

I pry open the lid and grin. It's not at all what I was expecting.

This changes everything.

LEVEL 15: RAMPART

I run back into Sarah's office and do a double take when I see Carlos. The corner of my mouth curls up. "What on earth are you wearing?"

He's decked out in an entirely leather outfit, including leather trousers and what can best be described as a bodice. It's decoratively embossed and would look more at home on a stout lady at a burlesque show. He completes the ensemble with a quiver full of arrows, a longbow as tall as he is, and a pointed hood. I can't help but laugh. "Mate, you look ridiculous."

"Laugh all you want, this is decent gear! This chest plate is level 23."

"Yeah, and size double D. Does it come in men's?"

He adjusts his bodice. "Piss off. I don't care how it looks. It is the optimal combination based on my current inventory. Speaking of which, how did you get on at the blacksmith's? Get anything good?"

I point at my waist and his eyes grow wide. "No way! You have guns?"

"I sure do. Check this out." I quick draw both of them from their holsters and spin them around so the handles are facing Carlos. One is a stout black pistol, the other is a silver revolver with an extra-long barrel. He takes them from me gingerly and examines them, reading the names etched into the handles. "Waterfall and Agile. Those are some pretty awful names for pistols. Have you tested them out yet?"

"No, I didn't want to run down the street randomly shooting people. I figured we could wait for a big battle. I'm still not entirely sure what shooting someone is going to do to them, I'm not sure if I want to find out."

"Only you could get two awesome weapons and then worry about the implications of using them. If you're not going to use them, you're still not going to be much use in a fight."

"I thought of that."

The blacksmith was more than happy to sell me a weapon, although it did require a trip outside to pickpocket the mound of unconscious people I left in the park. Those yoga pants don't leave much room for pockets and I felt more than a little awkward patting them down for coins.

I pull out the six-foot bo staff from my pocket like a magician with his line of hankies. I twirl it around and then slide it carefully back in.

"Looks like we are all set then. Let's go rescue your girlfriend."

"She's not my girlfriend!"

"Sure sure, I meant your friend, who is a girl, that you fancy."

"I'm reconsidering my stance on using the pistols..."

"You'd have to hit me first." He somersaults around the room like an acrobat, running along walls, doing back flips and swinging from the light fixture.

"How are you so nimble?"

"Easy, I put all my points into agility. Who needs health and strength?"

I glance at my health bar which is at least twice as long as when I started. I can't help it if I play a little more conservatively.

We set off in the car, following the green arrow. It only points in the direction we are supposed to be going, so it is the worst GPS ever.

"So what's with the bow? I figured you'd be more up close and personal, like a rogue or an assassin," I ask.

"You know how it is, no matter what character build I go for, I always end up being a sneaky archer."

"I suppose. What have you unlocked?"

"A bunch of cool stuff, including a very interesting spell."

"Awesome! Wait, how do you have magic?" I glance at his stats. "You're level 19 already?"

"I told you, I found a few gaps in the game's logic. Enemies will revive each other if you leave them prone long enough, and you get more EXP if you take them down again."

"You just sat there almost killing a couple of guys over and over again for an hour didn't you."

"Something like that." He smirks. "How far until we get to Sarah?"

I check the distance reading under the arrow. "It is still a couple of miles away."

"I don't get it, we are almost out of the city. What is even out here?"

We both share a glance and say in unison, "The castle!"

There's an old abandoned castle on the outskirts of town, not nice enough to be considered a tourist spot but still robust enough to make a half-decent defensive position. It would be the perfect place to lure us.

As soon as we pull up, I know we are in the right place. For reasons unknown the castle is now filled with waist-high walls, perfect for vaulting over. Those definitely weren't there the last time I came here on a school trip. There are also roving gangs of guards, walking similar looped patterns from the bank earlier, only this time with flaming torches and swords.

I pull Carlos aside, "Ok, here's the plan. We'll split up, you take the higher ground, see if you can setup a sniper perch. I'll sneak past the guards undetected and try to make it to the keep, which is where they would be holding Sarah. Once there, I'll try to get her out without raising the alarm. If we time it just right and coordi- nate our..." I turn and Carlos is gone. He's running full speed at the enemy guards, his bow drawn. He's emitting an obnoxiously loud battle cry that would wake the dead. So much for sneaky archer. He's gone full Leeroy on me.

I curse under my breath and run after him. He's taking cover behind one of the waist-high walls and eating a fistful of chocolate bars. I skid into place beside him just as a volley of arrows clatters off the wall behind us. My voice comes out a little louder than I intend, "What was that?"

"You think too much. I didn't have time for one of your intricate battle plans that fall apart ten seconds into the engagement. We play better when we improvise."

"This isn't a game, it's real life!"

Carlos stands, fires off three arrows, and then ducks back behind the wall. "Is it though? None of this is real, at least not in the traditional sense. Makes you think huh, perhaps all that nonsense about heaven and hell and the afterlife is legit after all, it's just on a different server with different rules turned on."

"I'm planning on not testing that theory any time soon. Let's just concentrate on staying alive. So now what?"

"How would I know, you're the planning guy."

I really hope they have friendly fire on in this game so I can hit him in the face with a table.

I'm still dreaming of beating up my teammate when I spot the two guards trying to flank. We can't let them get behind us, we'll get stuck in a crossfire. Time to test out my new purchase. I equip my bo staff. It is thick enough that it should be heavy, but I twirl it around effortlessly. I use it to vault over our cover, landing on top of the two guards and knocking them out cold.

The noise of me crashing to the ground has drawn every guard in the vicinity and they pour out of every doorway. It's ok though, there are two of us now. Carlos has already taken several of them out with headshots. I shout at him over the ruckus, "what are you doing? You can't just kill these guys! They could have families."

"Remember the Drunken Hedgehog? They will probably respawn when we leave."

"Probably?"

"Do you think they are concerned for *our* general wellbeing? Would you prefer me to fire arrows with boxing gloves on the end, like a cartoon?"

"Yes!"

"Well too bad. I'm here to win, not get pwned. If you're going to make it through this you are going to have to do some things you might not agree with. Now stop yapping and start fighting."

I peek my head over cover. Thanks to Carlos there are only a handful of guys left. We should be able to take them down easily enough. That's when I feel the ground quake. The biggest guy I have ever seen comes around the corner. He's at least seven feet tall, probably more, but with the build of a brick outhouse. He speaks in a booming voice. "You're mine!"

His health bar is massive, but it's the level above it that concerns me. He's a level 22 Bruiser. Even combined we are going to have a hard time taking him down. Carlos immediately switches his arrow fire to this new threat, but each arrow only takes off a sliver of his health. My hands reach for the guns in their holsters, but I'm still not sure I am willing to cross that line until I know the people will be ok. Instead I speed boost in and smack him with my bo staff. It vibrates in my hand as if bounces off his thick skin. I dart away before he can take a swipe at me.

Carlos continues to chip away with arrows, but he's running out of places to evade. I watch as he throws something down on the ground and a large bubble appears around him. He stands in the centre, firing arrows out. He must be safe from attacks inside.

Nope. The Bruiser plucks him out of the bubble and dashes him against a brick wall before tossing him across the map. I wait for Carlos to get up, but he doesn't.

This can't be it, I can't have lost him already.

This is my fault. I brought him into this. He'd be alive if it wasn't for me adding him to the game.

Anger takes over. I want this guy to suffer, to feel the pain that I am feeling. My hands shake as I draw both the pistols. I'm too mad to aim, I just point Agile in the general direction of the Bruiser and pull the trigger. It fires all of its bullets at once. They fly out like a sand storm. I wasn't prepared for the recoil and the gun bucks upwards, shooting down a passing pigeon in a poof of feathers. In my rage I scowl at the notification.

1 of 200 pigeons killed.

Now is not the time for bloody collectibles. I am mad enough already.

I try to reload, and that's when I realize I don't have any more bullets. All I have done is get the Bruiser's attention. He stomps towards me, ready to finish the job. I point my other pistol, Waterfall, and cringe as I pull the trigger. The recoil is enough to lift me off my feet. At first I think I have missed as there is no gaping bullet hole in the Bruiser's chest, but when I check his health bar I see that just over half of it is now missing. At least now I know I can shoot him.

One more shot should finish him off. I steady myself and point the gun, ready for the recoil this time. I pull the trigger and hear the *click.* I try a few more times with the same results. One bullet? What use is a gun with one bullet? I stare at my useless new weapon and get a notification.

Deploying next projectile. ETA 2 minutes.

2 minutes! We'll be dead by then. I have a gun that fires bullets so quickly I can't keep it loaded, and I have a gun that has the firing rate of an antique musket.

Bloody marvellous.

I stare around the girth of my attacker and see Carlos still laying prone on the ground. I have to get to him, but if I try to do it with the Bruiser on my tail I am going to get us both killed. If he's not dead already.

In my rage I almost forgot about my magic. Unfortunately there are no tables out here, so that leaves cream pies. I fling one his way with very little expectation, but it hits him right in the face. He angrily flails around while trying to clear his eyes. It is just the window I need.

The path to Carlos is too cluttered with walls, I need a straight shot to take advantage of my speed shoes. That's when I notice the castle walls. They have a narrow path that is heading in the right direction, I just need to get up there.

There is a convenient set of pillars of varying heights right next to the wall, I just need to gauge my jumps right. After the first couple I feel more confident, but the Bruiser bellows below me. He charges full speed, hitting the pillar I am standing on, sending it crashing to the ground. I only just leap to the next pillar in time. I watch as he clambers out of the rubble. I drag myself up onto the path and taunt the Bruiser, who doesn't take too kindly to it. He picks up the guy standing to his left and tosses him at me, narrowly missing. The poor guy hits the stone wall with a crunch. He's going to feel that tomorrow. Hopefully.

I crank the turbo shoes and bolt down the length of the wall, putting some distance between me and certain death. I leap down next to Carlos and check for a pulse. The moment I touch him I get a countdown from 10 seconds. I glance up to see the Bruiser picking his way across the courtyard, batting away anyone that gets in his way. This is going to be close. I keep my hand placed firmly on Carlos' neck and hold my breath.

Another gaggle of guards appears from a doorway. Just what we need, more people trying to kill us. That should be enough to doom us both, but they make the mistake of getting in the way of the Bruiser. He bats them out of the way and they scatter like pins at a bowling alley. Not only does it even up the numbers, it slows him down.

Carlos opens his eyes with a gasp and stares up at me. He says, "Is this heaven? If so, I want a refund."

Apparently his sense of humour died alongside him. "Now is not the time for chit chat, unless you want to get back to heaven in a hurry."

"Don't blame me, I thought that bubble shield blocked all attacks. Guess it only works on projectiles."

He ninja flips back onto his feet like it's no big deal. A few hours ago he couldn't even do one sit up.

The Bruiser pauses as he sees Carlos get back up. Two against one. Checkmate.

Apparently he doesn't agree. He scoops up a wooden barrel from an abandoned cart and tosses it at us. We both instinctively jump over it. He tries again, throwing it a little harder this time. It clips my foot as I leap and I crash to the ground with a thud.

There's a small chirping sound and Waterfall vibrates on my hip. Apparently it is ready to fire again. I sit up just in time to see our muscular friend picking up a bright red barrel. I glance at Carlos and he says, "you know what to do."

I aim up and shoot the barrel. It explodes in a fireball that almost singes our eyebrows right off. Nobody is surviving that, not even the Bruiser. A notification appears, but I'm too blinded by the flash to read it.

We both dust ourselves off and Carlos pulls a couple of burgers out of his pocket. He hands one to me. I try not to notice that it is warm. Each bite fills up a chunk of my health. It's not enough to get me to back to full, but it drags me off death's door.

We take a moment to survey the destruction. The walls are torn to shreds, with thick stone chunks laying everywhere. This is going to be a nightmare scenario for some poor janitor. English Heritage certainly won't be too happy with us. I'll have to donate them some gold pieces when this is all done.

I shout out, "Sarah!" but there is no response. We just assumed that she was here due to the guards. I flip on my speed shoes and do several laps of the castle, but there is no sign of her. When I get back, Carlos is kneeling over one of the guards, who is coughing. Carlos says, "Where is she?"

The guard chuckles, his voice a faint whisper. "She's dead."

My heart races but then I notice the bullshit detector is flashing. I reach down and grab him by the collar, resting Waterfall on his lap. "Want to try that one again? I'll know if you're lying to me."

"Your princess is in another castle."

No BS detected this time. He's telling the truth. I pistol whip him with Waterfall to finish him off.

I pull up the menu and see that the old quest is marked as complete. There's a new one:

Quest: Another Castle

I try to select it and get a new message:

Must be level 20 to start this Quest

You have got to be kidding me.

LEVEL 16: FUDGE

I deliver the pile of wolf pelts to the old man and he smiles before handing me my reward.

Legendary Trousers of Stand Sure. + 20 Defence + 10 Speed - 10 Attack

I slip them on and Carlos applauds. "Nice work! Now all you need is a legendary helm and you have the whole set. Not bad for a night's work."

There's a nagging feeling, like I am forgetting something. I can't quite place it though.

I'm not even quite sure how we ended up here. I know there was a castle, and then that creepy guy approached us about his vampire problem, which led us to the undertakers, which is where I met the vampire hunter who gave me that bitching silver dagger, which I had to use to slay the werewolf and his pack that was terrorizing the village, which gave me a stack of wolf pelts, which old man Peters traded me for these awesome trousers.

I feel like I'm forgetting something important. What was I doing again?

I check my watch. It's 8 a.m. I should be exhausted, but I feel totally fine.

Carlos stretches, flexing his new arm guards. Thankfully he managed to find some more appropriate gear that doesn't make him look like a backup dancer at a burlesque show. He lets out a yawn and says, "I guess we should get back to rescuing Sarah now."

Sarah! How on earth could I forget? I haven't paid attention to my level all night. I check to find I am level 23. I also have a stack of skill points to spend. "Carlos! Why didn't you say something?"

He stares at me confused. "You know how this goes, you start on one quest and you end up getting distracted by every side quest you find along the way. I just figured you were getting into the spirit of things. It's about bloody time. You're not her guardian. Heroes have to prioritize."

"Prioritize? I was trouser shopping! She's going to kill me if she finds out."

"In that case you may want to change before we rescue her, those things are pretty eye catching."

I click on the quest and the arrow appears. I already know where it is pointing. There is only one other castle in town.

We've barely gone three feet when an old lady with a blue dot above her head appears from behind a tree. She says, "How fortunate that I should bump into you. I am in need of assistance..."

"Nope. Not going to happen! We have somewhere to be."

"But young man, I have this rare amulet that..."

"La la la la." I jam my fingers in my ears and get out of there as quick as I can.

I don't like what this game is doing to me. The real Marcus would never forget about his friends and gallivant around town doing his own thing. He certainly wouldn't forget about Sarah, the girl he has been obsessing over for the last five years. Most importantly of all, real Marcus would never refer to himself in the 3rd person.

I race back to the car, then tap my foot while waiting for Carlos. He takes his sweet time about it. I should try and get him a pair of these fancy turbo shoes.

We drive straight to the other castle as it starts to rain. This castle is less majestic than the previous one, it is more of a ruins. There's a large mob of enemies sitting around a campfire, including three Bruisers, just waiting for us to trigger them. For no obvious reason there is also a crane, with a pallet of red barrels swinging in the wind above the mob. I pull Carlos aside. "Ok, are you going to listen to my game plan this time, or are you going to go charging in again?"

He stares at the three hulking Bruisers and says, "What's the plan?"

I point at the barrels. "If you can shoot out the rope those red barrels should topple into the group and explode, saving us the trouble of taking them on in hand-to-hand combat."

He draws an arrow but shakes his head. "I don't have a good angle from down here. I need a higher vantage point."

He's right, there's a risk of triggering a barrel from shooting upwards like this. Something is nagging at me. Games don't offer a setup like this unless there is a payoff. That's when I notice the strategically placed handholds around the perimeter. I follow them all the way to the other side of the campfire. "Ok, I need you to stealth your way around the outside of the camp and climb up that tower. That will bring you level with the crane and give you a perfect shot. You have to make it all the way there without being spotted. The moment they see you they will scatter and we'll have to fight each and every one of them."

He looks positively thrilled at the thought. His instincts are always to choose the impossible odds. I place my hand on his shoulder. "Please mate, I don't know what stands between us and rescuing Sarah, I just know that I don't want to be limping in there with no health. Can you at least try and do this the easy way?"

His shoulders sag and he nods sagely. "I'll give it my best shot."

I'm going to have to trust him on this one. I watch him run off and find myself hoping for both our sakes that he can control his impulses.

It is hard to follow his progress. He does an expert job of sticking to the shadows. I only catch glimpses of him as he darts from darkness to darkness. The guards on the perimeter vanish one by one as Carlos takes them down.

I lean out of my hiding spot to try and keep track of Carlos and a patrolling guard walks round the corner. We both startle. He opens his mouth to shout and I realize I am not going to be able to shut him up in time. I tense up, ready to fight, when there's a loud *thwack* and the guard falls to the ground face first, an arrow sticking out the back of his head. I look up and see a hand sticking out of the shadows with a brief thumbs up, before it disappears again.

After a few more minutes Carlos is in position at the top of the tower. I can't believe he's made it. This may be the first time he has ever resisted temptation and not intentionally kicked the hornet's nest. He fires an arrow and it severs the rope, dropping the barrels onto the group perfectly. I wait for the explosion, but nothing happens. The guards all pick up their weapons and start to fan out.

I think fast and shoot the nearest barrel with Waterfall, triggering a fireball explosion and sending guards flying everywhere. Most of them drop to zero health instantly, and the ones that don't are set alight and are running around while their health plummets. They are easy pickings.

Carlos appears back by my side without a sound. I give him a nudge. "Nice shot! I never doubted you."

"Sure, sure. Now let's go find Sarah, that explosion is going to attract a lot of unwanted attention."

Right on cue five guards come running, splashing through the growing puddles and brandishing swords and shields. We haven't fought shielded opponents yet. Carlos says, "You get the three on the left, I'll take out the two on the right."

"Why do I get three?"

"You're the hero. I'm just the sassy sidekick."

"Ok fine."

My combat skills have slowly been improving, especially with the bo staff. I step into the centre of the guards as Carlos hangs back, lining up a shot. Everyone waits for someone else to make the first move. Eventually the guards can't take it any longer. One of them steps forward to attack me and Carlos immediately shoots him in the leg. As he reaches down to try to pull out the arrow I take advantage of the distraction and thrust at him with my staff, catching him right under the chin and knocking him out. The guard on my left lunges in, his sword held high, but I duck under my own bo staff and his attack lands on the staff, which buckles but holds. I flip the staff up into the air and take advantage of my free hands by grabbing the guard and throwing him over my shoulder, crashing him into one of his friends that is charging at me. I leap into the air, narrowly avoiding a sneak attack from behind, and catch my staff at the apex of its flight, landing gently with it held behind my back. I hear another guy running up behind me, but I don't need to react, I can see Carlos already has him lined up. The arrow just misses me, the flight tickles my cheek on its way past, and I hear it embed in the guard behind me as he slumps to the ground with a groan.

The three remaining guards scramble to get back to their feet. Two of them are already at half health. Carlos says, "You want the easy pair or the healthy one?"

Better to fight one on one. "I'll take the healthy one."

The guard immediately rushes me. The bo staff is a great long-ranged weapon, but it is lousy in a sword fight. I swing at my opponent, but it bounces ineffectively off his shield with a clang. He reaches me and takes a swipe with his sword. I roll just in time, his sword carving up the ground where I was just standing. I can't let him get close to me like that. That is when I see them laying on the ground. I slip my bo staff back into my pocket as I roll again, this time standing up with the swords of the two fallen guards. I go back on the attack, alternating swipes from each sword, which the guard blocks with his shield or parries with his sword. I swing particularly hard and shatter his shield, breaking the sword in the process. Now it's a straight up sword fight.

The guard hangs back, wary. I turn to check on Carlos. He's sitting eating a burger, the other two guards nowhere to be seen. I shout over, "What are you doing?"

"Taking five. I'm hungry."

"I'm engaged in a fierce sword duel here. Could you maybe help me out?"

"Why? You need the practice."

"Seriously?"

The guard lunges at me and I block the attack, taking a small amount of chip damage. I try an overhead swing and it crashes down, almost connecting, until he blocks at the last second. He counterattacks and I parry, doubling my damage. Now if I can just get a solid hit in.

He's keeping his distance, but I can't figure out why. Quick as a flash he pulls out a throwing knife and tosses it at me. I don't even see the prompt, but instinct kicks in and I select it, catching the knife in the air and flinging it back at him. It hits him squarely in the chest and he falls to the ground.

"You couldn't have just shot him with an arrow?"

"And ruin the show? You had it under control." He finishes his burger. "Nice move with the throwing knife by the way."

"Thanks. I didn't know I could do that, it was a prompt. You think there are any more guards?"

"Unlikely. We've made enough noise that I can't imagine nobody knows we are here. I think that must be all of them."

"Ok, so let's go find Sarah."

We round the corner and that's when we see her. She is being held by a single guy, who is hiding behind her with a gun to her head. He says, "You might have taken out my mates, but I'm not going to give you a chance to do that to me. If you ever want to see your girlfriend again you will need to pass the trials of the Sigma Seven.

You will almost certainly die trying. Firstly, you will need to fight the dragon of..."

Thwack. An arrow appears in his right eye socket and he collapses in a heap, the gun going off when his body hits the ground. Sarah stands there shaking in the rain as I turn to Carlos. "What the fudge was that?"

Wait, why did I say fudge? That certainly isn't the word I was planning on using.

"I saw an opening and I took it."

"What if you'd missed!"

He shrugs. "I don't miss. I figured if we could kill him before he gave us the quest it wouldn't register. Am I right?"

I check and he's right, there is no new quest. I run over to Sarah. She's shivering. I shrug off my hoodie and wrap it around her shoulders. She hugs me tight. "My hero. What can I do to repay you?"

The look she gives me almost stops my heart. There is a deep longing in her eyes, like I have never seen before. What is she doing? I push her away. "No thanks necessary."

She sniffs the hoodie and smiles. "It smells like you."

It smells like charred nylon and the sweat of a dozen rugby players. Did they hit her in the head? "Are you feeling ok?"

"No, I'm cold and damp. Let's get me out of these wet clothes."

Quest complete: Earn the love of a fair maiden. +1000 EXP.

Well this is certainly not how I was expecting to complete that quest.

I pull Carlos aside. "We have a big problem. I think Sarah is trying to seduce me."

"I don't see the problem. You like her, now she likes you."

"But that isn't her! Whoever *that* is loves me because the game is telling her to." The words sting as I say them. I can't let her be manipulated like this. I have to think. I need to break her programming. How can I change her from being a trophy to being a fully fleshed out person again?

Carlos says, "She was a damsel in distress and you rescued her. You've made her your love interest. Now she's going to throw herself at you. The only way to stop it is to give her a new role."

"You're a genius!" I stare at Sarah and pray the option pops up. It takes a few seconds, but then it appears and I select it.

Just like that Sarah shakes her head and says, "What happened? I blacked out for a moment there."

"You were in trouble, but don't worry, you're safe now."

She sniffs the air and says, "What on earth is that stench?"

I smile. "That's my hoodie."

After a few more seconds she blinks and her eyes widen. "Why can I see a health bar? What did you do? Oh my god, I'm in the game aren't I? Fudge!"

Carlos says, "Why do you guys keep saying fudge?"

"Because of the game's rating there is no cursing allowed." Sarah replies.

Carlos is suddenly paying attention. "Wait, what the fudge? Fudge, fudge, fudge. Are you fudging kidding me. I can't say fudge anymore? This is an outrage! You didn't tell me about this. Is it too late to make it an 18 rating?"

"Shut the fudge up." I turn my attention back to Sarah, "About what I said in the bar..."

She blushes slightly. "Let's talk about that later, it feels like the kind of thing that should be discussed over a coffee, not a pile of corpses."

She has a point, this isn't really the ideal location for a heart to heart. Instead I say, "I'm sorry, I had to add you as a party member. You were in danger and the only way to save you was to make you part of the game. You weren't safe as an NPC."

"But it says I'm level 1. That must be some kind of mistake, don't they know I'm a developer? I've never been level 1 before!"

Carlos slaps Sarah heartily on the arm. "Welcome to the party. Now you're just as fudged as we are."

LEVEL 17: THE HOUSE ALWAYS WINS

"We need to get Sarah levelled up, she's not safe as a level 1. We should stick together," I proclaim.

Sarah shakes her head. "No, with the EXP split that doesn't make any sense. It will only slow down my progression. Not to mention the fact that the enemies scale with the highest-levelled character, so hanging out with you guys would put me in considerably more danger."

Carlos nudges me. "See, I told you!"

I stare at her. Something looks different, but I can't quite place it. "At least check if you have any weapons. I want to make sure we aren't sending you out there defenceless."

"Good point." She stares blankly and then says, "Interesting. I'm classed as a magic user, so I have two spells right now. Fireball and Ice blast."

"Try one."

Carlos and I take a step back. Sarah holds out her hand and a tiny ember appears on the ground. We all wait for something else to happen, but instead it flickers and goes out. Sarah stares at her hand before shrugging. "Well that was pretty pathetic. That's not going to be much use unless they want me to light their cigarette."

"Guess you need to level it up."

"I guess. It's going to be hard to take out many enemies with that. I always said the magic users were underpowered in the earlier levels."

Sarah stares off again. "I don't even have a base weapon. Guess I'll just have to disarm someone."

"No problem." I try to hand her Agile and Waterfall, but as she reaches over to take them she hesitates. I say, "It's ok, I can show you how to use them."

"It's not that, it won't let me take them. Magic users can't use ranged weapons. Do you have anything else?"

I scan my inventory and we try the bo staff, but that won't transfer either. She says, "It won't let me take it. I have to have a strength skill over 3 to use it."

Carlos reaches into his pocket and pulls out a stick. Sarah jumps when she picks it up. He says, "Take good care of it. That stick and I have been through a lot."

Sarah sighs and puts the stick in her pocket. "Thank you, it's a good start. I will meet up with you guys back in my office in a couple of hours. That should be enough for me to catch up on levels. Then we can travel together."

She turns to leave and pauses. I think she's going to say something else, maybe mention our conversation in the bar, but after a glance back in my direction she smiles and walks away.

Carlos waits until she is for sure gone before he says, "You guys are so cute."

"What are you talking about?"

"She likes you. It's obvious."

"Since when are you such an expert on women?"

"I'm in sales, my job is to know when someone is ready to buy. She's still hurting from her breakup, but she has feelings for you. You just need to make the first move."

"I tried remember, she almost got killed. I can't risk losing her."

He stares at me. "You lost her once already. Not many people get a second chance like this. Stop thinking so much, you can't plan your way into a relationship. Just go with the flow."

"If we get through this, I promise to try again."

"Thank god. I can't listen to you moping around for five more years." He cracks a smile. "Now let's stop standing around gossiping like a couple of bored housewives and go kick some arse. What's next?"

I'm checking the quest list when a new menu catches my eye. I say to Carlos, "There is a whole menu in here dedicated to our home base. What's that all about?"

Carlos groans. "I'd forgotten about that. The game has a tacked on base builder. It is pretty bare bones. It does come with some major advantages though. Visiting your base immediately heals all damage, restocks all ammo and opens up more inventory spaces. It will become more important as the game gets harder."

"That sounds pretty handy. Can we buy a base, or do we have to capture one? How does it work?"

"You have to buy the initial base and then I think all the upgrades are through resources. Like I said, it didn't appear to be very fleshed out. I'm sure someone in their focus group told them they should have it and it got plonked in."

"Ok, so how do we buy one? Is there a virtual estate agent we need to visit?"

"No, you have to find the base locations yourself. They were really expensive though. It is meant as end game content, they don't want players too OP in the early game."

I look at my measly balance of gold coins. "Doesn't sound like we'll be getting a base any time soon then."

"Nonsense, we just have to find a way to make lots of money quickly."

"I'm not robbing another bank!"

"Don't be silly, I would never suggest you rob a bank. It's too risky," says Carlos.

"Ok phew. For a moment there I was worried."

"Why take the chance when we can just walk into people's houses and take all the gold we can find." He follows this up with his innocent grin, the one that always gets me into trouble.

I groan. "That is *so* much worse than robbing a bank."

"Nonsense. No armed security guards, no cameras, no five-inch thick safe doors. We can just stroll right in."

I open my mouth to argue and stop myself. I wouldn't think twice about doing this in a game, so why am I overthinking it here? I need to embrace my situation.

"Ok fine, let's do it."

Before I can change my mind I run up to the nearest house and kick the front door in. Thankfully no-one is home. I start smashing up anything breakable, looking for gold coins. Teapot? Smashed. Decorative vase? Smashed. Espresso machine? I pick it up and smash it on the ground. Gold coins fly out everywhere.

Carlos runs in behind me. "Holy crap! Easy there tiger, I said let's rob them, not let's burn their house to the ground."

"You told me to find loot, so I am finding loot."

"I guess. Just try to leave the walls standing."

I scour the rest of the downstairs as Carlos works on the upstairs. When I am sure there is nothing left I shout up to him. "Ready to go next door?"

"Yep, hold on one second." There's a loud crash, followed by the sound of several things breaking. He leaps down the stairs three at a time. "Ok, I'm good."

We do three more houses in quick succession. All is going great until I open the door to move on to the next house and hear sirens. I glance down the street to see three police cars approaching at high speed. I turn and run straight into Carlos. "Change of plans, we are going out the back door."

He hesitates and I grab his arm. "No. We aren't getting into a punch up with the police."

"But, they probably have really great gear!"

There's only one way to convince him. "What happens in the game if you attack the city guards?"

He mumbles, "Every guard immediately recognizes you as a bad guy and you have to fight the guards everywhere you go."

"Does that sound like a fun way to spend the rest of our game? On the run from the cops?"

"Point taken." He doesn't look happy about it, but at least he is agreeing with me for once.

We run out the back door and leap over several garden fences. Once we are a safe distance away we switch to walking. We aren't exactly inconspicuous, what with me wearing a bright purple hoodie and pistols hanging off my belt. We have to circle back to the castle to pick up the car, but we don't encounter any trouble on the way. As we drive away several more police cars race past us on the way to a very confusing spree of break-ins, where houses were trashed and nothing valuable was taken.

I should be angry, or annoyed, but instead I feel exhilarated. "Wow! That was a close call."

"Nah, we were fine. What was our final haul?"

I check my inventory. "Just over 500 gold coins. I can't imagine it is enough to buy us a base."

"You're right about that. Bases start at 50,000 gold. We have enough to kick into phase 2 though."

＊

We sit in the smoky tavern that I am sure wasn't here a couple of days ago. The gentleman sitting opposite us is of short stature and has a long flowing beard. He sports several items of jewelry, including a very unusual black ring. The battle hammer he is holding completes his ensemble. I'm not sure what the etiquette is of calling someone a dwarf when they aren't one. I don't think I want to find out.

Carlos leans forwards. "I hear you're the man to talk to around here about gambling."

The dwarf eyes us both suspiciously. "You guards?"

Carlos looks deeply offended. "No sir, just weary adventurers looking for a way to make some easy gold."

"How do I know you ain't guards?"

Carlos sighs. "We don't have time for this." He draws an arrow and shoots the nearest innocent bystander. The poor guy hobbles off screaming for the guards, an arrow sticking out his arse. Several of the other patrons draw their weapons, but the dwarf waves at them to sit down. He says, "What are you going to do when the guards get here?"

There is a muffled thump from the other room and Carlos says, "Arrow dipped in sleeping potion. He'll be fine by morning. So are you the guy to talk to, or should we carry on to the next tavern?"

The dwarf grins. He taps on the ground three times with the handle of his hammer and a trapdoor opens just to the left of us. It looks very dark down there and smells like wet socks. Who knows what is waiting for us at the bottom. If I wasn't packing several sharp objects and two firearms I would definitely be aborting this mission right about now.

I gingerly climb down the ladder and find myself facing another door. Carlos doesn't bother with the ladder, he leaps down and lands without a sound.

He bangs on the door three times and a slot opens, "Password."

"Your bearded mate sent us down here."

"Password!"

Carlos reaches for his bow, but I place my hand on it. I take a out a gold coin and hold it up to the slot. A small hand snatches it. After a few seconds the door creaks open to reveal a full-sized casino. There are scantily clad women everywhere and several large bouncers with swords on their backs. This looks like the kind of place that sees its fair share of casual murders.

A wizened old man squints at us and says, "Leave your weapons on the table please."

He gestures to the large mound of random weapons heaped onto a rickety metal table. I hand my bo staff and pistols over and Carlos reluctantly places his bow and quiver down. He squints at the old man. "I've counted my arrows, so I suggest none of them go missing."

Carlos heads straight for the card table. He pats the seat next to him and I sit down. I'm not much of a card player, but I at least understand the basics. He says, "Gubbins is the fastest way to earn the money that we need for our base."

"Gubbins?"

"Yep. Don't worry, we'll pick it up as we go. Pay the gentleman."

I take a single gold piece out of my coin purse and hand it to the dealer. He bites it and places it on the betting square. He says, "Draw your cards." I stare at him blankly. Carlos reaches into his pocket and pulls out a deck, so I check my own inventory and find a flashing submenu called Gubbins. I flip through my deck. The cards depict all manner of colourful creatures, along with a raft of stats. I lean over to Carlos and mumble under my breath. "What the heck is this?"

Carlos says, "You know how it is with games these days, always have to have an opportunity for spinoffs."

"Wait, do you actually know how to play Gubbins?"

"Not exactly. I found the casino when I played, but I didn't want to waste time on a silly side game. How hard can it be?"

The dealer says, "Don't worry, it is very easy to get the hang of. You'll be winning in no time."

My bullshit detector goes into overdrive. That's not exactly reassuring.

I reply. "Any chance you can refresh us on the rules?"

If his grin was any wider he would turn into a cat and disappear. "Of course. You start with four heroes, each with their own lane, which are defended by their minions, which have a health indicated by the blue circle, an attack stat shown in red and a defence stat shown in yellow. You can then equip weapons and spells, which have a compound effect on the overall board and can be used to buff stats or affect the opposition's minions. When attacking, the target's defence number is subtracted from the attacker's attack stat and the difference is removed from their health points. Heroes have special abilities which charge with activity points, which are earned by defeating the enemy minions, but spent when you utilize deflect abilities. The goal is simple, kill all your opponent's heroes. I kill yours, I keep your money. You kill mine, I double your money. Would you like me to go over that again?"

I blink a few times. Perhaps it is one of those games that will make more sense when we have played a few hands.

Nope.

Now we are down ten gold coins and I still have no idea what is going on. The dealer's cards feel a lot more powerful than ours. He has mounted cavalry and archers with much better stats than our foot soldiers and donkeys. After a few more hands Carlos says, "I think I know the problem here."

"Yeah, we don't know what we are doing, the rules make no sense and the dealer is openly cheating."

"No, that's not the problem. The issue is that we're playing with a default deck."

"What are you talking about?"

"These games are always the same. Give me a moment, I'm sure it will be in here somewhere."

He blanks out and I am left to make small talk with the dealer. "How's your day going?"

"Not bad, only been one fight so far this shift and even that was a small one. There were only three bodies to clean up. Managed to snag myself these new boots." He hefts his foot up onto the table to show me.

"Lovely!"

I nudge Carlos and he says, "Hold on, almost got it. Do you know how hard it is to enter a credit card number with your mind?"

"Credit card?"

"Yep. Ok, I'll just get us a couple of booster packs... wait, that didn't quite do it. I'll just grab another couple...ok, give me a minute here."

He stares off for what feels like a long time, while making increasingly angry noises. Eventually he says, "Finally! Ok, let's do this. Check your deck again. I've bought us a few upgrades."

I take a peek and see some new cards. I have dragons, wizards, a couple of giants, all with much larger numbers than the previous ones. Some of them are shiny. "These must have cost a fortune!"

"Yeah, wouldn't you know it, most of the packs I bought were full of crap. Damn loot crates. I had to buy a few more than I anticipated."

"How many more?"

He mumbles a number that sounds suspiciously like five hundred and thirteen.

"I don't want to know how much that cost."

"You certainly don't. I'll send you the bill if we manage to survive this." He leans closer to me and whispers, "We have to capitalize on the dealer thinking we are total idiots."

That won't be hard. I'm about to formulate a slow and steady plan to recoup our losses when Carlos grabs the coin purse and empties it onto the table. "We're all in."

"But..."

The dealer deftly scoops it all over to his side. "Bets are now closed."

Bugger.

I needn't have panicked. Our new decks steamroll his cavalry and eat his cannons for breakfast. He nods as we slaughter his heroes and he pulls out a stack of gold coins. I reach out for them but Carlos says, "leave it. We'll go again."

Several rounds later, the pile of gold coins is starting to get peoples' attention. I say, "Ok, this has to be the last time. That should cover the cost of our base." The dealer looks over at the pit master, who nods ever so slightly. With a crooked grin the dealer turns over his cards, and wouldn't you know it he suddenly has a kraken and several Greek gods. Some of his cards have triple digit stats.

We get absolutely pounded. Entire rows of the board are decimated with a single attack. One by one our heroes fall, until only one remains. I'm all out of cards, and Carlos only has three left.

It's not looking good, until Carlos plays his next card. It is black and it seems to be emitting its own dark mist. He places it on the table and the onlookers gasp. I read the card and see why.

Death. Kills every card on the board instantly. Single use only.

The dealer chuckles. "Nice try, but that also kills your last hero. In the event of a tie the house wins." He reaches out to grab our coins but Carlos says, "Not so fast." He plays another card.

Extra turn. The player may use this at the end of their turn to gain an additional turn.

The crowd around us starts to chatter. What could Carlos possibly do to an entire board of dead characters?

With a cheeky grin he plays his last card.

Zombie. Bring one hero back from the dead.

Carlos smirks at the dealer as the crowd erupts in cheers. "Would you look at that, our hero is feeling much better. Now pay up."

I optimistically wait for the dealer to bring a wheelbarrow full of gold to us. Instead four very large gentlemen appear behind us. The widest one says, "May we have a word with you gents in the back room?"

I sink into my chair, but Carlos is having none of it. He says, "Unless the word is 'congratulations' we aren't interested. We won fair and square. Now pay us what you owe us, or else."

I straighten up in my seat and add, "Yeah. What he said!"

I need to work on my smack talk.

Two of the guys reach out and grab us, lifting us up out of our seats. They aren't exactly going for gentle. It's hard to get words out when your ribcage is being slowly crushed. "We haven't done anything wrong!"

The dealer smiles. "Sure you did, you won. These gentlemen will escort you out back and make sure that you don't make the same mistake again."

He eyes my outfit and says to one of his goons, "Those are nice shoes. Bring those back to me when you're done."

It's not a promising sign that we won't be needing shoes after our little chat. Now would be a really great time to have our weapons. If only they weren't sitting on that stupid table across the other side of the room.

Wait a minute. Table!

My left hand twitches. I can feel the table right at the edge of my reach. I concentrate and there's a squeal as the metal legs drag across the floor, and then just like that it is airborne. There is a loud crash as it smashes into the back of the guard holding me, which might not have been so bad for him if it weren't loaded up with sharp instruments. There's a nasty squishing sound and his grip loosens. I capitalize, wriggling free and dropping to the ground. There are weapons scattered everywhere so I scoop up a dagger and jam it in the foot of the guard holding Carlos, who screams and drops him.

Carlos has barely hit the ground when he rolls, picking up his bow and quiver in one swift motion. He stands and fires an arrow into the foot of the guard standing next to us, pinning him to the ground. The next arrow hits a guard in the shoulder and he slumps to the ground immediately. Must have been a sleeping arrow. Then he turns to the dealer, an arrow quivering in his bow, and says, "We'd like to cash out please."

I pick up my guns and keep them drawn, ready for anything. Two more guys appear from a back room, but unfortunately for them they are running into a room full of very large, very heavy tables. With the flick of my hand two roulette tables sandwich them with a crunch. I'm busy smiling to myself when the pit master pulls a throwing dagger from under his jacket and tosses it at Carlos. I don't have time to think, I just react. I shoot it out of the air with Waterfall.

We both wait a moment for more guards, but none appear. I start scooping our winnings into my pockets, watching the counter ticking up. That's when Carlos says, "might as well keep going. Where's the safe?"

I glare at him. "We can't rob the place!"

"You think they are going to kill us less because we only took *our* money?"

He has a point. The dealer gingerly points towards the back room that the large guards charged out of. My bullshit detector goes off again and I point Waterfall at him. He doesn't need to know it's going to be a couple of minutes before I can shoot him. "Would you like to rethink your answer?"

He reluctantly swings his arm across to point to a rickety wooden door that looks like a cupboard.

Carlos says, "I'll hold the fort here, you go see what you can get."

I slowly work my way across the room, several patrons cowering as I pass them. I reach the door and open it slowly. It squeaks on its hinges. I am coiled up, ready to strike anyone daft enough to try and get the jump on me, but there's nobody inside. There is however a very large safe door with an electronic keypad that has space for an 8-digit code. Next to it is a small keyhole.

I get out my trusty lock-picks and pop them in the keyhole. I twist once, and they immediately snap in half. I guess it was a tad optimistic to think I could break into a safe using twigs. I'm not exactly a safecracker.

Hold on though, perhaps I could be?

I hop into my skills menu. There's a dexterity skill branch which I have barely looked at. The first upgrade is picking advanced locks. I'm going to have to spend some of my hard-earned skill points to unlock it, but there must be something good inside or they wouldn't have this bloody big safe. On the other hand, what if I need those points for something else? Who knows what we are going to go up against.

Choices, choices.

Carlos shouts at me from the other room. "Whatever you are doing in there can you speed it up, the guards in here are getting a little twitchy."

That settles it. I cash in 5 of my skill points and get a notification that I am now a master locksmith. I step towards the lock and the electronic screen changes into something else. I squint at it and smile. It's a match 3 puzzle game. Spread across the board are three key tiles, which I guess I am trying to get together.

It takes me a couple of tries to match up the keys, but the moment I do there is a loud rumble as the locks disengage. I drag the door open with a grunt and the shimmer of expensive metal catches my eye.

I stare into the vault and my mouth falls open.

LEVEL 18: TOTALLY NUTS

The pile of gold stretches to the ceiling, but that is not what catches my eye. The long, sleek, shiny blade of a sword sticks out of the pile of treasure. It is simple yet elegant, built for combat, not decoration. That is a legendary sword if ever I saw one. I want it.

I reach out to take it and a voice behind me says, "That's not yours."

I turn around to find a small pointy-eared creature staring back at me. An elf perhaps. Definitely a game character. I give him my most innocent smile. "I'm just going to borrow it. I'll bring it back as soon as I am done."

"I can't let you take that. My employer would not be happy, and it's bad news for everyone if he's unhappy." The elf shudders at the thought. I hope I never run into his boss.

"I need it to save the world, so I'm afraid your employer is just going to have to suck it up." I reach out to touch the sword and a whip wraps around my wrist with a snap. I try pulling on it to topple the little guy, but he stands resolute, immovable. Then he gives it a tug and it feels like my arm is being ripped out of the socket. I fall over hard and the whip untangles itself. I hear a sound and roll at the last moment, which is a good thing as the whip cracks the spot where I was just laying, sending coins flying.

The elf's health bar appears. Level 30 High Elf. He doesn't look like any high elf I have ever seen. He looks more like a Christmas elf.

He pulls out a large joint and takes a drag. He blows a smoke ring and then suddenly cracks the whip again, catching my cheek. It immediately starts to sting.

"You little bastard!"

I run at him, ready to punch him right in his tiny face. He dodges and the whip wraps around my feet, tying them together. I wipeout into a pile of very sharp crowns and lose more health. I hear Carlos shouting from the other room, "What's taking so long?"

"Nothing, just a small hitch. I'll need a minute."

"A minute? May I remind you there are several very large and angry guys in here. This is supposed to be a robbery, not a tea party. Get a move on."

I hop back to my feet and equip my bo staff. I start swinging it at him. One moment he is there, the next he is not. He flips around like a tiny acrobat, cartwheeling and somersaulting over the piles of coins. He swings from a light fixture using his whip, spinning around me like an angry piñata. I flail at him several times, but he's always just out of reach. He lands back on the ground and I thrust my bo staff at him, but he dodges my attack and runs right up the staff. He punches me in the face before flipping over me and whipping me in the back.

I'm being slow and predictable, and he's kicking my arse because of it. I'm going to have to mix things up.

I break off my attacks and run straight for the sword. I reach out to grab it, but then I feel a tug on my belt. I look down just in time to see the whip pulling Agile right out of its holster.

Disarmed.

It flies straight into the elf's hand and he grins. Good thing it's all out of bullets.

He reaches into a nearby box and pulls out an extra-long golden magazine. He slams it into my pistol and cocks it.

Bugger.

He's smart enough to burst fire, so he doesn't blow through the entire mag in one go. I dive left as bullets fill the air around me. I slide as I hit the ground, ending up behind a mound of gold coins. He fires again and coins rain down around me.

Getting shot with my own gun is not high on my list of things to do today. There's a brief pause while he reloads and I seize my opportunity. I flip on my turbo shoes and close the distance between us in an instant. I'm still going very fast when I drop kick him. He is a lot lighter than I was expecting and the sheer velocity launches him out the door and into the next room. There's a loud crash as Carlos shouts, "Bloody hell. What was that?"

"It's a long story."

"Looked like a short story to me. We need to get out of here right now. Grab what you can and run!"

I grab the sword and try to put it in my pocket. Instead it sticks magically to my back.

Acquired New Weapon. Legendary sword - Showstopper. Doubles Parry damage. Unbreakable.

I stuff as many armfuls of treasure into my pockets as I can as I am running towards the exit. Thankfully the extra weight doesn't slow me down and I sprint out of the vault to find Carlos holding a guard, an arrow to his throat. He says, "Everyone just stay calm. My friend and I will be leaving now. No need to chase us."

I run past the High Elf, who is currently stuck face first in a dustbin. Annoyingly Agile is stuck in there with him and I certainly don't want to let him out to try and get it back. Shame.

I scurry up the ladder before backup arrives.

I'm in the process of lifting the hatch when it shatters in my hands as a hammer crashes through it. Another second and that would have been my head. I dive up through the hole before the dwarf has a chance to swing again. He spins the hammer around like a cheerleader with a baton. He snarls at me, "Who do you think you are, coming in here and messing with the Black Ring? Do you have any idea who you are stealing from? You should drop your weapons and let me kill you quickly, you won't like what happens if our boss gets hold of you."

He looks like big trouble, but his stats say otherwise. He's only a level 8 dwarf. As he hefts the hammer above his head I draw Waterfall and shoot him in the leg. It's enough to take down all his health and he falls to the ground with a whimper.

Carlos' head appears through the trapdoor. He looks at the dwarf and says, "You made short work of him."

"He brought a hammer to a gun fight."

We bolt out of the door and into the car. My sword gets stuck and I have to take it off and slide it onto the back seat. I reach into my pockets to get my trusty sticks and remember that they are laying broken on the floor of the vault. I turn to Carlos. "I can't start the car. I need two sticks, now!"

"You've got to be kidding me!" He pulls an arrow out of his quiver and snaps it in half as a very shiny axe slams into the car bonnet. The guy wielding it looks less than happy as he tries to tug it loose for another go. I fiddle with the lock, trying to line up the arrows, but they are moving slower now due to me upgrading my lock-picking skills. Now is not the time for slower. Carlos yells, "Not to rush you or anything, but in about three seconds we're both going to be dead."

Got it. As the arrows land in the sweet spot the engine roars to life and I floor the accelerator. The wheel spin leaves a cloud of black smoke behind us. The axe is still firmly embedded in our bonnet. I laugh manically. "I can't believe we got away with that!"

An arrow smashes through the back windshield and embeds itself in the cars dashboard between us. Carlos says, "You might want to postpone that celebration..."

He unbuckles his seatbelt and opens the sunroof. His top half disappears and I hear the twang of his bow. He shouts down at me, "We've got three cars after us. Looks like a classic chase mission."

Urgh. Chase missions are the worst. I'm far from a good driver. I failed my test five times. It normally takes me twenty minutes to parallel park the car. This may be the shortest car chase in history.

No. Not today. I'm the hero. This mission requires me to be good at driving, so that is what I am going to be.

I watch carefully in the rear view mirror. Carlos peppers one of the cars with arrows until their bonnet looks like a hedgehog. Smoke starts pouring out of it, then fire, before it explodes in a ball of fire so large you'd think the car was made entirely out of dynamite.

I'm breathing a sigh of relief when our car gets shunted from the left, spinning us around. Without thinking I flip it into reverse and stare out the rear window, dodging left and right between parked cars. This definitely wasn't part of my driving test. Carlos manages to get an arrow through the driver's window of one of the chase cars, taking out the driver and flipping them over a parked car. Two down, one to go.

The other car gets stuck behind his upside-down comrade. As we screech around the corner he becomes a dot in my rear view mirror. I'm so busy looking at that I don't see the brown blur that runs out into the road until I feel the thump of it under my tires. I instinctively slam on the brakes and Carlos says, "What are you doing?"

"I hit something. An animal I think. I need to check if it's ok."

"Now? We are in the middle of a bloody car chase!"

I leap out and see the small brown fur-ball in the middle of the road. I run over and see a twitch of movement. I scoop it up to find a tattered squirrel. It is missing patches of fur on its face and its tail looks like a frayed rope. I'm not sure if he looks this beat up because he was just hit by a car, or if being hit by the car is only the latest in a long line of tragedies to befall the little guy. It looks like the latter. Suddenly a countdown starts.

I can hear Carlos screaming at me from the car. "What is taking so long?"

"I hit a squirrel. Apparently I can revive him."

"Revive him? I'm not dying so you can save a fudging tree rat."

There's only a few more seconds to go when the enemy car skids sideways around the corner. There's the ping of bullets hitting the ground around me as I run back to the car, clutching my new furry friend. As the timer reaches zero he jumps to life in my hands.

Pet selected - Squirrel

What? No! I don't want a pet squirrel. What use is a squirrel? Before I can do anything he runs up my arm and nestles in the hood of my hoodie. I'm barely in the car when I hear snoring. There's no time now to fix this, I'll have to deal with it later.

Carlos scowls at me. "If we survive this car chase, I'm going to murder you."

"Take a number."

I floor it, the tires squealing in protest. The Mustang strains but accelerates forwards like a roller coaster. The other driver pulls alongside us and points a machine gun at us. The side of our car is instantly riddled with bullet holes and the passenger side window shatters. I slam into his car, knocking the gun from his hand. He immediately retaliates, slamming his car into ours, almost ploughing us into a red phone box.

I check for a side street that we can escape down, but there is nothing. That's when I realize we are running out of road. There's a bridge under construction ahead, and there's a construction zone blocking the lane we are currently in. The other driver spots this at the same time and shunts us, making sure we stay in our lane. There's no time to stop. I'm going to have to go for it. I punch it and Carlos screams, "What are you doing, we're never going to make it!"

The nose of his car inches ahead, blocking our escape. Carlos is right, we're not going to make it.

We both watch in horror as the High Elf clambers out of the car next to us and surfs on the roof. He pulls Agile out from behind his back and starts firing, filling our bonnet with bullet holes and causing smoke to pour out of the engine.

I shout, "Why aren't you shooting back?"

"I'm all out of arrows."

Without saying anything Carlos grabs the wheel. I immediately know what to do. I draw Waterfall, aim out the front windscreen and fire.

The noise is deafening and my ears start ringing. All the windows in our car shatter simultaneously, blasting us with cold air and smoke. It's not a great shot, it's not even a good shot, it misses the High Elf by a country mile. Luckily the noise is enough to make the other driver turn around for a fraction of a second. That's when I fling the pie at him. It splats on the inside of his windscreen, completely blocking his view. As he desperately tries to wipe it away I nudge the back of his car and he spins out of control, flipping end over end until he crashes into the portable toilet in the construction zone. It was apparently packed to the brim with explosive diarrhea as the resulting column of fire almost reaches the moon. We drive right through it, the flames briefly filling the car. Ahead is a conveniently placed ramp. I punch the accelerator, giving it all we've got. As we hit the ramp the engine finally gives in and dies with a sputter.

I hit the ramp at an angle and we fly through the air, doing a barrel roll, before landing with a thud on the other side. All four wheels fly off the car, smashing into shop windows, parked cars and a run down old house. The chassis skids to a halt, leaving a cascade of sparks in its wake. When it finally stops Carlos stares at me. He says, "How did you know we were going to make that jump?"

"I didn't! I just went for it."

I'm expecting him to be mad at me, to scream and shout, but instead he nods. "Finally! It's about time you got into the spirit of things. Nice work."

As I clamber out of the car the door falls off. I survey the wreckage. There's a long piece of rope dangling from the golden axe in our bonnet. That's strange. I didn't notice that before. As I get closer I realize it is a whip.

I barely have time to warn Carlos when the High Elf jumps on his back, holding Agile to his head. He says, "You're going to return that sword and all that gold, or I'm going to turn your friend's head into a cheese grater."

I hold up my hands. "Let's not do anything hasty. We can talk this through."

"Actually, I'm not sure why we are discussing this at all. You're just as good to me dead as you are alive." He swings Agile to face me. There's no time to dodge. I close my eyes as I hear it firing.

After a second I open my eyes. There is a shimmering light in front of me. Is this heaven? I can still see Carlos and the elf through it, but they are iridescent, as if I'm staring at them through a bubble. That's when I realize that Carlos cast his bubble shield on me. The click click click is the familiar sound of Agile running out of bullets. The High Elf squeals as Carlos grabs him and flings him into the air, shouting, "PULL!"

I crank the turbo shoes and grab my new sword out the back of the car. As I race towards the high Elf I make a decision. No sense in cleaving the little guy in two, he's just doing his job. I equip my bo staff instead. It connects like a baseball bat and our would be murderer goes flying over the horizon. Agile clatters to the floor by my feet, a parting gift.

"Well that went about as well as could be expected. What are we going to do for transport?"

A guy pulls up in an identical car to the one we were previously driving. I recognize him as the guy we stole the car from previously. He doesn't appear to recognize us though. He says, "Are you guys ok?"

Carlos grins. "Hooray for asset reuse! Make sure you get the keys this time."

LEVEL 19: CHOP CHOP

"We need to get out of here, before the Black Ring find us."

"Moving around with this kind of loot is a risk. We need to buy a base as quickly as possible."

I check my inventory. There's a lot of loot. "I have no idea how we are going to sell this stuff."

A familiar creepy voice behind me makes me jump. "What are you selling?"

I spin to see the merchant gurning at us. I say, "We have a lot of merchandise that is less than..."

"Expensive!" Carlos nudges me. He mutters, "Let's not put off a potential buyer."

I start emptying my pockets, pulling out gold crowns, sceptres and jewels as big as apples. It was as much as I could grab. The merchant keeps a completely neutral face as I pile everything up in front of him. When I am finished he says, "I'll give you a great price for it."

A number appears on the screen. It's a very large number. I act casual as I keenly accept the offer and my gold balance jumps to five figures while the pile of stuff instantly disappears. I'm about to leave when the Merchant says, "Got lots of things on sale."

Carlos runs over like a kid in a sweet shop. Before I can stop him he says, "Nice! There's a legendary bow. I'll take it!"

Just like that ten thousand gold vanishes without me getting a say and Carlos' bow is suddenly jewel-encrusted. He twangs the string and says, "Got any special arrows?"

"Indeed. I have ice, fire and sleeping arrows."

"I'll take as many as you have."

Two thousand gold goes poof. I try to drag him away, but he says, "What is that?"

The merchant pulls out a golden arrow. "This is the legendary arrow of..."

"I'll take it."

Another five thousand gold disappears.

"Hold on a minute! You don't even know what that does."

"I don't need to, just look at it." He holds it up to the light and it glistens.

"We're supposed to be buying a base, not decking you out in fancy gear!"

"You know how I get when I see decent loot. Tell me fine shop-keep, do you have any..."

I punch him. Right in the face. I didn't mean to, but he's being a selfish dick and I'm not in the mood. He instinctively reaches for an arrow and I place my hands on my guns, ready to go, but he slowly lowers his hand and smiles. He wipes blood from the corner of his mouth. "Sorry about that, I got carried away. It's nice to see you again, old Marcus."

I smile back. That was surprisingly satisfying.

I turn my attention back to the Merchant. "We are looking to buy a base."

The corner of the Merchant's mouth twitches up into a half smile. It's the most expressive I have ever seen him. He says, "You need base? I sell you base."

He doesn't exactly look like an estate agent. Unless he's got a base stuffed in his jacket, I'm not sure quite how he is going to sell us one. Still, it's worth a try. "Ok, I'll bite. Where is this base?"

"Right behind you."

I turn around to see a ramshackle hut. There's a still smouldering tire embedded in the front wall. The only thing living there is mold. One side of the roof is missing and there is a tree growing out the hole. I shake my head. "Do you have anything that is less of a fixer upper?"

"Nope. That is only base. Take or leave. It's good price. Fifty thousand gold."

"Fifty thousand! For *that*? You've got to be joking."

"It just needs a few upgrades." Says Carlos.

"Upgrades? It needs to be burnt to the ground and the ashes shot into space. That place is basically a bioweapon factory."

Carlos says, "We'll take it thanks."

Before I can protest the 50k disappears from my account, totally wiping out the remaining balance. The merchant hands over a set of rusty keys and says, "No refunds." Then he disappears in a puff of smoke.

I turn to Carlos. "Why on earth would you buy this dump?"

"A quick lick of paint and a good cleaning will make a world of difference. We can fix everything with a bit of elbow grease."

"Are you forgetting who you're talking to? Don't you remember my shelf in woodworking class."

"Remember it? I still have the scar on my head from when it fell on me. Thank goodness there weren't any books on it at the time."

"So what makes you think that I'm suddenly capable of fixing *that*." I gesture at the rubble that is our new domicile.

Carlos just smiles. "You'll see. Go get some wood."

"Wood? Where am I going to get wood?"

"Where do you think you're going to get wood from? Go chop down some trees."

"With what?"

"With the bloody big sword on your back you pillock! Honestly, it's a miracle we've made it this far."

Oh right. I'd forgotten that it was there. I can't even feel the weight of it. Luckily there is a park right across the road, so I jog over and get to work.

The first tree falls down after a few swipes of my sword. The moment it lands it vanishes, leaving behind a pile of neatly bundled two by fours. I touch them and they leap into my pocket. Easy!

After the seventh tree I hear a loud wailing. A woman comes running up to me, her face bright red with anger. She screams, "what on earth do you think you're doing?" She points her phone in my face.

I stare around sheepishly and notice for the first time the trail of destruction I have left through the park. There is a line of stumps in my wake. I mumble, "I'm getting wood."

"You're waving a sword around in a kids' playground and destroying public property! I've got the whole thing on video. I'm calling the police."

"Wait! Don't! I know this looks bad, but it's for a good cause."

"What?"

"I'm upgrading my base..." Now that I think about it, that's not a great reason. She apparently agrees with me. She waves the phone at me. "You're going to jail buddy."

I'm forced to consider my options. Is knocking her out an option? I feel bad even considering it, but it's going to be hard to save the world from a cell. She puts the phone to her ear and says, "Hello, is that 999?"

I clench my fist. Can I really do this? Hit a poor defenceless woman? I don't suppose I have a choice. It's for the sake of the whole world. I can't fight the entire police force on top of every-thing else. I pull back my hand...

"Yes hello. There's a guy in the park that is...OW!"

Ow? I haven't touched her. She spins on the spot and there's an arrow sticking out of her arse. She slurs, "What the F..." and collapses.

Carlos appears by my side. "Sorry to step in there. Looked like you were having a spot of trouble."

"Sleeping arrow?"

"Yep. She's going to be a bit sore tomorrow, but I think she'll forgive me. You get wood?" He sniggers.

"Sure did. I'm still not sure what exactly I am supposed to do with it."

Carlos sniggers some more before regaining his composure. "Come on, I'll show you."

I follow him back to our base. It looks even worse than I remember and it has only been five minutes.

Carlos says, "Go on then. Fix it up."

"Did you forget the conversation we had all of ten minutes ago? I don't even have a hammer or nails."

"Doesn't matter. You should just be able to upgrade it. Maybe try getting closer."

"Do I have to?"

He nudges me forward and a new option appears.

Upgrade base to level 1? Requires 30 wood.

I select Y and in an instant the base doubles in size. I didn't have to lift a finger. It looks like an actual house now, not just an abandoned bonfire. There is a front door and everything. Also windows. Not too sure how I made those with a large stack of carved-up trees, but who am I to argue. The tire has even turned into a quaint swing.

I tentatively try the key and the front door swings open. There is furniture in here. It is best described as functional, but it also exists, so it is a major improvement over the furniture situation ten seconds ago.

We do have a few more unusual additions, one being the large green ammo crate in the corner of the living room. I open it to find it packed to bursting with standard arrows and mags for Agile. I put several mags in my pockets.

Carlos says, "Not a bad start. What do you need for the next upgrade?"

I check. "To upgrade to level 2 we need 50 wood and 20 stone."

"What does that get us?"

The list is long. I pick out some of the highlights. "Level 2 brings common level automated defences, a forge to make our own weapons, a 20% EXP boost and a pizza oven."

"Automated defences sounds pretty handy. I wonder why we would need that?"

That's when we hear the battle cry outside. I stick my head out the window and pull it back in slowly. "You had to say it."

"How many?"

I do a quick count. "Twenty guys, half with bows and half with swords."

"Sounds easy enough. You take on the close quarter guys and I'll snipe the ranged ones."

"You want me to fight ten guys armed with swords single handedly?"

"Of course not. You can use both hands." He winks and starts immediately firing arrows out my brand-new bedroom window. He could have at least opened the window first.

A life bar appears above my usual one, with the title *BASE*. It is already starting to shrink and when I look out the window the swordsmen are hacking up my new fence. I shout, "Oy! Get off my lawn!" Then I somersault out the window, drawing both pistols and shooting three of the swordsmen before I hit the ground. Agile is much more useful when I don't hold down the trigger. I pull out Showstopper, eager to try out my new weapon, but the guys don't charge me. Instead they keep hacking away at my house, whittling away its health bar. Damn, it's a base defence level. I hate these.

I spin the blade around in my hands. It is perfectly balanced, it feels as if it has no weight at all. It feels a little cheap to attack someone that doesn't appear to intend me any harm, but we nearly died earning the money for this base and I'll be damned if I am doing that again. I rush over to the closest guy and take a swing at him. I cringe as it connects, concerned I am going to chop his arm off, but the blade passes straight through his limb and the only thing it takes a chunk off is his health bar. Perfect.

He keels over after two more swipes. His friends seem unperturbed by the fact I just killed their mate right next to them, instead they keep hacking away at the fence. So be it. They quickly go the same way as their friend, until there is only one left. He at least puts up a modicum of a fight with a feeble attempt to block my attack, but Showstopper carves right through his sword, shattering it in his hands. He looks sad about it so I put him out of his misery.

I clip Showstopper to my back just as Carlos fells the last of the archers. I can't even see the guy he took out, I just heard the scream a few seconds after he fired an arrow at the horizon.

I survey the damage. "Well that could have been worse."

Carlos says, "You mean like a couple of Bruisers and a trebuchet?"

I don't even need to turn around.

Most homeowners have to worry about mortgage payments and their furnace breaking down. I have to worry about freaking trebuchets.

***

There are bodies everywhere, strewn liberally through the front garden. Carlos walks amongst the fallen foes, retrieving arrows.

I glance at our new base. It's a smouldering crater filled with shards of broken wood and glass, reflected by the sliver of health remaining in the base bar. The ammo crate exploded after the third wave, which didn't exactly help matters. My new tire swing is on fire. Somehow our base looks even worse than before the upgrade.

"One more wave to go. We can do this." Says Carlos.

"Honestly, I'm not sure we can. There were already too many of them for us to handle in the last wave, and you know the final wave is always the biggest. What do you think happens if we lose?"

"Our base will be destroyed and we will have to start again from scratch."

My shoulders sag. "We don't have time for that! I can't face trying to raise another 50k."

"Then we have to beat this wave."

He makes it sound so simple.

There's the sound of horns on the horizon. They start to appear, one by one, until they are all we can see. Fifty knights, all heavily armoured and on horseback. There's no way we can take them all on without at least a couple slipping through and finishing off our base.

I shout, "How many arrows do you have left?"

"Fourteen. That last wave really wiped me out."

"You're going to have to make them count."

"You think?"

"What about that fancy gold one you bought?"

"If you think I am wasting that on low-level knights you're having a laugh."

A battle cry drifts across the park and just like that, the knights charge us.

Carlos fires a volley of arrows, but they bounce off the knight's armour. He switches his fire to their horses, but they are wearing expensive-looking horse armour and his shots are equally ineffective.

I burst fire Agile, taking a few knights down, but then there is the familiar sound of Agile running out of bullets.

It's no use. We are screwed. Our only hope is that when they have destroyed our base they don't decide that killing us would make a nice encore.

The knights are closing the distance fast when an explosion rocks the park, scattering them everywhere. Several more get frozen in a block of ice. There's a flash and lightning arcs between the knights, their armour doing a wonderful job of conducting the charge.

A solitary figure appears, riding on a glistening white stallion. I can't make out their features, but they are wrecking shop. They are coming right at us. I really hope they are on our side.

The horse pulls up and Sarah jumps down. She's not wearing much. I can't help but stare at her chain mail bikini. It might just be my imagination, but I swear her boobs are bigger.

Carlos confirms my assessment. "Holy chesticles, what happened to you?"

Sarah gives him a withering glance. "Apparently I need to have a word with the art department. Female heroes in the game are slightly curvier than your average woman. It seems to have affected my physique."

He raises his eyebrow. "I'll say. It's not exactly helped by your outfit..."

"Yes, that's something else I need to discuss with them. All high-level gear for female characters is on the skimpy side. Believe it or not, this offers the highest level of protection." She hikes up her bikini and her new assets jiggle for what feels like a long time. What was I doing again? Oh right!

"Guys, can we save the catch up for after the battle?"

Sarah holds out her hands and more lightning arcs out, shocking a dozen knights. The survivors rush to take off their armour, which is a big mistake. Carlos picks them off with arrows and I charge in with Showstopper, carving down the rest.

I'm just about to relax when I see a group flanking around us to get to the base. "We've got trouble, northeast."

Sarah glances in their direction and with a flick of her hands a pillar of ice blocks their path. As they try to scramble around it I turbo dash over and finish them off.

The dust settles and there are no knights left standing. I run over and hug Sarah for a little longer than is strictly necessary. "You really saved our bacon. How did you know where we were?"

"I got a big flashing arrow and a message telling me our base was under attack." She looks at the flaming wreckage and says, "Is that our base?"

Carlos waves his hands, "It's fine, we'll get that fixed right up." He kicks the tire swing and the rope snaps, sending the tire rolling away. He says, "Those were some pretty kick arse spells Sarah, care to teach me a couple of those?"

"No can do, they are reserved for strict magic users. Speaking of which, I need a potion, my MP is totally tanked." She pulls a glowing blue bottle out of her pocket and chugs it like a student on a Friday night.

"Can't you just wait for your MP to recharge?"

"I could, but it takes forever when you're a magic user because of the length of the MP bar. Potions are kind of essential because all my spells are so powerful they use up a lot of MP."

I check her stats. No that's not a euphemism, I mean her actual stats. I can hardly believe what I am seeing. "Sarah, how are you already a level 22 Mage?"

"Carlos isn't the only one that knows how to cut corners around here. I found a few new exploits we can all take advantage of."

I feel a scratch on my neck and my new pet crawls out onto my shoulder. Sarah immediately holds up her hands, ready to zap the little guy. I shout, "Wait! He's with me."

"What is that?"

"Apparently he's my new pet squirrel. I almost killed him with the car."

Carlos mutters, "Death would have been the merciful option. That thing looks like a chipmunk and a rat had a baby, and then tried to eat it."

"Don't say that!"

"Ok fine, I was wrong." He waits a few seconds before following it up with, "He looks like a wrinkly old man's hairy nutsack. Hey, that's what you should call him. Nutsack."

"First of all, I'm concerned about your seemingly deep knowledge of old man balls. Secondly, no, I am not going to call him Nutsack."

There is a chime and I get a message:

Pet name accepted.

Wait, what? I glance at the squirrel and above his head it now says *Nutsack.*

Marvellous.

I have bigger problems to worry about right now. I walk over to the nearest tree and try to scoop Nutsack onto a branch. He clings to me as if his life depended on it, his tiny claws digging into my arm. I try pulling harder when he turns and nips my finger. I instinctively let go and he runs back up my arm and back into my hood. Within moments the snoring starts up again.

"Looks like you've got a new friend." Sarah says. "Hey wait a minute, what's that on your back? Besides Nutsack."

"That's Showstopper. It's my new sword. Check it out." I draw it and hold it out for her to inspect. She runs her hand slowly down the blade.

"This is a legendary broadsword. Where did you get this?"

"Carlos and I borrowed a few things from an illegal gambling den."

Her expression immediately shifts. "Please tell me it wasn't run by the Black Ring?"

"Now that you mention it, everyone was wearing matching jewellery, and I vaguely recall someone mentioning the name Black Ring. Is that a problem?"

"Well that depends on your definition of a problem. Do you consider an ever growing bounty on your head that will attract everything from the lowliest scum to the most ruthless assassins a problem?"

"Yes, that definitely sounds like a problem. How do we make it stop?"

"There are only two ways in the game to stop the Black Ring bounty. Die, or kill the leader of the Black Ring."

"Let's go with door number 2. Let me guess, the leader is some ridiculous mid-game boss that will chew us up and spit us out?"

Sarah sighs. "Something like that. Let me ask, how do you feel about vampires?"

LEVEL 20: YOU SUCK

We sit in our newly repaired living room. Carlos has thoughtfully made us all a cup of tea, even though he didn't need to, due to the base regenerating our health. The windows are open and birds are chirping outside. It sounds peaceful, even if they are probably saying 'who cut down all the bloody trees?' For a moment it is easy to forget that none of this is real, that we are still stuck in the game.

I look at my two companions as they talk animatedly about games they have both played. They compare funny stories of last-minute clutch wins and unexpected glitches. They barely know each other, but when it comes to games they have common ground, a shared language. Even in the face of all this danger, they are both still laughing.

I've been going about this all wrong. I've been approaching this whole thing like a job. I hate my job. This isn't some torture to be endured, or puzzle to be solved. It is a game to be played. I never play my best when I am not enjoying myself.

I need to get the fun back.

I jump up out of my seat. "Ok, let's go kill us a vampire!"

Carlos and Sarah stop talking and look at me like I've grown another head. Sarah says, "I'm afraid it's not going to be that easy. We need a plan. I've never fought him myself, a different team was working on the area he resides in, but I've heard the horror stories from the QA testers. He always manages to bite the players, and if he does there's a 10% chance you become a vampire."

"No problem, that means there's a 90% chance we'll be fine. I like those odds!"

"Are you feeling ok?" Carlos looks worried.

"Yes, I'm fine. Better than fine. So where might we find a vampire in the middle of the day?"

"In the game he lives in the rafters of an old playhouse, but there's nothing like that around here. Sunlight eventually kills him, so he'd have to stay somewhere dark, but where the members of the Black Ring could come and go without raising suspicion. Any ideas?"

Carlos is the first one to figure it out. "The cinema! No-one would notice large groups of people and there's not a sliver of sunlight to be seen."

"That is as good a place to start as any. Let's go to the cinema and see if we can find him."

"Is there anything else that can hurt him? Apart from sunlight?" I ask.

"I don't actually know. They were always changing his weaknesses based on beta player feedback. We should stop and get some provisions on the way, just in case."

We head to the car. Sarah climbs in the passenger seat and sniffs. "Did you guys have the car cleaned? It's got that new car smell."

***

We pull up to the cinema and immediately know it is the place. It looks exactly like the kind of building that would house a resident evil spirit or two. It could be the fact it is decorated for Halloween, with cobwebs, spooky flashing lights, and eery music, despite it being July. It could be the vampire double bill that is advertised as today's movie. Or it could be the large mob of angry-looking Black Ring members loitering in the car park that gives it away.

In the centre of the pack is a large stone golem, with a black ring painted around its arm. It is at least 8ft tall. It looks like it will be a nightmare to fight. What weapon is going to touch a creature made entirely out of stone? Only one way to find out!

Sarah says, "Ok, we're going to have to be careful because that gol..."

I turn to them both, "No time for plans. Let's do this!" and then I charge. I'm bringing the fun. Carlos and Sarah will be right behind me.

I get some pretty strange looks from the Black Ring as I run right into the centre of their group and leap through the air, Show-stopper held high. I bring it down with an almighty *clang* and it bounces harmlessly off the golem's thick rocky chest. A health bar appears that informs me he is level 43. He looks mildly annoyed, his small, black, coal eyes shrinking in confusion at the puny human with the death wish.

I hear the sound of a dozen weapons being drawn.

No problem. I do my best to sound like a hero. "We've got this, right team?"

I turn and my backup is nowhere to be seen.

Bollocks.

This was a very bad idea.

I crank the turbo shoes and leg it. Arrows and gunshots rain down around me and I feel the ground shaking as the golem starts to pick up speed. The time between thuds shortens and any second I am expecting him to flatten me.

It doesn't happen, and just like that the pounding stops. I run straight past Carlos and Sarah, who are still huddled behind the car. They stare at me utterly befuddled. When I glance over my shoulder I am relieved to see I am no longer being pursued. I slowly make my way back to my team.

"Where were you guys?"

"Standing here waiting to make a plan!"

There's something I am happy to be confused about. "Why did they stop chasing me?"

Sarah says, "They are currently guarding that entrance. That means unless they are attacked they won't pursue, and if they do, it won't be beyond a certain range. What were you thinking rushing in like that?"

"I was keen to get stuck in."

"To a level 43 golem? He can kill us all in one stomp. We are going to need to work together if we are going to go up against an opponent like that."

Ok, so I chose a bad time to go rogue. Carlos jumps to my defence. "It was a solid effort mate, but even I'm not convinced we can win this fight. We need to find another way."

The world has officially gone mad.

I need to redeem myself. I scout the area and spot something promising. I point at it. "That looks like a side entrance. Think we can sneak over there without alerting the cronies out front?"

Sarah points upwards. "You've got half a dozen security cameras covering the car park. It's going to be nigh on impossible without triggering an alarm."

Carlos pulls his hood up. "Sneaky archer, at your service. I'll be right back."

He makes it look easy. Carlos merges with the shadows, flowing from one to the other like a fluid. He doesn't make a sound. At one point he climbs up the security camera pole so he can hide in its blind spot. As soon as the camera turns around he drops down and continues on his way.

When he reaches the side door, he presses a large red button which turns all the security cameras off. They make a powering down noise and droop forwards, like a drunk Grandma falling asleep after Christmas dinner.

Sarah and I sneak across the car park, avoiding line of sight to the guards out front. When we reach Carlos he says, "this might be a waste of time. Look at the lock on this thing."

There's an advanced lock with an electronic keypad. I step up and crack my fingers. "Stand back, I've got this."

I managed to look cool for at least a couple of seconds, but it's hard to maintain when you're playing a match 3 puzzle game.

Once I line up the key tiles the door slides open. Sarah stares at me. "Impressive. Master locksmith?"

"That's me."

We step through the door and hear whirring as a security camera inside the room turns towards us. There's no time for us all to get back out the doorway. Sarah holds out her hand and an arc of electricity fries the camera, which lets out a puff of black smoke to let us know it is done for the day.

"Nice work team! Now let's find us a vampire. If possible we should try to kill him quietly, so we don't get a visit from his friends outside."

A chandelier crashes to the ground just left of us, showering us with shards of glass. This is followed by a loud cackling laugh.

"I think it is safe to say he may already know we're here," says Sarah.

"Even better. Let's get stuck in then," replies Carlos.

I glance at Sarah. She looks worried. I place my hand on her shoulder and can't help but notice how soft and warm it is. I say, "Is everything ok?"

"I don't like this. I know most of the game really well, but I always knew better than to piss off the Black Ring, so I never did. I'm going into this just as blind as you guys. I'm scared."

"Don't be. Whatever happens, we will face it together."

There's a moment, just a moment, when she smiles at me and I feel something. Then just like that, it is gone. She says, "One thing I don't understand. Why aren't there guards inside?"

"I'm afraid I killed them all. I never have been very good at impulse control. You'd think I'd have learned it in 500 years!"

We all turn around to see a morbidly obese teenager wearing all black staring back at us. He's sipping from a gigantic drink cup. I can hear the slurping from back here. I don't want to know what he's drinking.

"What the hell? I thought vampires were all skinny? How can you be this fat on a liquid diet?" says Carlos.

"Just because I don't have a soul, doesn't mean words don't hurt." He surveys us and says, "You must be the idiots that robbed me. Are you here to save me the trouble of hunting you down? That's honestly rather considerate of you."

"Considerate enough that you will leave our friend out of it? She had nothing to do with the robbery." I gesture to Sarah.

"Oh ok, sure, I can do that."

My bullshit detector starts flashing. "You're lying!"

"Well duh!" The vampire turns to Carlos and waves his thumb at me, "What's with your friend? Is he always this naive?"

"'Fraid so. He's something of an optimist. So are you seriously the leader of the Black Ring? You look like you came straight from a mosh pit."

"Mosh pit? Is that like a dungeon? I'm afraid I haven't gotten out much in this new world. That's something that I am planning to change, now that I have run out of guards to eat."

Carlos nods at me and I slowly pull the water bottle out behind my back. I toss it at the chubby vampire and shout, "Now!"

The arrow slices it clean in half, showering the vampire in water. I wait for the screaming, or some kind of reaction, but instead he looks mildly annoyed. He wipes up some of the water and puts it in his mouth. "Let me guess, holy water?"

"Yes, fresh from a church! Shouldn't you be writhing around in pain or something?"

"Yeah, I'll get right on that. Seriously, this shirt is dry clean only. If

I wasn't going to brutally murder you guys before, I certainly am now."

We all look at each other. I turn to Sarah. "Any other ideas?"

"Try the garlic!"

I toss a garlic clove at him like a hand grenade. As it lands by his feet Sarah vaporizes it with a fireball, showering him with garlic mist.

He coughs a few times. "Ok, now you guys are starting to piss me off. It's not bad enough to soak me, now you've made me smell like a French kitchen. You guys are so dead."

A health bar appears above the vampire's head. It is surprisingly small. He's only a level 7. That's not the only thing to catch my eye. I have to read his name twice. I can't help but laugh.

Carlos sees it too. He says, "Your name is Roger?"

Roger looks surprised. He stammers, "No! I am Tungsten, lord of the Black Ring. Prepare to die!"

Carlos turns to me. "We don't have all day here. Can we kill him now?"

"Fine, but make it quick."

Carlos draws one of the arrows he made for just this occasion, with no steel tip and a sharpened wooden end. We're not entirely sure if it will count as a stake, but there's only one way to find out. He fires it straight at Roger's heart, and the moment it reaches him he screams and disappears in a cloud of black smoke.

"Well, that was easier than I expected..."

Sarah says, "Something isn't right. The QA guys would complain about this fight continually, there's no way it should have been this easy."

"Maybe we are just that good?" Carlos swaggers around and we are all smiling when Roger leaps out of the shadows and bites Carlos on the neck. He screams, "Bloody hell! Get him off me!"

I draw Waterfall but there's too big a risk of hitting Carlos, who is frantically trying to prise Roger off his neck. His health isn't draining nearly as quick as I thought it would. I thought this guy was supposed to be hard to beat?

After a few more seconds Roger disappears in another cloud of black smoke and reappears on the other side of the room, wiping his mouth with his sleeve. Something is different about him and it takes me a moment to spot it. "Hey guys, it looks like he just jumped 10 levels..."

"Yeah, he nicked them from me!" says Carlos. I glance at his stats and he's right, he's dropped down to level 16. Oh dear. That complicates matters. We have to kill him quickly, before he turns us all into level one grunts and murders us with a light breeze.

I point Waterfall at him and pull the trigger. He smiles and a bubble shield appears around him, the shot bouncing harmlessly away. Carlos shouts, "he's stolen my spells too! Someone kill this thieving bastard."

Sarah throws a few fireballs his way, but they are also absorbed by the shield. The bubble bobbles under the onslaught and disappears with a loud pop. Roger is nowhere to be seen.

"Ok, keep your eyes open, he can reappear anywhere!" I say, but no-one answers. I turn around and Roger is already biting Sarah. She is trying to shout, but no sound is coming out. I turn on my turbo shoes and run into them both, knocking them to the ground.

Roger scrambles to his feet and vanishes again. Sarah puts her hand up to her neck. "He'd only just bitten me, he didn't get much. Just a couple of levels. All my spells are still here, so that's a relief. How are we going to deal with this guy? He'll just continue to pick away at us."

"We need a plan!" I stare at Carlos and he nods while holding his neck. He says, "No arguments from me."

"Ok, he's moving too quick for us to use ranged weapons, so we are going to have to close the distance. Sarah, your freeze spell is our best bet. If we can just get him to hold still for a few seconds I think we have the firepower to take him down, but that only works if we can stop him moving."

I pull out my bo staff and use Showstopper to shave the end of it. It's now an extra-long stake.

"Ok, we are going to need bait, someone that can coax him down here and get him to stop moving long enough for us to freeze him."

Both of them stare at me.

"Ok fine, but be ready to hit him the moment he gets me. I don't want dinner and a movie."

A voice echoes from the rafters. "I'm looking forward to getting my legendary sword back. Those pistols will go nicely with my collection."

I pull out Showstopper and twirl it around. "You're welcome to come get it over my dead body."

There's suddenly a voice behind me and cold breath on my neck. "Deal!"

"Now!"

I hear the sound of the ice blast, but it is muffled. The walls are shimmering. Roger says, "This shield thing is very handy. Where were we?"

I try to get away, but my legs won't move. I wait for the pain in my neck, but it feels more like a scratch. Actually, lots of scratches. After a few seconds Roger makes a retching sound and I turn to find him with a limp Nutsack in his mouth. Yeah I know how that sounds, but it's not funny.

Roger spits out my pet and picks fluff from his teeth. "What the heck is this thing doing in your hood?"

I don't know how, but Nutsack is suddenly looking much better. I watch as new fur sprouts on his face. It is lighter than the existing fur, creating white stripes. Even his tail is getting bushier. He looks like a brand-new squirrel.

Roger on the other hand is not looking so good. His hair falls out in clumps and he starts scratching at his skin. His health bar starts to deplete. He yells, "What have you done to me?"

Nutsack bites Roger on the hand and jumps across to my shoulder, straight back into my hood. It is just the distraction I need. I thrust the bo staff into Roger's chest. He screams, but it doesn't kill him. I'm running out of weapons here. I draw Agile and pause. Is shooting him going to do anything? The bullets are dipped in holy water, but we already established that is useless.

Maybe there's another way. I point Agile at the ceiling. "Holy water may not have worked, so let's try holey ceiling." I spray bullets, turning the roof into a sieve. Sunlight comes pouring in. The moment it touches Roger's skin he wails. He tries to vanish, but there's a whooshing sound and his legs turn blue. I look to see a blue stream emanating from Sarah's hands that freezes him in place. He pleads with me, "Ok, your debt is forgiven, let's just call it quits!"

"Sorry Roger, you had your chance."

His arms catch on fire and he wails. "You'll regret this! The prophecy states that whomever should strike the final blow will become the l..."

Thwack. The arrow hits him in the head and a big chunk of his life disappears. There's only a fraction left, but then it blinks and the bar empties. Roger turns to ash with a final groan, taking my bo staff with him.

Sarah and I both glare at Carlos and he says, "Yawn, backstory. Let's get back to the fun."

"You idiot! That could have been really important. Now we won't know what terrible curse may be inflicted upon us."

"Sounds good to me! Hey, what's that on the ground?"

At first I think he's just trying to change the subject, but when I look there are three icons shimmering in the pile of ash. I check each of them.

Bubble shield

Blink

Mange

"I think these are spells and status effects. Carlos, see if you can get your bubble shield back."

He bends down. The moment he touches the icon it vanishes and he says, "Yep! That did it, I got my shield back. I still don't have my levels though, looks like I'm going to have to get those back the hard way. What about the other two?"

Sarah says, "Blink is that teleportation spell he was using. I'm not sure about Mange though. Isn't that something foxes get?"

"I think that's what he got when he bit Nutsack." I feel a little nudge in the back of my neck when I say his name. He wiggles around until he gets comfortable and then the snoring promptly starts up again. "Let's leave that one alone. The question is, who wants Blink? I already have the speed shoes, so I am good for getting around quickly."

I'm expecting a fight, but Carlos says, "Strategically it makes sense for Sarah to take it. I have a better range and I should never be close enough to the enemies to require a quick exit."

Well that was easy!

Sarah touches the icon and says, "I should test it out."

In a puff of smoke she is gone, reappearing over the other side of the room. Then she does the same in reverse, materializing so close that it makes me jump. She says, "Wow, that's pretty cool, but it really eats up MP. Maybe if I level up it will become more efficient. We should test it out in combat."

"Yeah, speaking of which, we need to practice fighting together. We were a bit all over the place against Roger, and that was one fat emo kid. If we're going to fight an army we need to be a well-oiled machine."

Carlos says, "Before we march off into combat, I need food badly. I think there's a fast food place just around the corner."

Sarah evaporates and after a few seconds she reappears holding a brown paper bag. She hands out burgers. She washes hers down with a potion and says, "I agree, we need to learn to fight together. Our skills are complementary, we can do a lot more damage if we can coordinate attacks. We just need to find a low-level mob to practice on."

There's a thump on the door that is loud enough to rattle the hinges. We all share a look as the door comes crashing down and the Black Ring guards from outside come charging in. The golem stands at the head of the group, ready to take us down. They all glance at the pile of ash on the floor that used to be their boss and look none too pleased.

We instinctively group up, backs together, ready to fight. This is going to be rough.

That's when they kneel, heads low and hold their weapons out towards me.

Carlos says, "Well, I need a new pair of trousers."

It looks like I'm the new leader of the Black Ring.

"Seriously, could you all leave us alone for a minute? Go do whatever it is that you do. With less murdering."

The mercenaries stare at me coldly. Nobody moves.

I turn to Carlos and Sarah. "So I guess that is what Roger was trying to tell us. Whoever kills him becomes the leader of the Black Ring."

Carlos scowls. "But I'm the one that killed him! I should be their leader."

"The sunlight must have finished him off. Who really knows. The point is, now we have thirty additional mouths to feed. What are we going to do with them? Could we use them to fight for us?"

Sarah shakes her head. "They'd get all the EXP."

"There must be something they can do that would be useful."

A new message flashes up:

Your Base is under attack. Protect your base!

Oh god, we're going to have to keep doing that?

Wait. "I command you to go guard our base."

They continue staring. It's so quiet I can hear Nutsack squeaking just behind me. It's probably a mating call. Just what I need, a love nest in my hoodie.

Suddenly the mob dissipates without warning. I have no idea if they are going where I asked them to, or if they just got bored and left to go on a rampage. The important thing is, they didn't mutiny and immediately murder me. Bonus!

Carlos says, "Back to the matter at hand, can we go find a mob? Preferably one that won't kill me immediately. I can't face the final boss as a measly level 16."

**

"Are you sure this is a good place to be?" asks Sarah.

We stand in the Kasbah car park. The remains of Carlos' car are still there, only now they are smouldering from the fire that several homeless people are currently gathered around.

"Yes, this was the first place we encountered an enemy, so it is kind of like the starting zone. We should get some easy pickings here."

I wait for Carlos to agree with me, but he is too busy searching for targets.

There is a gang of youths loitering in the far corner of the car park. They look like perfect fodder for us to test our teamwork. I say, "I'll engage them. Get ready to fight."

I stroll over and say, "Afternoon chaps."

I'm expecting it to be enough. Around here a wrong glance can get your teeth kicked in. However, these young men apparently missed the memo. One of them says, "Good afternoon sir, I hope you are having a nice day. Is there something we can help you with?"

I'm not really sure what to do with that. One of them is on his phone. I slap it out of his hand and the screen shatters as it hits the ground. Now I'm ready to rumble.

He says, "Oh no, what a terrible accident! Good thing I got the extended protection plan with zero deductible."

What is with these kids? How am I supposed to start a fight if they are all so darn reasonable?

I turn to leave and a burger wrapper falls out of my pocket and onto the ground. As I step away there is a gasp and one of them proclaims, "Sir, are you going to pick that up?"

I bend down out of habit and have to stop myself. I slowly straighten up. "Actually no, I am just going to leave it there. I'm a big fan of littering."

That has got them riled up. I go in for the kill. "I also drive a car with terrible mileage, and I like my food stuffed full of GMOs, and I only buy my dogs from puppy mills."

Yep, that did it. Health bars everywhere. They are only level 3, so they will be perfect cannon fodder for us to practice.

I am about to grab Carlos and Sarah when a shadow blocks out the sun. I turn and have to crane my neck to see the three guys that are towering over me. One of them says, "Everything alright little bro?"

"Actually, this guy is being very insensitive towards the planet and refuses to pick up his litter."

"Is that so?"

I get hefted into the air. I just have time to see that my opponent is a level 35 Big Brother before he tosses me over to where Carlos and Sarah are standing. They help me up. Carlos says, "I thought this was supposed to be an easy fight?"

He has a point. All three of them are massive. It's a bloody bonanza of bros.

"I tried, ok. Just follow the plan and we will be fine. Sarah, get behind them and cause a distraction. Carlos, suppressive fire. I will get in close and see if I can wear their health bars down. Let's do this. Go team!" I hold my hand in the centre, but the other two just stare at me like I'm an idiot.

Sarah teleports closer to the attackers just as Carlos fires his first volley of arrows. One of them hits Sarah square in the shoulder, chipping off her health. Friendly fire is still on. She says, "Hey! Watch where you're aiming!"

"Sorry, I didn't know that's where you were going to be."

Carlos pulls out a blue arrow and fires it at one of the larger guys. The moment it hits he starts to shiver and he freezes on the spot, but just then Sarah tosses a fireball into the group and the blue slowly fades away again as he warms up.

Sarah is trying to pull the arrow out of her back when one of the big bros charges at her. I zoom in, planning to intercept him and save the day. Instead, he scoops her up and throws her right at me. I'm going too fast to course correct and we collide head on. She pins me to the ground, her bosom landing squarely on my face. The chain mail is scratchy, but for some reason my brain isn't too focused on that fact right now. She says, "what is that sticking in my hip?"

"Sorry about that. It's my gun." I draw Waterfall and aim it at the nearest Big Bro. I'm hoping it is enough to scare him, but he stands there unperturbed. I have him lined up in my sights, but just as I pull the trigger he takes a hit from an arrow and staggers backwards, out of the line of fire. This is getting ridiculous. We are supposed to be on the same team!

The big bro stalks towards me, ready to teach me a lesson. I wield Showstopper, expecting him to back down, but he keeps coming. I take a swing and he deflects it effortlessly and punches me hard in the face, taking my life bar down by almost a third. We can't get into a fistfight with these guys, they will eat us for lunch. That goes double for Carlos.

Speaking of which, he's not looking too hot right now. Two of the big bros have broken off to go after him. They must sense he is the weakest. He's firing arrow after arrow, but they aren't doing much good. One of them lunges at him and Carlos rolls out of the way just in time as the fists crash into the spot where he was just standing. He shouts, "Little help here guys?"

Sarah flicks her wrist but nothing happens. She says, "Weird, my spells aren't working?"

I try to run over to help Carlos, but I run straight into an invisible wall. I try to go around it, but I bump straight into another one. I run in a circle, but my new invisible prison is only a few feet wide. It wasn't there a second ago? Is this some kind of magic? The Big Bros certainly don't look like magic users.

I look up and Carlos is doing a very convincing impression of a mime, pressed up against a wall that isn't there. Sarah is too. What is going on? Are we just going to have to stand here, trapped, while the Big Bros beat the snot out of us?

Just like that, the Big Bros freeze. Then one of them runs at Carlos and swings at him. Carlos doesn't even try and block it. The punch hits him hard, but he stays in the same spot, losing most of his health in the process. I watch as the second big bro does the same thing and Carlos falls to the ground. There is nothing I can do while I'm stuck here.

The third Big Bro runs straight at me. I cower, waiting for the attack, but he stops a foot away from me and just stands there. None of this makes any sense. That is when the message pops up:

Player's Turn

The floor is suddenly covered in a white grid that wasn't there before. As I move my gaze around, the square I am staring at is highlighted. If I stare at the spot next to Carlos the square lights up red. I try several other squares around him, but it doesn't change to green until I am only halfway. I can't get to him this turn.

At least I can do some damage. I pull out Waterfall and check. It is ready to fire. I aim it point blank at the Big Bro right in front of me and pull the trigger. I feel the recoil, but he doesn't go down, or even show any damage. Instead I get a notification.

Miss

Miss! It was pressed against him. How the heck did I miss?

I shout over to Sarah, "Can you hear me?"

I'm expecting it to echo off my invisible walled chamber, but instead she shouts back. "Yes. Can you move?"

"I can. What is going on?"

"I think the game has glitched out. The game used to be a turn-based strategy game before we moved it to VR. It looks like it has flipped back into the old rules. It's a known issue."

"Turn-based? Awesome!"

I love turn-based games. No reflexes to worry about, no pinpoint accuracy required, just a distilled set of rules that determine the optimal strategy.

"I don't know how to make it stop. In the game it usually resolves itself if you get to the end of the battle. I have no idea what it will do in the real world."

"Ok, well there's really only one way to find out. Step one is to get to Carlos. Can you check your movement? You should have a grid on the floor that changes from green to red."

"No, nothing like that. Have you handed the turn over to me?"

"Handed it over?" I stare at Sarah and with a chime the grid disappears. She says, "Ok, I see it now. What do you want me to do?"

"Can you make it to Carlos?"

"No, but I may be able to protect him. Hold on."

She waves her hands and projects an ice spell towards Carlos. At first I think she is going to freeze the Big Bros, but instead a pillar of ice forms, lifting him up off the ground. When he is several feet in the air she says, "That won't hold them forever, but it should let you get to him. The problem is, now I can't attack, and you already attacked this turn. We are sitting ducks. I'm going to get as far away as I can, but we need to take these guys out."

She turns and runs in a straight line away from the Big Bros, but it's not very far. The grid reappears as she hands the turn back to me.

We need to revive Carlos. Without him we are losing out on an entire attack every turn. If only there was a way for me to move quicker, to get to him this turn.

Wait, move quicker? Why didn't I think of this sooner? I flip on my speed shoes and my movement range doubles. There's even space at the top of the ice pillar for me to stand. I select the space and without conscious effort my legs start pumping and run me right up next to him. I skid to a halt the moment I reach him. It's almost as if someone else has control of my body. Creepy!

An option appears to revive him. Apparently it will use up the rest of my action points for the turn. I click on it and place my hands on his chest. There's nothing more I can do, so I select *End Turn*.

The Big Bros immediately start punching at the bottom of the ice pillar. The sounding of cracking ice fills the air and the pillar starts to tilt, but it stops moving just before it topples. I'd love to dart away, but I couldn't run off even if I tried. I am stuck in my invisible cube.

The other Big Bro runs towards Sarah. I'm hoping he can't reach her, but at the last moment he lunges and gets to the square next to her. He pulls back his fist in a leisurely haymaker. I just have to stand here and watch, there's nothing I can do. I don't even want to think about how much damage it is going to do. Am I going to be reviving Sarah next turn?

The punch misses. I have no idea how, but he whiffs it over her head and *Miss* pops up. That was close. Too close.

It is our turn again. The moment it starts Carlos opens his eyes and leaps to his feet. He says, "What happened? Why can't I move?"

"It's a long story. Somehow we are in a turn-based fight."

"Turn-based? You must be thrilled! So how do I attack?"

"I just have to hand control over to you." I'm just about to do that when I say, "So what is your plan exactly?"

"I'm not sure yet, I will figure it out when I get there. I just know I really want to punch the guys that knocked me out."

I take a deep breath. "That didn't work out so great for you last time. You need to keep your distance. They don't have ranged weapons, you can sit back and pick them off."

"But that's no fun. I want payback. Those guys killed me!"

"You were barely dead, it doesn't count. You need to think more strategically. Whether we like it or not, we have a lot of time to make our decisions at the moment. Let's practice working together."

I'm expecting a fight, but Carlos starts to nod. After a few moments he says, "We can totally humiliate these guys!"

"Sure, if that will make you happy. So how do we get off this ice pillar without taking a beating?"

He thinks for a moment. "Let's bring it down on top of them." He shouts, "Sarah, can you get a fireball this far?"

I hand her control and she says, "Yes, only just. Where should I be aiming?"

"Bottom of the ice pillar, between the two Big Bros. Can you get them both in the area of attack?"

"Yes I can, but won't you two get burned?"

"I have a plan for that. Fire away."

She runs away from the Big Bro next to her. As soon as she is in range she throws a fireball and it immediately engulfs the bottom of the pillar. The two enemies start losing health and the ice pillar drops, bringing us level with them. Carlos says, "Ok, let's focus fire on the guy with the lowest health. Can you reach him?"

"I can, but he's currently on fire. Won't that be a problem?"

"Trust me."

The grid reappears and I run up to the guy. I take a swipe with Showstopper and it removes the rest of his life bar. He immediately faints, but my arm bursts into flames where it touched him. It stings, but my arm stays intact. I'm pretty sure I don't want to leave it like this. I shout, "Now is a good time to fill me in on the rest of that plan!"

I hand him back the turn, hoping he has something up his sleeve. He pulls a blue arrow out of his quiver and turns to face me. Before I can ask what he is doing he fires it right at me. I flinch as it hits me in the shoulder, but the flames are immediately extinguished and I haven't lost any health. Then he moves several squares away from the remaining Big Bro.

It's a great start. Now we are only facing off against two enemies, so we already have the advantage. The first one runs over to me and punches me, which unfortunately connects. I'm back down to one hit. I don't know how we eat in this game, and if it will take up my turn.

I wait for the other Big Bro to chase Sarah, but instead he moves over and picks up a dustbin, hiking it above his head. He looks ready to toss it, but instead he freezes.

It's our turn again. Sarah eyes the guy behind her and says, "Can one of you take him out? I'm out of MP and it will use up my action points to drink a potion."

I try aiming Agile. It can reach him, but it's not going to do enough damage to finish him off. I shout at Carlos and he checks too. "Looks like I can take off about half with a fire arrow. If we both concentrate our fire on him then it might do it, but we'd both have to hit. It's risky. What about the other guy?" says Carlos.

I check his stats. "I can take him out with Agile in one burst, but then we'd be leaving Sarah vulnerable."

"Ok. Take that shot. If you miss I can try instead. If you hit I will make sure Sarah is ok. If she gets taken out we'll easily be able to revive her next round."

"Guys, I am right here! You're talking about me getting killed like it is a mild inconvenience." She doesn't look super impressed.

Carlos is right though. We have to play the odds. I line up my shot and pull the trigger. The hail of bullets whittles away the Big Bro's health bar and he drops to the ground, with a whoop from Carlos. I turn my attention to him, "Ok, now what?"

"Do you think that bin counts as a projectile?"

Before I can answer he flicks his hand and a bubble shield envelopes Sarah. Then he moves to make sure he can get a shot off next turn, and just like that our turn is over.

The Big Bro springs to life and immediately throws the bin at Sarah. It bounces harmlessly off the bubble shield. He stares as it rolls away, and then turns and runs right at me, but he has no attack points left. There's no-one else left to move, so it is back to us, and I smash the Bro with a swipe of Showstopper.

Carlos says, "Ice or fire Sarah?"

"Let's ice him."

Sarah flings an ice blast his way. Carlos follows it up with an ice arrow, freezing him solid. He skips his turn due to his convincing impression of a popsicle. Our turn pops up again and I say, "Do the honours Carlos."

A headshot finishes the Big Bro off with a satisfying twang. The moment he falls to the ground, we can all move freely again. I take a deep breath. It feels nice not to be cooped up in an invisible cell. Sarah strolls over and says, "It is a good job that worked! I thought I was in big trouble there."

"Did you ever doubt us?" says Carlos.

"Of course not." If her tone was any more dripping with sarcasm we'd need a lifeboat.

"Question, what are you both spending your skill points on?" I ask. I'm really tempted to put them all into my health bar, but that's not very exciting.

Carlos leaps into the air, then jumps again mid-air as if there is an invisible springboard. He throws in a flip in for good measure. "Agility all the way baby."

"That's really impressive and utterly pointless, unless we have a quest to grab something off a really tall shelf."

"I can't lose health if they can't hit me."

"If only that were true. Literally all I have done all day is revive you. A fat vampire caught you and the only thing he ran for was the mobile blood bank."

"We'll see who gets the last laugh on this one."

Perhaps he's right. Sarah says, "Magic is obviously my focus. It's hard to choose between making my current spells stronger or buying a new spell. I think I'm going to increase my fireball."

Ok, well that settles it, everyone else is getting cool stuff. I browse through my skill tree. There are all kinds of new combat moves I can get. I see a really cool one and purchase it before I can change my mind.

Move unlocked - Flaming Uppercut.

That's surely going to come in handy. I test it out and leap into the air, my fist suddenly ablaze. The moment I land the flames go out. Carlos says, "Wow, pretty cool! I can't wait to see that one in action."

"Speaking of action, that went pretty well. At least we worked together. Now if we can just learn to do that in a real-time fight." I give Carlos a glance so he knows who I believe to be the key barrier to that particular milestone.

Instead of acknowledging it, he changes the subject. "Ok, so what is left? We must be getting pretty close to the end game now."

I check the timer. We only have five hours left.

"The only quest item remaining is to face a final fear, but I don't know which one that is. I also haven't completed my legendary armour set yet. I am missing a legendary helm. Any idea where I might pick one of those up?"

Sarah thinks for a second and says, "Actually I do, but you're not going to like it."

"Why do you keep saying that?"

LEVEL 22: HATS OFF

"Are we absolutely certain that this is our best option?" I stare down the open manhole cover and try to hold my breath.

Sarah nods, "It is the only legendary helm that I know for sure was implemented. We were still building out a lot of the armour sets. We decided that the dwarves would be the race responsible for crafting the best helms."

Carlos' voice sounds funny as he pinches his nose. "Makes sense, but why exactly are we jumping into the sewer?"

"Dwarves live underground. This is the only underground area in the city, so by that logic, this is where they would live."

"You're certain? Some of the older pubs in the city have cellars, perhaps they would live there?"

"Not big enough. Trust me, this is where we are going to find them."

There's no time for further debate, the clock is ticking. I tuck my arms and legs in like a pencil and jump into the hole, landing at the bottom with a splash. It's dark down here and hard to see, but I hear a lot of critters scurrying away.

There's a loud splash and some sputtering and I say, "I think I swallowed some water." This is followed by dry heaving.

Sarah lands far more daintily. After a few seconds a small flame appears in her hand and the tunnel lights up. It stretches as far as I can see. We look both ways down the tunnel, but there is no obvious sign of which way to go. I pick a direction and set off walking.

We've gone round a few blind corners when we round one and I almost fall off a very steep drop. Carlos bumps into the back of me and we both teeter, but a prompt flashes up and I select it quick enough that I manage to right myself, dragging him off the edge in the process. I carefully peer down into utter darkness. "That doesn't look promising. Sarah, can you get the light up here? I think I can see something out there."

As Sarah gets closer the outline of a ledge appears. I could leap up, but I have no way of knowing what I am letting myself in for. Sarah realizes the same thing and casts the fireball onto the ledge, illuminating it. It's a tiny platform, barely big enough for the three of us. I can't see where it is being held up by anything, it appears to be floating unsupported in the air. Just as quickly the fire goes out.

I turn to Sarah. "Do you have platforming in your game by chance?"

"Only in a few of the temples. The beta players hated it, it was horrible to play in first person. We had to implement a 3rd person view just for the platforming sections. We were actually considering dropping it."

Carlos sighs. "Sarah, we really need to talk about your game. I'm starting to worry that you've just chucked anything and everything in there. Where's the thematic consistency?"

She shrugs, "Who cares as long as people are enjoying themselves?"

Something is bugging me. "3rd person in VR? How does that even work?"

I've no sooner asked the question than my vision starts to slide backwards. At first I think I am falling and I take a step back, but then I see something black and furry appearing in my vision. I move my head instinctively and the furry object moves in perfect tandem, until I realize I am looking at the back of my own head. I immediately feel sick and lean forward to throw up, but instead of my view tilting I watch as my body bends over and heaves onto the ground. I wave my hand in front of my face, but I don't see fingers, instead I watch my body wave at thin air as it gets smaller. When I am several feet in the air I stop moving. I'm definitely going to puke again.

I see Sarah and Carlos twirling sporadically and call out to them, "did your viewpoint just get messed up too?"

Carlos says, "Yep. This is weird."

After a few moments Sarah says, "Is my arse really this big?"

That earns a chuckle out of Carlos. I am smart enough to keep my mouth shut. My brain is having a hard time reconciling this out of body experience.

At least from up here it is easier to judge the distance to the platform. My body jumps up and grabs hold of the ledge, pulling itself up with little effort. Sarah does the same and Carlos somersaults up with a smile. We all huddle together, trying not to nudge each other into oblivion below. I can't see the next platform in the darkness. "Any chance we can get a bit more light?"

Sarah casts another fireball, but this one drops into the nothingness below. After a few seconds there is a loud whoosh and the whole room goes bright red as a blast of heat knocks us off our feet. I peer over the edge of the platform at the raging inferno below. Apparently sewer gas is flammable. We now have our very own fire level.

At least now we can see through the darkness. Unfortunately it is not all good news. The next platform is several feet above us. "I don't see how we can get up there."

"If only you had some points in agility," says Carlos with a smirk.

"Shut up."

"Maybe you should re-spec?" He runs straight up the wall and back flips onto the platform above us.

"Wait, can I do that?"

Sarah nods. "Yeah, we left it open as a last resort, but there is a penalty of 25% of your skill points. We didn't want players reassigning their skill points every five minutes. It is supposed to be for emergencies only."

I don't want to lose my health upgrades and lose 25% of my skill points in the process for one stupid platforming section. There must be another way. I turn to Sarah. "What's your plan?"

She smiles and blinks out of existence, appearing above.

Hmmm. It's fine, I can figure this out, I just need a little bit of time.

There's a loud creak and a crack appears in the platform I am standing on. Sarah shouts down, "In some levels the platforms don't last very long. We wanted to keep it exciting."

Exciting! That's the wrong word for it. A chunk of the platform crumbles off and falls into the raging inferno below. I shout back up, "How am I going to get up there?"

I'm going to have to re-spec, I don't see any other choice. I pan around frantically from above the action, looking for any other solution. That's when I see the frayed rope sitting on the corner of the platform that Sarah and Carlos are now on. "Hey! Toss that rope down to me."

Carlos runs over and grabs it. There's nothing to attach it to, so he braces himself and throws it over the edge. It misses me by several feet and dangles in thin air.

"What was that throw?"

"Sorry, it's hard to aim when you can't see your own hands!"

He's right. I try to steer my body towards the rope, but it's not entirely clear if I am pointing in the right direction. It's going to need a leap of faith. I back up until I am out of platform and as I start to run the ground gives way beneath me. I'm suddenly airborne, my arms flapping like a newborn chick trying to fly. There's a scratch on my hand as it brushes against the rope and I grab onto it with all my strength.

Carlos grunts as the rope slips through his hands. "I'm really regretting taking you to all those drive-thrus."

"Should have put your skill points in strength Mr. Twinkle toes."

With help from Sarah he manages to haul me up onto the platform, just as the first cracks appear. I say, "Well this is bloody ridiculous. Is it going to be like this all the way up?"

The axe lands at my feet with a thunk, sticking in the ground and making me jump. I spin my detached viewpoint around to find where it came from and see the dwarves coming out of holes all the way up the tower. They are clutching bags of small throwing axes.

"Carlos!"

"Yep, I see them too. I'm on it."

He starts firing arrows. The first few clang off the walls, but once he gets the hang of aiming dwarves tumble from their perches into the flames below. He doesn't stop shooting as he leaps on thin air, double jumping his way up to the next platform. There is no way I am going to make it.

Sarah says, "I've got it."

She blinks up to the platform. There's an electrical panel on the far wall, which she zaps with electricity. A platform above starts to descend with a groan, closing the distance. Just as I am about to jump, it stops and starts heading back up. I'm going to have to time it perfectly.

There's a thud in my back and I reach around and pull out an axe. "You missed one Carlos."

"Kind of got my hands full here. Feel free to help out."

"Yeah, I've got my own problems." I watch as the platform turns and heads back down towards me. Three....Two....One....

I jump up. My fingers wrap around the ledge as it starts to ascend. I'm about to pull myself up when an axe sticks into the ground between my hands. "Seriously!"

"Don't get your legendary knickers in a twist." There's a scream as a dwarf falls from his perch. He lands on the platform I am currently dangling from with a crash and hops to his feet. I scramble up as quick as I can before he can kick me into the inferno below. He shakes his head, his helmet rattling with the effort, and then he takes a swing at me with his axe. There's no room to dodge so I block at the last second, and with a *ching* it parries. Now it's my turn. I take a heavy swing of Showstopper. He blocks, but the double damage is enough to nudge him off the edge. He teeters precariously, before falling with a scream. It's not much, but it is enough to earn me a new skill point.

I've learned my lesson. I pull up the menu and put my new point into agility. The first skill unlocks with a chime. Wall run. That's going to be handy. At least I will get to try it right away. I look at the wall and run straight up it, leaping off it at the pinnacle and grabbing the platform that Carlos and Sarah are standing on.

"Any more dwarves?" I ask.

"No, I think we got them all for now."

That's a relief.

I wall run up to the next platform and find a large wooden gate blocking the way. I try hacking at it with Showstopper, but nothing happens. I mean like actually nothing, not even a scratch. I would ask Sarah to burn it down, but I already know it won't help. It is one of *those* gates that is impervious to damage. On the floor several feet away is a pressure pad that glimmers yellow. I step on it and the gate trundles open just enough for them to duck under it. Sarah and Carlos squeeze through, but the moment I take my foot off the pad the gate comes crashing down with enough force to shake the platform.

I try again, this time with my turbo shoes on, but the gate is too far away and closes too quickly. I crash into it with a thud.

Sarah appears back next to me in a puff of smoke, making me jump.

"Don't do that!"

She says, "I'll stand on the button and once you're through I'll just blink back through the gate."

"Good idea!"

I take my foot off and am about to stroll through when the gate comes crashing back down. I turn to find Sarah jumping up and down on the pressure pad, which is stubbornly refusing to budge. "Damn button won't let me push it."

"You're not heavy enough." I scan the room looking for dwarf bodies, but we've chucked them all into the inferno. There has to be another solution. "What if I give you all my gear?"

"It doesn't affect your overall weight."

"What about a spell? Could you cast an ice tower on it? Or zap it with electricity?"

She tries both of them with no effect. She squints at the pressure pad, "I think yellow means it isn't affected by magic. We need a different solution."

I could try rolling through, but it's a high-risk strategy that is likely to get me cut in half.

I jump on the plate again and the gate opens. The moment I lift my foot it crashes back down. It definitely isn't a timing issue. "Carlos, be a gent and stand under the gate for me."

"No chance! Have you seen the spikes on that thing?"

"I just need you to slow it down for a moment so I can roll under it."

"So then there can be two dead bodies crushed under it instead of one?"

"Wait, that gives me an idea! Raise the gate." Sarah waves frantically and I comply. She runs back to the other side of the gate and casts her ice spell, forming a tower under the gate. I can see where she is going with this. I say, "We should test it to make sure it holds the weight."

I take my foot off and the gate crashes into the ice tower. It only stays open a couple of seconds longer before it carves through the tower, scattering ice chunks everywhere. It's not a lot of time, but it's the best we've found.

I re-raise the gate and Sarah rebuilds the ice tower. I crank my turbo shoes, run at the gate and roll forward with my eyes closed, half expecting a wooden spike to land on my face. Instead there's a loud crunch and I get a sprinkle of ice on my face. I open my eyes to find Sarah smiling back at me. "Nice work!"

Something is wrong. It takes me a moment to realize what has changed. I can see my hands again! I wave them around. It feels good to be back in my body.

I stare around the room. I can barely make out the walls. They really need to pay their electricity bill around here. The only light is from the frosted glass case in the centre of the room. That must be where the helm is. I start walking towards it, but Sarah grabs me. "This is too easy. I don't like it."

"Too easy? I almost got guillotined by a gate not even twenty seconds ago."

A stone doorway opens with a rumble opposite us, the light briefly casting a short silhouette, brandishing an axe bigger than the person. Then the door shuts and we are plunged into darkness even worse than before, because now my darn eyes won't adjust.

I fumble around in the darkness. "Are you guys still there?"

Carlos replies, "Yep. I've got a bad feeling about this."

There is the sound of running and then without warning I get head-butted in the face and lose a third of my health. I don't even have a chance to retaliate. Blood pours out of my nose and a female voice echoes around the room with a thick Scottish accent. "You've come to the wrong place if you think you're taking my helm without a fight."

"We just need to borrow it. I promise we'll bring it back." Why does no-one even believe me when I say that?

More running, and then Carlos says, "What the bloody heck is that?" This is followed by a sound best described as oomph, followed by whimpering. I hear Carlos mumble, "She headbutted me in the nuts! Someone kill her please."

"Kill her? I can't even see her!"

Sarah throws a fireball, and for the briefest moment I catch a glimpse of her. At least I think it's a her. There's a rather thick red beard, but also long hair in ponytails. It's not entirely clear. Before I have a chance to attack, she disappears into the darkness again.

"Sarah, can you throw a few more fireballs so we can see what's going on?"

"Sure, just let me drink this potion. Hey!" There's the sound of smashing glass and Sarah says, "She just knocked my last potion out of my hand! I've got enough MP for maybe one or two more fireballs, and then that's it."

"Carlos, are you back in action yet?"

"Yep, but that is going to hurt tomorrow. I may have to get some frozen peas."

"We need a plan, some way that we can work together to solve this problem. It must exist, the game wouldn't put us in this situation if there wasn't a solution. Carlos, do you have any more fire arrows?"

"Fraid not, I used them all up."

There's a long silence, punctuated by a cackling laughter. Something says, "boo" behind me and as I spin around I catch an axe to the chest, knocking me to the ground. It doesn't do much damage, but if we can't hit her then it is just a matter of time before she picks us off.

"I've got it!" exclaims Carlos.

I've got a good feeling about this. Perhaps he's secretly a strategic genius.

"Set me on fire!"

Perhaps not.

"What are you talking about? How does that help?"

"I have an entire quiver of wooden arrows. If I'm on fire they should all be instant fire arrows. You guys can stand next to me and we'll be able to see her coming."

"But you'll be on fire!"

"It's not a big deal, just revive me if I run out of health."

I can't believe that our best option is to set a member of our own team alight. Still, I don't have any better plans. "Ok fine, let's do it. Sarah, can you find Carlos?"

A small fireball appears in her hand and sweeps until she finds him, "Are you sure about this?"

"Do it."

The fireball arcs through the air and lands right on Carlos' head, setting his hood on fire. He says, "that's not too bad..." Then his whole torso bursts into flame. He runs around screaming, "Bad idea! This was a bad idea!"

"Focus! Use your arrows, we don't have much time."

He stops circling and says, "Sorry about that, just a bit of a shock, what with all the burning pain. Let's turn on the lights." He starts firing arrows, which arc through the air and stick into walls, the floor, pillars, anything at all. He slowly turns until we are standing in a circle of fire. There's a cackle and a shadow appears, running towards me. I have just enough time to step aside and take a swing with Showstopper. It does some damage and the dwarf roars, "You top-siders will never have what is rightfully mine. I am unstoppable!"

That is when the flaming arrow lands in her beard. She lights up like a vodka-soaked Guy Fawkes, running around patting at her face. At least now she is easy to see. I run over and take a few more swipes, even Sarah gets in on the action with her very last fireball. It is enough to whittle down her health and with a final scream she collapses. An icon is left showing a picture of a helmet. I'm studying it when Carlos says, "Guys, little help here?"

I spin back and Carlos is still very much on fire. I rush over and help to roll him around on the floor until the flames go out. His health bar is red and flashing. "I can't believe that worked!"

"The next Sun Tzu you most certainly are not."

"Meh, strategy is overrated." He gets up and brushes ash off his jacket. "So what upgrade did we get?"

"Check it out for yourself. You earned it."

He ambles over and says, "Cool! Hard head, do triple damage with head-butts. I'm not sure it makes the most sense for me to have this one, if I am head butting someone I am a pretty crappy sneaky archer."

"All the more reason for you to have it. If someone gets the jump on you it will help you to defend yourself."

"Works for me!" He picks it up and smiles. "Now I want to go test this out."

"Not so fast. We have to get our prize." I walk over to the glass case and squint inside. I am not sure what I was expecting, but it certainly wasn't what I find.

"A traffic cone? Are you kidding me? Are you sure this is right?"

Sarah scans the cone. "Yep. Says it is the legendary helm of Bakrus. + 50 defence, but -10 reaction speed for some reason. Try it on."

I pick it up and place it carefully on my head. It fits perfectly. I say, "how does it look?" Both Carlos and Sarah stifle sniggers before telling me how great it looks. The message flashes up:

Quest complete: Completed a legendary armour set. +1000 EXP.

Nice!

I finally have everything I need to face the final boss.

LEVEL 23: THE LUKTO HOTEL

"We're running out of time. We need to get levelled up as fast as we can." Carlos taps an imaginary watch.

"Do we absolutely have to be at max level?" I ask.

Sarah says, "The final boss in the game is designed to test you to the very limits of your abilities. If we go in there with anything other than maxed out stats we'll be dead within 30 seconds. We have QA guys that have never beaten him even with a fully levelled character, and these guys play the game for a living."

"Yes, well we already established your QA guys suck." Carlos sees the look on Sarah's face and says, "Ok fine, I get it, the big bad is a big bad. So is there a way to speed this up or not? I don't think we have time to go rescue someone's garden gnome or fetch their poodle from the groomers."

Sarah thinks for a moment. "There may be a better way. It's risky, but it will be the fastest way to get us all to max."

Carlos' ears perk up at the word risky. I take a deep breath. "Just how risky are we talking here?"

"Very. There's a heroes fight club where you can fight one on one and bet levels. The more levels you bet, the tougher your opponent. If you win you get all those levels at once."

"And if you lose?" I'm willing to bet I already know the answer.

"You lose those levels."

Carlos jumps around excitedly. "I can get to the max level in one shot!"

Urgh. I already know this is a terrible idea, but there's no turning back now. "Where exactly can we find this heroes fight club?"

***

"Are you sure this is the right place?"

"This is what the old man in the sketchy pub said. The Lukto Hotel."

I was expecting a run down, abandoned building on the outskirts of town. This place looks like it belongs in Vegas. The golden pillars at the entrance must be fifteen feet tall. The cars parked outside are all worth seven figures.

"This does not look like an underground fight club."

"Exactly! Here it is, hiding in plain sight."

We head inside. The reception is even grander. There is a crystal chandelier, several expensive-looking vases and a lift with shiny gold doors.

A man in a top hat and tuxedo greets us. He looks at us as if we are disturbing his very important task of standing around doing nothing. "I'm afraid we have no reservations."

"We are just here to check out the facilities."

"I'm sorry, but we have a strict dress code." He surveys our outfits. Sarah tries to cover up her bikini, but it doesn't do much to help.

Carlos pulls out his bow. "Does this meet it?"

His expression changes from dismissive to neutral. Without a word he flips a switch under the podium he is standing behind and the lift doors slide open. We stroll over to find it is not a lift at all, it's a corridor. As we walk down it there is a rumbling, as if a train is passing overhead, but there are no train lines out here. I push open a heavy set of wooden doors and the sound transforms from a rumble into the roar of a crowd. We are standing in what can best be described as a coliseum. There are all manner of creatures in the crowd, not just humans. In the centre is a dirt circle, where a knight in a suit of armour is engaged in a fierce battle with a minotaur. I watch as the knight is skewered and flicked forcefully into the crowd, where he lands in a heap and doesn't get up.

"This looks fun!" exclaims Carlos. Only he could be excited by a place like this.

"Who wants to go first?" I don't know why I even bothered asking. Carlos sprints down to the arena and talks to a very shady looking individual who gives him a thumbs up.

"Do you think he's going to play it safe and only gamble a few levels at a time?" says Sarah.

I don't need to answer. A black shadow appears on the ground and blocks out the sun. We watch as a dragon the size of a small aircraft carrier lands in the arena. It barely fits, its tail swishes in and out of the ring. Several people in the front row wisely decide now would be a good time for some refreshments and vacate their seats en masse.

Carlos doesn't look fazed at all, he hops up and down on the spot. The sketchy man walks out to the centre of the arena and holds his hand in the air. He slowly backs away towards the edge of the ring before dropping his arm and shouting "Fight!"

Carlos immediately starts firing arrows, which the dragon blocks with its leathery wings. The dragon spins and whips its tail, but Carlos somersaults over it just in time. He looses another couple of arrows, catching the dragon on its underside. They actually manage to stick and do a modicum of damage. This causes the dragon to screech and take flight, hovering a few feet over the arena. It opens its mouth and a jet of fire comes out, completely engulfing the entire arena.

"Well that took longer than expected. Let's go get Carlos' ashes." I take a step down but Sarah grabs me by the arm and says, "Look."

As the smoke clears I see the shimmering of Carlos' bubble shield. It pops and he stands up triumphantly. The crowd goes absolutely wild, hollering, cheering and stomping their feet.

The dragon looks less impressed. It dives and tries to devour Carlos, but at the last second he steps aside and grabs it by the ear, pulling himself up onto its back. It tries to buck him off, but he holds on tight, waving his free hand in the air.

Sarah says, "I think Carlos might actually be crazy."

"Yep," is the best I can manage as I watch my friend flailing around. I've seen him do a lot of stupid things, but this takes the biscuit.

Eventually the dragon shakes him loose and he lands back in the arena, rolling the moment he hits the ground. This has been a very impressive display, but he still hasn't done any meaningful damage. The dragon is too big, too strong and too fast. Carlos has nothing that can hurt it.

Except maybe he does. He pulls out the golden arrow. He draws back his bow and waits. What is he waiting for?

The dragon is becoming increasingly agitated, its attacks more wild and desperate. It rears up again, its mouth open, ready to cook Carlos alive. I don't know if it has been long enough, is his bubble shield back up yet?

A lick of flame leaves the dragon's mouth as Carlos fires the arrow. It goes straight down the dragon's throat, but nothing else happens. The crowd goes silent. Carlos turns his back on the dragon and crosses his arms. He's given up. The dragon sees its chance to finish the job and raises its claws to cleave him in two. That is when it explodes in a flash of blue flames, raining chunks into the audience.

Everyone is on their feet now. Several pairs of underwear, men's and women's, get thrown into the arena. Carlos swaggers off the stage like a rock star. He struts up to Sarah and I, brushing chunks of dragon off his shoulder.

"You are certifiable! Did you gamble all of your levels?"

"Don't be silly, I saved a couple. Had to have something to gamble with if I lost."

I check his stats. Level 50 Stealth Archer. He's grinning. "Oh man, what am I going to spend all these skill points on?"

"I think you have luck levelled up enough. Maybe try bumping up your common sense stat."

"Boring! So which of you is going next?"

Sarah and I both hesitate. After watching that display I am in no rush. She says, "I suppose I can go."

"Are you going to do it sensibly over a few rounds, or do it all at once?" I ask.

"I haven't decided yet."

She strolls down to the arena and Carlos pats me on the shoulder. "Way to be a modern guy, letting the woman go for the fight to the death first. I'm sure you're going to be able to just sit here and watch her without interfering."

Uh oh. He has a point. I'm not sure if my nerves can take it. I guess I know which way Sarah went as a hulking Centaur steps into the ring with her.

What follows closely resembles a small child watching a horror movie. I spend the next ten minutes occasionally peeking through my fingers and making strained faces.

Sarah is ok, she is keeping it at bay with fireballs.

She's chugging a potion behind a wall made of ice.

She blinks out of the way just as the Centaur charges.

She blasts it with lightning, leaving a static charge in the air of the arena.

Carlos doesn't help, with the occasional teeth sucking or near miss groan.

I feel heat on my face and I peek through my fingers to see the blazing corpse of the Centaur collapse on the ground. Carlos says, "What a fight! I don't think we'll see another one like that again. She has really levelled up that fireball, that last one was like a meteor! You're up bud."

I walk past Sarah on my way to the arena. She smiles and says, "Don't worry, you'll be fine."

Will I heck! Dragons, Centaurs, what am I going to be pitted against? A giant scorpion, or perhaps a gorgon.

When I reach the sketchy guy he says, "Ah fresh meat. How many levels would you like to bet?"

I really want to say one, but we don't have time for me to fight twelve times to get to max. I swallow hard and say, "Twelve please."

"Ok. Step into the arena and I will choose a suitable opponent."

I walk into the circle and the crowd hushes, waiting to see what foul creature will be brought out to face me. I hear clicking and scraping coming down the hallway. A giant centipede? Some kind of killer robot?

A sweet old granny hobbles into the arena with a walker. Is she lost? Perhaps she is trying to get to the stands? I walk over to her, speaking slowly and loudly, "Are you ok ma'am?"

I hear "Fight" behind me. I turn around, but don't see my opponent. When I turn back I get a walker to the temple and the crowd bursts into laughter. I back away, clutching at my face. The old lady says, "In my day sonny, we showed our elders some respect!" She starts to stumble towards me and I don't know what to do. I can't exactly shoot an old lady. I back away, holding my hands out in front of me. "I think there has been a misunderstanding. I was looking to fight some kind of creature."

She darts forwards with surprising speed and does a handstand onto her walker. Then she does a spinning helicopter kick, her wrinkly ankles flapping in the wind as she kicks me repeatedly in the face.

My health has already taken a beating. She hits with the force of a wrinkly bag of hammers. I hear Carlos shouting from the stands, "Hit her!"

"I can't!"

"You have to!"

Get my arse handed to me by a granny, or kick the snot out of an old lady in front of a crowd. I'm not loving these options.

Now she is swinging her purse around like a bola. It connects and sends me flying across the arena. She must be carrying around a set of free weights in that thing.

I have to make a choice. Am I going to be the good guy, the softie, the paladin? Or is it time for a dash of renegade?

I'm going to have to hit her.

She reaches into her purse and tosses out handfuls of something onto the ground. I have no idea what it is, but as I run towards her to hit her I step on one and stick to the ground. It's a god damned toffee sweet. As I try to wrench my foot free she dashes towards me and does a combo of punches on my face. I'm stuck here like a punching bag, my head bobbing back and forth with each punch.

I draw Waterfall and shoot at her, but she rolls out the way. She's got the reflexes of a fifteen year old FPS player.

I finally manage to get my foot free. I make a mental note to avoid the rest of the toffee landmines.

"Do you want to see some pictures of my grandkids?" She pulls out a photo album the size of a phone book and hits me in the face with it.

That's it. It's on.

I grab Showstopper. With a quick flick the photo album is cleaved in two. Pictures of ugly infants rain down around me as Granny screams in rage and barrels at me faster than the damn Centaur.

I fling a pie in her face and drop for the leg sweep. It's hard to sweep two legs and a walker, but I manage it. Granny crashes to the ground faster than a set of dinosaur bones without the pins.

Now she's really pissed. She staggers back to her feet and sticks her hand in her bag. I'm ready for more toffees, but she pulls something else out that I can't quite make out. As I dash in to hit her again she points it at me and my eyes turn to fire. It's flipping mace. I fall to the ground clutching my eyes and she rushes over and starts kneeing me in the face, blowing a rape whistle for added effect. I try to open my eyes, but they are already swelling up. She moves in for the kill, I can hear the clink, clink as she gets closer. It's all I need. When she is almost on top of me I unleash the flaming uppercut.

It's super effective!

She must be doused in gin and hairspray. It sends her flying into the air, her frail body limp. Her grey hair is still smouldering when she lands and I get a message:

K.O. - Winner

+12 levels

Level 50 - Senior Business Analyst

I want to go and help her, but there are already crowd members rushing over to her. Some of them start walking towards me, looking less than thrilled. Carlos appears by my side, wiping tears from his eyes. "Oh mate, that was classic. I never thought you had it in you to uppercut a granny into next week."

"I think now might be a good time for us to leave."

"Are you sure? We still have some time. Maybe you can beat the crap out of a box of puppies."

"Seriously, we need to get out of here."

Carlos finally pays attention to the group of angry people stalking towards us and says, "Ok, point taken. I was bored of this place anyway. Time to skedaddle."

We run back through the doors we came through. Sarah throws up an ice wall, blocking the doors before anyone can follow us. She turns to me. "That was...surprising."

"Look, I don't want you to think I'm some kind of granny-bashing psycho. I was just defending myself."

There's a hint of a smile as she says, "I just didn't realize you had a dark side."

Carlos tries to help. "What, Marcus? Yeah, he can be a real arse-hole when he needs to be, isn't that right mate." He winks at me. He thinks he's helping.

Worst. Wingman. Ever.

LEVEL 24: TEAM BUILDING

"We should head back to base and stock up before the final show-down. How long do we have left?"

I check the countdown. "90 minutes. We are cutting it pretty close."

"It's on the way, it won't add much extra time." Carlos lays across the back seat and chuckles. I don't need to ask what he is laughing about. I'm going to be called Granny basher for the rest of eternity. Is it weird to hope that maybe the world ends after all?

I almost drive right past the base. I have to do a double take. It looks a lot different from when we left it. For one, it is now 10ft up in the air.

"Guys, why is our base a tree house?"

They both stare up at the three story house that is suspended in the air by a tree that is almost certainly not structurally sound enough to hold that kind of weight. The only way in is a rope ladder, so I reluctantly climb it. There is no sign of the Black Ring anywhere.

I pull myself up onto a nice porch and open the front door. I can hardly believe my eyes. This place looks straight out of a magazine. There is a huge kitchen with stainless steel appliances, a TV the size of a wall and a games collection that spans generations. It is my dream home, in tree house form.

I walk through the living room and find myself in the armoury. It is an unusual addition to the house and doesn't really fit in with the modern vibe, but I'm not complaining. The walls are covered in every manner of weaponry you can think of. I reach up and pull a pair of nunchucks down off the wall. Was it really only yesterday that I wielded these for the first time? I spin them around without thinking and then slip them into my pocket. I also grab a handful of throwing knives, for old times' sake. I add several mags of Agile ammo while I am at it.

There are lots of other items. I see golden samurai swords, jewel-encrusted battle hammers, a shield that appears to be made of solid diamond, but I can't bring anything else. I need all my remaining inventory spots for food. Something tells me I'm going to need healing in the final battle.

I hear a commotion and go to investigate. Several members of the Black Ring are engaged in a heated debate around a pool table. As soon as I walk into the room they all stop what they are doing and stand to attention. I say, "carry on," but they don't move.

I find Carlos and Sarah raiding the cupboards, stuffing food into their pockets. I tell them both about the armoury and Carlos runs off, coming back momentarily with a full quiver.

"So why is our base now a tree house?" asks Carlos.

"It makes literally no sense, but I suppose strategically it is harder to attack now." I do a quick check. "Wow, it says the base is level 5. These guys have been busy. The weird thing is I didn't ask them to do any upgrades. I guess they took the initiative."

Carlos says, "What do you think this button does?" He's pointing at a large red button on the wall. Before I can say anything he's pushed it. A blaring alarm sounds and metal shutters immediately descend over all the windows and turrets drop down from the roof. It's enough of a racket to wake up Nutsack, who appears on my shoulder. He looks terrible, his eyes are bloodshot and he keeps scratching at his mouth. Black Ring members come running, weapons drawn. I hold up my hands, "False alarm, please go back to what you were doing."

They stare at Nutsack like they have never seen a squirrel before. He yawns and goes back into my hoodie. After a few seconds the Black Ring disperse. I turn to Carlos, "You just can't help yourself can you? You see a bloody big red button on the wall and you have to push it."

"What can I say, I am curious."

"That is a much politer way of phrasing it than I would have chosen."

Something starts blinking in my peripheral. I look and the timer is now flashing, counting down from 60 minutes. "Ok team, I think it's time. Is everyone ready for the final showdown?"

They both do a check of their armour and gear and nod. I pull up my quest menu and click on the very last one. The green arrow appears. "Ok. Let's do this."

***

As we get closer to the location Carlos says, "I think it's taking us to Master Systems. You think Jenkins is the final boss?"

"A fat middle-aged balding guy? Wouldn't be much of a challenge."

"Says the guy who almost got killed by a Granny an hour ago."

"Well luckily for me I have Carlos the dragon slayer with me, so he can do some actual work while I take a break. Will be a nice change."

Sarah says, "You two are like an old married couple. We are all on the same team here. Like I said before, the end game boss in the game is tough as nails, so if it turns out to be your boss then consider yourself lucky."

We pull up outside the building and the arrow points towards the entrance. Looks like we might have hit the jackpot.

As we stroll into reception the security guard jumps to his feet. He reaches for his walkie talkie and it shatters in his hand as Carlos shoots an arrow through it. He turns to run and gets a sleeping arrow in the arse for his trouble. The receptionist doesn't even look up from her game of solitaire.

As the three of us ascend in the lift I say, "Just act natural. I'll see if I can get Jenkins out of the building and away from innocent people."

The lift doors open and a photocopier flies towards me. I roll out of the way as it crashes into the back wall of the lift.

"Looks like they are expecting us."

We step out of the lift and they are all waiting for us. Brad, Jim and Cindy. They form a line between us and Jenkins' office, like a football team trying desperately to block a free kick. They are all level 20, with the weedy health bars to go with it.

I smile. "Hey team. I don't suppose you fancy moving out of the way?"

Cindy steps forward. "We know what you're doing and we can't let it happen. If you want to get to Jenkins, you'll have to go through us."

"Fine by me." I turn to Carlos and Sarah. "I have a few long-standing issues I would like to resolve with my team, why don't you two take five."

Carlos nods but Sarah looks worried. "There are three of them, are you sure you'll be ok?"

"You have my blessing to step in if things get bad. Here, please hold on to these for me." I hand over Showstopper and my pistols. I don't want to make it too easy and besides, these are the kinds of issues that need to be resolved with bare hands.

Jim is the first one to rush me. It's the most enthusiastic I have ever seen him. He takes a wild swing and I step out of the way, sticking my foot out to sweep his legs. He crashes hard into the cubicle wall behind me, knocking it over. I can't capitalize though, Brad has picked up two staplers. I hold my hands up in the air. "Oh no. Please, don't shoot." He squeezes one of them and a staple flies out at surprising speed, narrowly missing me. He grins and points them both at me as staples fill the air. I roll under the blizzard of spiky metal and get close enough to take a swing at him. He evades, so I swing again, and he dodges again. Of course his evasion skill is high, he's been avoiding work for months. I try a flurry of kicks. The first couple miss, but the last three connect, whittling away most of his health bar. He starts to plead with me, "Wait, please don't. I didn't mean to leave you high and dry like that."

I almost fall for it, but I see that he's reloading the staplers behind his back. He swings them back around to face me and I duck under the shots and flaming uppercut him into the roof. He gets stuck in the roof tiles, his legs kicking frantically.

I turn to find Jim storming towards me again, his upper body covered in staples, tiny red blotches forming on his white shirt. He looks pissed. He scoops up the photocopier and holds it above his head. I slide a pie along the floor just as he steps forward, ready to throw. He steps in it and his leg goes from under him, tossing the photocopier up into the air as he lands on his back. It lands with a crash on his head and he's out for the count. Two down, one to go.

As usual Cindy was happy for the others to do her dirty work. Now she's all alone. She smiles at me smugly. "I can't wait to kick your arse. Then we'll know who really deserves that promotion."

She moves effortlessly into a fighting stance and darts at me, her leg flying. I duck, sidestep and roll just in time. She's a lot faster than I was expecting. She says, "Surprised? Five years of boxercise." She is dancing on the spot to a beat that only she can hear. She picks up a handful of highlighters, throwing them like darts. I snatch them out of the air one by one.

She tries again, punches flailing, but it's as if she is moving in slow motion. She is all bark and no bite. That's when I realize the truth. She always has been. I have spent the last year being afraid of her, when I should have been feeling sorry for her.

I could end this with one punch, but I hesitate. She laughs and says, "what's the matter, afraid to hit a girl?"

"Actually, I recently got over that particular fear. However, I'm still not sure it would be right for me to hit you."

She smirks, ready to attack again, but I say, "Luckily, this desk doesn't have those same reservations."

The puzzled look on her face is priceless. "What?"

Her desk flies over a little quicker than I planned, knocking her out cold in one glance and showering her with pens and highlighters.

Perfect fight! +100 EXP

Carlos pats me on the back. "Looks like you enjoyed that."

"Yeah I got a few things off my chest. There's still one more person I need to deal with." I glance over at Jenkins' office.

Sarah says, "Want some backup?"

"I don't know yet. Let's see what we're dealing with. Be ready for anything."

I stroll over to Jenkins' office and pound on the door. After a few seconds I hear, "Come in."

I'm not sure what I was expecting, but it wasn't Jenkins in a power suit. He looks ridiculous, like a dog wearing a tuxedo. I'm ready for a fight, but he sees me and says, "Nice of you to show up for work today Marcus."

"Yes, well, I had to work through a few things. We need to talk."

"I am in the middle of something. Put something in my calendar for later in the week."

"I'm afraid it has to be now. It's important."

He adjusts his tie. "I decide what is important around here, not you. I'm docking you a week's pay as punishment for your behaviour. Now get back to work."

"I'm afraid that's not going to be possible. I quit."

Stick up for yourself - 4 of 4 Fears conquered. 100% complete.

There's a momentary flash of panic before he wrestles it under control. He knows that I do most of the work around here. Perhaps this is it, this is the final battle that I have been building up to. It was never about reaching level 50, it was about understanding my worth and not letting this petulant man child push me around. It's a philosophical victory. How profound.

I'm not paying attention, which is a mistake. A health bar appears above his head, far larger than any I have seen before. The title says *Level 100 Middle Manager*. I have barely had time to process it when he lunges at me. He moves far quicker than a man of his size should move. Before I know what is going on he scoops me up off the floor and slams me against his desk. Then he kicks open his office door, drags me up by the scruff of my hoodie, and throws me straight through the window.

I hurtle towards the ground, screaming as I go. The fall damage alone from this height is likely to kill me. What a stupid way for the world to end, from a fat guy throwing me out a window. I've defeated Bruisers, Carnies, Football Hooligans, killer elves and a geriatric, and it's going to be gravity that kills me.

I'm 8ft from the ground, my teeth clenched, when Sarah appears in a puff of smoke, her arms outstretched. She catches me with little effort and I hang there in her arms like a newlywed. It goes on a little too long before she places me on the ground. "Thanks for that, I thought I was a goner."

"Oh you totally were."

How reassuring.

I can hear Jenkins roaring above, his little piggy face glaring down at me out of the broken window. He storms towards Carlos, ready to fight. Even Carlos knows better than to take on a level 100 end game boss by himself. He fires an arrow through the closest window before running and leaping out in a swan dive. At the last moment he flips himself in the air and lands in a superhero pose, cracking the pavement and kicking up a cloud of dust. I run over. "How are you not dead?"

He stands up casually. "What? Oh that? I maxed out my agility skill tree. I don't take fall damage."

"Do you think Jenkins will come after us?"

"Absolutely. I've never seen him so pissed. What did you say to him?"

"I quit."

Carlos beams at me. "Finally! No wonder he's so mad, now he might have to do some actual work."

I turn to both of them. "This is going to get ugly. That wasn't normal Jenkins, it is some end boss equivalent. Who knows what tricks he has up his sleeves."

"Whatever they are, we'll face them together," says Carlos.

"We've got this," says Sarah.

I hold my hand out and they both place theirs on top of mine.

At least I can tick that off my bucket list before the world ends.

"We don't have long, he's going to be here any moment. Here's the plan..."

***

Jenkins bursts through the fire escape doors, red and wheezing. He must have taken the stairs. If this was the real Jenkins he'd be dead already. He scans the Master Systems car park for us, but we are all safely out of sight. We need him in the middle, where we can surround him.

I left a little something to tempt him out into the open.

He's wary as he walks towards the burger lying on the ground. He picks it up and sniffs it before taking a bite. That's the signal.

I open fire with Agile, keeping it firmly aimed at the centre of mass. He's a large target, so even with the recoil I manage to make most of the bullets land. It doesn't do much damage, but it sure gets his attention. He chucks the rest of the burger on the ground and charges towards me like a wounded rhino. That's when Carlos pops up and looses a few arrows into his back. The last one sticks and Jenkins stops to try and pull it out. That's when Sarah appears by his side, zapping him with lightning. As he turns to swing at her she vanishes again. I try a shot with Waterfall, and that one hits too. The damage is starting to show now, not a lot, but if we can keep this up we should be able to wear him down. We just need to keep him at a distance.

Jenkins apparently realizes the same thing. He picks up the car next to him and tosses it effortlessly at Sarah. I scream as it lands where she was standing seconds earlier, just as she blinks back into existence by my side. She says, "That was close. I can't keep teleporting everywhere, I'll run out of potions."

Carlos keeps a continuous stream of arrows flying, but Jenkins scoops up another car and uses it as a shield as he charges at Carlos' position. Carlos only just manages to roll out of the way as the car slams into the wall behind him. I reload Agile and try to provide a distraction, but Jenkins has figured out what we are up to. He ignores the flurry of bullets and chases after Carlos, who's slowly getting backed into the corner of the chain-link fence. In a few seconds Jenkins will have him trapped. There's no time to think, no time to plan. It's time to act.

I flip on my turbo shoes and bolt past Jenkins, grabbing Carlos on the way. The extra weight slows me down, but it's enough to drag him out of danger. I hear Jenkins roaring behind us. I drop Carlos next to Sarah and say, "It's a good start, but we need to keep up the pressure. Let's stay on the offensive."

I turn right back and sprint at Jenkins. Just as I reach him I pull out my nunchucks and run around him in a circle, flailing as I go, like a psychopathic tornado. He howls and takes swings at me, but I'm too quick. Eventually the nunchucks shatter in my hand. I'm about to dart away when he sticks his arm out like a clothesline and I run full speed into it, somersaulting across the car park and landing on the roof of a car. I'm down 90% of my HP with one hit. Not ideal, but it could be worse, I could be dead. I quickly wolf down burgers until I am back at full health.

I flip back onto my feet and check Jenkins' stats. He's lost a little over 20% of his health and we are still in pretty good shape. We can do this.

Sarah shouts, "Carlos, firewall."

She flings a huge fireball as Carlos makes it rain fire arrows. The flames engulf Jenkins, but he steps through them without damage. It looks like he's immune to status effects.

Carlos switches to normal arrows and peeks back up to fire when Jenkins flings something at him, hitting him squarely in the chest. It's not clear from here what it is, but Carlos looks really unhappy about it. He ducks back down behind the car, but I can hear him gagging from over here while he tries to force a burger into his mouth. What could it be? For some strange reason my bullshit detector is going nuts.

I find out why when I peek back up to see where Jenkins is. A dollop of bull shit lands on the bonnet of the car, inches from my face. The smell is wretched. Jenkins is flinging it like an angry ape, a constant stream of it. It must be his magic ability. Endless bull shit. This is going to make things harder.

If only I had projectiles. It would be handy if there was a stack of tables in the car park that I could put to good use.

That's when I realize the building behind me is stuffed to bursting with tables.

I concentrate hard. I can feel them all, right on the edge of my powers. I don't need many, just a handful. With a scream I coax them out of the building, raining glass as they come hurtling through the windows. I concentrate them all on Jenkins, piling them on top of him. Sarah spots her opportunity and chucks a fire-ball in the mix, setting them on fire. Carlos fires arrows through the gaps.

I keep dancing the tables in and out, crashing them together and pulling them apart, until my MP is completely depleted. As soon as it hits zero the tables fall to the ground and the others retreat as Jenkins picks himself up off the ground. His shirt is charred and untucked, his tie is loose and his dodgy comb-over is everywhere except where it is supposed to be.

He's down to half health. Just a little bit further. I check my inventory. Still lots of ammo for Agile, some throwing knives and several burgers. I reload and pull out both pistols. Time to get my Woo on.

I leap through the air as a barrage of poop flies at me. I aim carefully, taking my time, going for the extra damage of the headshot. It connects just as I land and roll, but I'm still out in the open. Jenkins turns and unleashes a literal shit storm. I hold my hands in front of my face, but nothing connects. I peek over my guard to see a wall of ice in front of me, blocking the poop. I glance over and Sarah nods.

I peek around the wall as Jenkins stalks towards me, maintaining fire, hoping to catch me stranded. If I step out I'm going to get hit, if I stay here I am a sitting duck. What's a guy to do?

I get ready to fight as he gets closer. I'm just going to have to hit him hard and move fast before he can counter. He lifts his arms up, ready to bring them crashing down. I'm going to have to time this perfectly.

Carlos appears on Jenkins' back, riding him rodeo style. He's got an arrow and he is going to town back there, stabbing with one hand and clutching the comb over with the other. Jenkins tries to buck him off, but he holds on tight, until Jenkins staggers away. I watch as Jenkins finally gets hold of Carlos and pulls him off his back. He holds him by his foot and slams him into a parked car, then another, before tossing him into the wall. I wait, but Carlos doesn't get up. He's out for the count.

Sarah shouts, "Go revive Carlos, I will keep Jenkins busy."

I run over and place my hand on Carlos chest. The timer starts, its slow steady countdown betraying the urgency of the situation. I watch, helpless, as Sarah dances in between attacks, throwing ice, fire and lightning before blinking away just as Jenkins lunges for her. She has the timing down perfectly. When he steps back to throw shit at her she deflects it right back at him, giving her just enough time to get in a free hit. If anyone could wear him down, it would be her.

Jenkins suddenly breaks off his attack. What is he doing? Sarah throws a fireball at him, but he leaps over it. At first I think he is dodging, but too late I realize it's an attack. She tries to blink away, but it doesn't work. She must be out of MP. She scrambles to pull out a potion as he lands on her like a beached whale. She's knocked down immediately, the potion rolling away.

There's still five seconds left on Carlos' timer, but now I'm all alone. Jenkins stalks towards me, a smug grin on his face. I'm in trouble and he knows it. If I take my hand off Carlos the timer starts again, and there's no way I'll get another ten seconds to revive anyone. I use my other hand to throw a few knives his way, but they barely slow him down.

That's when they appear. Dozens of them. They slink out of every shadow and drop down from the rooftops. The Black Ring is here to save their glorious leader. Jenkins hesitates, aware that he is now surrounded by a new threat. I shout, "Get him! Get Jenkins!" but none of them move.

Nutsack appears on my shoulder. Something is definitely wrong with him, wafts of smoke are coming off him and he's desperately trying to stay out of the sun. He points a furry paw at Jenkins and makes several squeaking sounds, and just like that the Black Ring attacks. That's when I realize I am not the leader of the Black Ring. Nutsack is.

That explains the tree house.

Jenkins swats away these new attackers like flies, but they keep coming. It's all I need, a distraction. The revival timer reaches zero and Carlos sits up. He opens his eyes and says, "Did we win yet?"

"We're working on it. You got one last push in you?"

"Always buddy. Always. What do you need me to do?"

"I need your mad archery skills. We have to hit him in his weak spot."

"Weak spot? I don't see a glowing red ball or gap in his armour. Where is his weak spot?"

"Where is every guy's weak spot?"

He cringes. "Dude, that is pure evil. If it was anyone but Jenkins I'd politely decline, but for him I'll make an exception."

"Think you can hit it?"

"Well it's an exceptionally small target, but you can rely on me."

"Wait for my signal."

I crank up the turbo shoes one last time. I dart over to Jenkins and unleash Agile on him. I follow up with a shot from Waterfall, right in the arse. He turns to swat at me, and that's when I shout, "Now!"

Carlos unleashes the arrow and it curves through the air. It hits Jenkins square in the crotch with a twang and his knees buckle. His face falls right into range and I hit him with a flaming upper-cut. It connects with his jaw with a crack and a lone tooth comes flying out as he topples to the ground, his health bar depleted.

We've done it!

I rush over to Sarah and bounce on the spot as the timer counts down. When she opens her eyes I smile. "We did it. We won."

She looks concerned. It's not what I was expecting. She sits up and says, "It shouldn't be this easy."

There's a noise behind me. I spin around to see Jenkins getting back to his feet. His laugh echoes off the building like a classic cartoon villain. Muscles tear through his shirt and his health balloons to a million HP. He grows to be twelve feet tall, his girth blocking out the sun. A new name appears for him. *Mega Jenkins.*

He turns and stomps on the remaining Black Ring. They scatter and run, bodies flying. One hit from him was enough to finish them. That doesn't bode well.

We all run in different directions, peppering him with bullets and arrows. There is no noticeable effect on his health bar.

I shout over to Carlos, "We need to focus on the weak spot again."

"I can try, but each arrow doesn't do a whole lot of damage."

"What about your head butt special ability? That does a lot more damage."

"You want me to head butt him in the crotch? Are you joking me? You're asking me to teabag myself!"

"For the sake of the world."

"Urgh. This better work. Sarah, can you ice me a path to Jenkins?"

She doesn't ask why, she just casts her ice spell across the floor, creating a runway. Carlos starts skating towards Jenkins, going faster and faster. He's really putting his max agility to the test.

Mega Jenkins swings for him, but Carlos effortlessly leaps over the attack. He ducks his head and barrels headfirst into Jenkins' crotch.

The effect is immediate. A huge chunk of Jenkins' health disappears and Sarah and I cheer.

Then just like that, Mega Jenkins' health bar fills back up. What is going on?

Sarah shouts, "He's regenerating health!"

"But his health bar is already ridiculous. How are we going to beat him?"

"Oh no! I think he has the regen bug. His health is filling up too quickly."

"What does that mean?"

"It means we can't win."

Well fudge.

Carlos is still running back to Sarah and I when Jenkins charges up an attack. My bullshit detector goes off and I shout, "incoming!" We are all out in the open. This is going to end badly.

The Mega Jenkins shitstorm is so much worse. Hundreds of projectiles fill the air, more than anyone could ever dodge. We are sitting ducks. That is when the world goes fuzzy again. Carlos has cast his bubble shield over Sarah and I, leaving himself completely exposed. The shitstorm knocks him down, pinning him to the ground as Jenkins whittles down his health bar. He turns to me and shouts, "You've got this." Then he is gone, buried in a mound of bull shit.

I scream and try to run out of the bubble, but Sarah holds me back. I finally stop and say, "How are we going to beat him?"

She says, "I'm not sure we can. I am all out of MP."

"I guess this is it then."

She hugs me. "I'm sorry. This is all my fault."

"I'm sorry too. I never told you how I really felt."

Her hug tightens. "You did though. I just wasn't ready to hear it. You know it's strange, I can barely even remember my fiancee. The more I think about him, the fuzzier he becomes. All I know is that he hurt me. I didn't want to be hurt again."

"I would never hurt you."

"I know that. You're the guy that stopped a car chase to save a squirrel. Of course, you're also the guy that set a Granny on fire..."

"That was self-defence!"

We both smile, lost in the moment. Then out of nowhere Sarah leans in to kiss me. I close my eyes. It's not exactly how I hoped we would get together, but at least I'll get in a kiss before the end of the world.

There's a scream and I open my eyes to find Sarah in Jenkins' hand. The bastard has scooped her out from the bubble shield. He grins at me. "You should have just kept your mouth shut and done as you were told. All this could have been avoided."

He claps his hands together and Sarah's health bar vanishes. He tosses her over his shoulder like a discarded coffee cup. That's when I really lose it. I fire everything I have, Agile, Waterfall, a table. He laughs as his health bar fills up instantly.

There is no way to beat him.

Nutsack appears on my shoulder again. He doesn't need to die here with me. I try to shoo him away, but he turns and looks at me, with his new red eyes, and then he smiles. Something is definitely different about him. Before I can figure it out he leaps off me, no doubt to run to freedom, but then he glides right up and lands on Jenkins. Apparently my useless pet is no ordinary squirrel, he's a flying squirrel.

Jenkins looks down and tries to swat Nutsack away, but he darts over his shoulder and down his back. When Jenkins tries to hit him again, he starts to bite. Not nibbles either, hearty bites that would strip bark off a tree. Jenkins howls and spins in a circle patting at himself, desperately trying to get the furry nuisance away. What's most interesting is just how much damage Nutsack is doing, Jenkins has lost almost a tenth of his health bar. I wait for it to regen, but it doesn't.

I'm just thinking maybe Nutsack is going to win the day when Jenkins finally grabs him. He spikes my furry friend into the ground and the little guy doesn't get back up. I use the only move I have left, I throw a cream pie at him. It hits him in the face. At least I get a chuckle before he kills me. That's when he starts to scream. He claws at his face and starts to vomit. "Get it off me! It burns!"

What the hell was in that cream pie? Oh right, cream! He's lactose intolerant!

While he's screaming I crank the turbo shoes and run over to the other side of the car park. Where is it, I know it is here somewhere. I find it wedged under a car tire. I pop the cork and down the potion in one go. I dash back over and start flinging pies at any exposed skin I can see, until I am all out of MP. It's still not enough, he's only lost 25% of his health, but at least now it stays lost.

I watch as Nutsack jumps back to his feet and runs over to me. How is that possible? His health bar slowly fills back up to full. He suddenly has the regen skill, but how? That's when I notice the new sharp teeth sticking out of Nutsack's mouth. The little guy is a vampire squirrel. He must have caught it from Roger. He looks at me and points up at the sun. Confused, I hold him up and he immediately starts to smoke. That's when I realize what he wants me to do. He is sacrificing himself so I can get the regen skill. With it I might have a chance of beating Jenkins.

Kill the squirrel, save the world.

He starts to smoulder and squeaks with the pain. It shouldn't be a difficult choice, but something in me snaps. I lower Nutsack down to the ground, being careful to put him in the shadows. His health bar fills up again. He protests, but then I give him a pet. "Not today little guy. I've lost enough friends. This is my fight, and I'm going to win it on my own terms."

Fudge this game. It keeps trying to make me be someone I'm not. Well it is time to start playing it my way. All I need is a plan.

Any second now Jenkins will be back on his feet. There has to be a way to beat him. I just need to do more damage. If only there was some way to multiply my damage output.

That's it!

I take off this stupid cone hat. I'm going to be needing my reflexes. I hop into the menu and reassign my skill points, putting them all into the skill I need. I'll take the 25% loss. It leaves me with no health, no strength, no offensive skills at all, but it doesn't matter.

Jenkins gets back to his feet. He still has 75% of his health, over 750,000 HP. With my new stats I only do 100 HP of damage per hit. If my plan works, it won't matter.

I draw Showstopper just as the music starts up. This isn't orchestral, it is fast paced electronic music, fitting for the final showdown.

Let's dance.

Jenkins hesitates. He doesn't know how weak I am. He wants to keep me at a distance. He points his hand and gets ready to blast me. My BS detector flashes. Perfect.

The poop flies at me. I don't dodge, or jump or roll. I take a deep breath and parry. 20X *damage* appears. My new stats are working.

Jenkins fires again and I parry. 40X *damage*. And again. 80X *damage*.

He starts rapid firing, one after the other, boom, boom, boom. Parry, parry, parry. 740X *damage*.

He goes for the kill. He fires the shitstorm. Too bad for him, I'm in the zone. I can't parry them all, most of them miss, but I get as many as I can. Showstopper whirls around like a helicopter blade, the *ching* sounds blurring into one long *chchchchchchchchchchchchchchchching*. When he is done I am 5120X *damage*.

It's still not enough.

He finally realizes what I am doing and stops firing. He only has to hit me once, and I can't attack him yet. If I do my parry multiplier will be reset and I'm as good as dead. He's expecting me to retreat, so instead I charge him. He takes a swing and I roll, that most basic of moves. He tries again, and again, and on the third time I stop suddenly and parry. It *chings* just as his strike connects. 10240X *damage*.

Now's the time. Any hit will do it, but I've come this far. This has to mean something. He swings at me again in desperation and I side step, hopping onto his arm. I run up it full speed and leap towards his face. Time slows down as we draw level and I see the look of fear in his eyes. I finally understand. He's always been afraid of me, that is why he kept me down. I was never more than a threat to him. Well, that ends today.

I can do anything right now, I could draw Waterfall and shoot him point blank in the face, I could chop off his head with Showstopper, I could head butt him into next week.

Instead I reach out and tap him on the nose with a "boop."

He looks confused, then relieved, then angry. That's when the shockwave hits him. He flies across the car park like a missile, crashing into the Master Systems building. His health bar vanishes and I see the words I have been waiting for.

Quest Complete: Defeat the Dark Lord

You win!

Play again? Y/N

I check and my health bar is still there. I'm still in the game. That means there is still time.

Not much though. The game timer only has thirty seconds left.

I rush over and revive Sarah. She's barely awake when I shout, "Help me get Carlos!"

We run over to the shit heap and start digging as the timer ticks away. I get a hand on him and the countdown starts. It is only a few seconds ahead of the timer. He wakes up and sniffs, "Where the fudge am I? Did we win?"

2 seconds left.

I hold my breath and select N.

There is a ripple that expands outwards, warping reality back to its previous state. The crushed cars all leap back to their parking spaces, the glass flies back up and becomes windows, and Jenkins is back to his usual rotund self. I walk over to find him laying on the ground. "What happened? Where am I? What are you doing here? Why do you have a traffic cone on your head?"

I laugh and take it off. It's just a plain old traffic cone now, there's nothing special about it.

Jenkins scowls at me. "Shouldn't you be in work?"

Oh goody, I get to quit all over again. "Actually Mr. Jenkins, I'm afraid I am tendering my resignation, effective immediately."

"What? You can't do that! No-one knows how to do half the stuff you do." He scrambles to his feet and grabs me by the collar. "You can have the promotion, effective immediately." He looks desperate.

I shrug his hands off me and say, "I'm sorry, but I'm not interested. You had your chance. You should give it to Cindy. Goodbye Jenkins."

He's still screaming at me when I turn and walk away. I don't have time to listen to any more of his nonsense.

I'm heading back over to Sarah when there is a familiar scratching on my leg. I look down to see Nutsack clinging to me. He's back to his tatty self, mange and all. I stop walking and say, "I couldn't have done it without you buddy."

He runs up my leg and straight up into my hood.

What the hell, I always wanted a pet.

I get back to Carlos and Sarah. Carlos says, "I really need a shower."

"Yeah, you do."

Sarah says, "I really need new clothes."

"No, you don't." I lean in and kiss her. I wait to see if she pushes me away, but she wraps her arms around me and pulls me close. It's everything I hoped it would be.

Carlos says, "About bloody time!"

LEVEL 26: AFTER THE CREDITS

I walk in the front door. My Mum takes one look at me and starts screaming, "Where in the bloody hell have you been young man? I have been worried sick! What on earth are you wearing?"

I run over and hug her as hard as I can. "It's nice to have you back Mum."

"It's those video games isn't it, that's what you've been doing. I told you they were bad for you."

"Actually, I think I'm going to be taking a break from games for a while."

"A break? But you love games."

"Yeah, I played a tough one recently and it has put me off them. Besides, I have a girlfriend now."

If Mum didn't look shocked before, she does now. "A girlfriend? When? Who?"

"She's right outside, you should come and meet her."

Mum immediately forgets she is mad at me. She follows me out of the front door to find Carlos and Sarah sitting in the Mustang. Sarah gets out, still in her chain mail bikini and says, "Nice to meet you Mrs. Kennedy. Apologies for my outfit, we were at a fancy dress party and I haven't had a chance to get changed yet."

Mum turns to me and smiles. "Well this is a lovely surprise."

I feel a scratch on my neck and Mum shrieks. "What is that in your hood?"

"Oh, that's Nutsack. He's my new pet."

"There is no way we are having a squirrel living in the house!"

"Yeah, about that. I have my own place now. It's a long story. I promise I will fill you in once I have had a chance to figure it all out myself. But don't worry, I haven't forgotten about the mortgage. I have a few items in my new house that I will be selling to avid collectors that should more than make up what you have left to pay."

Mum stares at me, astounded. "Did you win the lottery, or did Jenkins finally give you that promotion?"

"Actually, I don't work there anymore. I quit this morning."

"Quit? You can't quit. You need that job. Carlos, can you please talk some sense into him."

He waves from the passenger seat. "Sorry Mrs. K, no can do. Marcus has earned himself a holiday. We've been through a lot. You know, I had to go two whole days without saying fu…"

"Carlos! Language." She turns her attention back to me. "So what are you going to do now?"

I grab Sarah and kiss her for an inappropriate amount of time.

When I finally come up for air I smile and say, "Sarah and I have some catching up to do."

There's one item left in my inventory, I mean pocket, that I'm still hoping I might get to use.

Thanks Charles.

GAME OVER

Begin Encrypted Quantum Tunnel.

Connection Secured.

Chat link established.

PJ: Seriously, what are we supposed to be doing? This new AI fixes bugs before I even know they exist.

MK: We are just here to babysit. Like how old fashioned cars had steering wheels way past the point they needed them because all the old farts wouldn't trust the computer to drive for them.

PJ: Yeah my son bought one of those vintage Teslas. He swears by it, uses the pedals and everything. Kids these days!

MK: A couple more years and they won't need us any more. How's your pension?

PJ: Don't ask. My doc says he will have to euthanize me on my 120th birthday if I can't boost my contributions. Is yours any better?

MK: It will be when you pay up on our Super Bowl CLVI bet.

PJ: How much was that again?

MK: One bitcoin.

PJ: Shut up, that was a week ago, when one bitcoin was a beer. There's no way I am giving you a months wages.

PJ: 2 months.

PJ: 3 weeks.

PJ: Ok, I give up. I'll pay you back when the market crashes again.

MK: Oh no you don't. I need that money now. Pay up.

PJ: Double or nothing.

MK: Urgh, I don't know why I keep betting with you. You never pay.

PJ: It's something to do. Seriously, let's make it interesting. I'll make it fun for you. You like that new VR game with all the knights and magic and stuff right? The one that's in beta.

MK: I do. So what?

PJ: I found a way to merge it with a branch of the simulation...

MK: ARE YOU OUT OF YOUR MIND! The AI will find that in seconds and you'll be out of a job. You won't even make it to 110. Your wife will remarry some smoking hot 90 year old that your kids will have to call Dad.

PJ: Have a little faith will you. I'm running it on the backup backup server, which the AI only checks once a week. I've been messing around with it in my spare time, you should check it out.

MK: Don't the virtuals reject the new rules? Whenever we try and change something they always crash. They are so temperamental.

PJ: I found a way around it. I have managed to convince them that they are still in the real world, but the real world is broken. They genuinely believe what is happening to them. No desyncs at all in my last QA test. I just need to roll it out to the full server.

MK: Ok, now you've got me interested. Send me the link, but if anyone asks I'm denying this conversation ever happened.

***

MK: This is actually pretty cool. I like how you're merging the two rule sets. Very clever. I still don't get what this has to do with our bet though.

PJ: Simple. You just have to get one of the virtuals to win the game.

MK: I'm waiting for the but...

PJ: But I get to pick the virtual, and you can't make any alterations to them.

MK: No way. Never going to happen. You'll pick a guy in a coma, or a baby, or some other nonsense. Give me my bitcoin.

PJ: Ok fine, I'll make a list of everyone that is exactly average. Average height, build, looks, intelligence, the whole package. Then I'll let you pick one, so you know I'm not cheating.

MK: Speaking of cheating, how do I know you aren't trying to pull a fast one. This whole thing could be rigged.

PJ: You can check the code yourself. I ported it over exactly, bugs and all. So are we on?

MK: How many chances do I get? To win?

PJ: One!

MK: One hundred.

PJ: Fine, ten.

MK: Two hundred.

PJ: That's not how negotiating works.

MK: Sure it is. Three hundred.

PJ: Ok fine, you can have one hundred tries, but the sim gets reset each time so there is no cross contamination between runs. You can't alter any physical properties or the backstory of your virtual, they have to be exactly as they were when you pick them. I can't have you making them a super ninja. Deal?

MK: Ok. You're on!

***

PJ: Man, your guy nearly had it that time.

MK: Shut up!

PJ: Seriously, getting killed by the initial mugger is a new low. How many attempts is that anyway?

MK: You know full well it is seven. Still plenty to go.

***

MK: I found your little secret...

PJ: ?

MK: Professor Jasper?

PJ: Oh right, him.

MK: You put a virtual version of yourself in the game! What is the matter with you?

PJ: It was just a bit of fun, I was practising migrating a backup of my personality.

MK: Yeah, I was just going to say how realistic he is.

PJ: Thanks!

MK: He's a smug arsehole. Very authentic.

***

PJ: Are you breaking the rules?

MK: Whatever do you mean?

PJ: What happened to Shen?

MK: Who?

PJ: Shen Mue. The nerdy Asian kid that invites them to play the game.

MK: Oh him? Yeah, he won the lottery. I gave my guy an upgrade.

PJ: You replaced him with this Sarah chick. Who is she anyway?

MK: She's an old crush of my guy. You said I couldn't alter his backstory, you didn't say anything about changing anyone else. She had a sudden desire to move back to their home town.

PJ: You sneaky bugger! I'll allow it, it's not going to help. Your guy would need a million attempts to even get close.

***

PJ: AHAHAHAHAHAHA.

MK: It's not funny.

PJ: I think it is hilarious! Who could have possibly known that your guy would find a way to woo his long lost sweetheart and spend the last few days of his life in bed with her.

MK: It just needs more tweaking.

PJ: You'd better hurry up, only 82 tries left.

***

PJ: You gave her a fake fiancee?

MK: Turns out he was a real dick. Now she's too sad to jump into bed with my guy.

PJ: I worry about you sometimes.

***

PJ: You've got to be kidding me. There's no way you're not helping him out.

MK: Check the logs.

PJ: We both know the logs can be changed.

MK: I swear I'm not. It is no fun if I cheat.

PJ: Urgh, I see why you like this virtual.

MK: His fears are what are holding him back. I need to find a way to get him to conquer them. Am I allowed to add quests?

PJ: I don't see why not, as long as they don't break any of the rules of the game. The time limit still applies though. I can't have this taking too long.

***

PJ: I'm impressed. Your guy genuinely nearly had it that time.

MK: If only he would stop sacrificing himself to save Sarah.

PJ: Yeah, it's a real shame. Oh well.

MK: If only I could convince him that saving her would have wider consequences, like ending the world or something. If only there was a shallow exposition NPC that could randomly blurt that out to him...

PJ: Not a chance!

***

PJ: I hate to admit this, but I am rooting for your guy.

MK: I know right? It is hard to watch him dying in all these horrid ways. Are you sure we have to stop at 100? I want to see him finish this.

PJ: A bet's a bet.

***

PJ: Are you nervous? Last chance before my debt is resolved.

MK: Nah, my guy has got this.

PJ: He's going to destroy the world for some ridiculous reason, just you watch.

MK: No chance.

***

PJ: A vampire squirrel? Now I've seen everything!

MK: Why won't he kill it? Oh god, please no!

PJ: Told you! The whole world is ending because he won't kill a squirrel that is already dead.

MK: I give up. This guy is hopeless.

PJ: Wait, he's not done yet...

MK: OMG DID YOU SEE THAT!

PJ: WTF! You must have cheated. There's no way.

MK: Check whatever you need to check. That was legit. My guy for the clutch win. Now pay up! Two bitcoins.

PJ:.......

MK: Are you going to pay me or not?

PJ: Double or nothing?

If you enjoyed this book there's a pretty good chance you'll enjoy one of my others. Here is a quick overview of what they are.

Grow Up is the next book in the One Up Series, (of which Level Up is the start) although it follows different characters on their own adventure. It is better classified as GameLit, with a lot of gaming humour and strategies, but no direct levelling up. You can grab a copy here:

Amazon

If you liked the humour in Level Up, the **Lucky Beggar Trilogy** is the book for you. It follows a homeless man as he is infected with a concentrated form of karma, so his actions are judged immediately. There is lots of banter and shenanigans, and a fluffy sidekick. You can pick it up here:

Amazon

. . .

If you liked the action in Level Up, **TROJAN** is an action packed techno-thriller. It follows a rookie FBI agent on her first case, tracking down a dangerous hacker with the help of an outside consulting agency called Tempest. You can pick it up here:

Amazon

If you need something a little darker to balance things out, **The Colony** is the story of Ben, who is a clone born into captivity. He must fight for his chance to be released from his prison, but what lays beyond the wall may be even worse. You can pick it up here:

Amazon

If you loved the gaming aspects of Level Up and are hungry for more I heartily recommend **Ruins of Majesta: Volume 1 - Blood and Cupcakes** by **Taj McCoy El**. It's a fun filled adventure and suitable for anyone that loves a great story.

Here's the blurb:

M.I.T. calls her a genius, her mother calls her Cupcake, her buddies call her Princess Cuddle Fluff and she's here to kick butt and blow stuff up.

At least until she realizes she's stuck.

Eleven-year-old Mayah's just collateral damage in an investigation by a government agency that's intent on keeping control of its finances. Now she's trapped in the Virtual Reality game of Ruins of Majesta waging the war for her life the only way she can, by questing, leveling up and sewing.

You can check it out here:

Amazon

ACKNOWLEDGEMENTS

Did you know only 1% of readers leave a review on Amazon? Who doesn't want to be in the top 1%!

If you enjoyed the book please consider leaving a review. You just have to click here - My Book. It really is a huge help to discover-ability and lets other readers know about the book. It will only take a couple of minutes. Seriously, I'll wait...

Ok, you're back? Let's keep going!

This was a tremendously fun book to write. As a lifelong gamer I was excited when I heard that there was a new genre of books that was mixing gaming concepts with traditional stories. Finally, I could put the many thousands of hours of my gaming time to good use! Even better, I could tell my wife that my gaming time was now *research*.

The tricky part was making sure that I had hit the mark in regards to the genre. It feels like LitRPG is ever changing as more and more people release books in the genre. To do a decent market test I turned to Royal Roads Legends (https://royalroadl.com) where there is a bunch of avid readers and a large group of LitRPG fans.

I released a chapter every day and got a ton of really useful feedback that has helped make the book so much better. A huge thanks to everyone that took the time to suggest a change. Also, a special thanks to Mikkel, who gave me my very first review on the site after only 5 chapters. It really helped to encourage me that I was on the right path.

When I looked at the other books in the genre the thing that really jumped out at me was just how nice all their covers were. I usually make my own covers (and it shows!) but for this book I really wanted to go all out. While browsing deviant art I stumbled across the amazingly talented Sicarius8 (https://sicarius8. deviantart.com) who had not only drawn beautiful fantasy style settings, but had also drawn a totally badass picture of a squirrel. It was meant to be! I got in touch with three bullet points and a few weeks later I had the finished cover in my hands. It was so much cooler than I could have possibly imagined! I highly recommend her for anyone else looking to get a cover made.

I'd also like to give a shout out to Cel Rince (https:// celestianrince.com), proofreader extraordinaire, for catching a massive stack of typos even after I had read through the book a few dozen times. His work was detailed, prompt and very reasonably priced.

I want to say a special thanks to Laura and Aaron. You guys were my gaming buddies, always there for another game of MK2 or Soul Calibur. Many a sleepless night was spent in front of a Sega console. I have so many happy memories of the three of us huddled around a TV.

As always, a massive thank you to my wife, who suffered more than usual for this book as I wrote the majority of it during National Novel Writing Month. It was my first time doing NaNo-WriMo, but when I saw that several fellow Flashdogs were doing it (including the serial Nano superstar Brian Creek) I decided to bite the bullet. 50k words in a month was quite the challenge and ate up all my free time, which meant my wife spent November wondering if she was ever going to see her husband again. I hope the finished result makes it up to her.

Finally I would like to thank you, dear reader, for reading the acknowledgments section, because let's be honest, almost no-one does.

Looking for an excuse to read through the book again? I've hidden the names of my favourite games throughout the story. Some of them are obvious, others are homages or subtle references. Can you find them all?

ABOUT THE AUTHOR

Craig Anderson is a British Canadian indie author that is also a lifelong gamer. This is his sixth published book and his first attempt at a LitRPG.

He lives with his wife, two kids under four, and a veritable zoo of pets. His house always looks like a tornado just passed through it.

He really hates writing about himself in the 3rd person.

You can stalk him on twitter here: @todayschapter

You can like him on facebook here:

https://www.facebook.com/CraigAndersonAuthor

You can check out his website here: www.todayschapter.com

Printed in Great Britain
by Amazon

16166029R00174